A KILLER'S KISS

HELEN HARPER

For the Harparty people

CHAPTER ONE

.

I COULDN'T SAY FOR SURE WHEN I'D BECOME IMMUNE TO THE stench of death but, as I gazed down at the decaying corpse, I knew the reek no longer bothered me.

The pixie's skin was the colour of death but her lips were a slash of bright purple, her perfectly applied lipstick a stark contrast to the rest of her face.

'Is she there?' the anxious neighbour called from the doorway, his neat moustache quivering. 'Is she alright?'

I walked back out of the small, neat bedroom and into the hallway. Fred was in the kitchen, his head stuck in the fridge. I glanced at him, then lifted my head towards the pale-faced man. 'Do you know if Ms Thorn has any family?'

The man's shoulders sank. 'Oh,' he whispered.

I offered him a sympathetic smile, which he didn't notice. 'I'm afraid she's passed away.'

He started blinking rapidly. 'Oh,' he said again. 'Oh.'

I took his elbow and steered him gently away from the late Rosie Thorn's front door. His own flat lay opposite. He stumbled inside and into his living room. I followed, watching as he sank heavily onto a smart, velvet-covered sofa and buried his face in his hands.

I gave him a moment or two to compose himself while I looked around and wished my own flat were as neat and tidy as this one. Neither Lukas nor I were particularly messy but this place was on another level. 'Why don't I make you a cup of tea?' I offered.

'No.' He shook his head. 'No. I'm fine.' He gave me a watery smile. 'Thank you, but it's okay. It was a shock, that's all. I only saw her last week. I would have checked on her sooner but I've been on holiday up north. I didn't get back until this morning.'

'It probably wouldn't have made any difference, Mr Harris,' I said. 'A post-mortem will be conducted as a matter of course, but it looks to me as if she died quickly and peacefully. Do you know how old she was?'

'Seventy-nine. She was planning her eightieth birthday party next month. A glam-rock theme. She told me she was planning to dress up like Kiss. She'd already bought the make-up.'

Good for her.

Harris ran a shaky hand through his hair. He glanced at me, looked away, then glanced back again.

'What is it?' I asked softly. Clearly he had something on his mind.

'I'm a nurse,' he whispered, as if he were afraid of anyone else hearing even though we were the only people in the room. 'Rosie was fed up with going to her GP for check-ups. She hated hanging around, waiting to be seen. She always said the waiting room was full of too many sick people and she didn't want to catch anything.'

'Uh-huh.' I waited, aware that he had more he needed to say.

'I've been helping her out.' Guilt traced the lines on his face, deepening each one until he looked almost haggard. 'I took her blood pressure every month and recommended various vita-mins and food to keep her strength up. I kept telling her to go to her doctor and that I could only do so much, but she wouldn't listen.'

'Okay. Thank you for telling me that. You'll need to come into the Supe Squad station some time soon to make a statement about what you did for her.' I kept my tone sympathetic. 'You can't force anyone to go to their doctor, and it may not have changed anything if she had.'

Alan Harris choked back a sob. 'She was a nice lady, a great neighbour.'

'Does she have any family nearby?' I asked.

'She has a son and a granddaughter from her first marriage, I think,' he said 'They don't talk very often. One of her ex-husbands comes around now and then to check on her, though.'

One of her ex-husbands? A ghost of a smile crossed my mouth. 'Is he a pixie too?'

He shook his head. 'A werewolf.'

That was unusual, though not unheard of. 'Do you know his name?'

'Robert Sullivan.'

I raised an eyebrow. The only Robert Sullivan I knew was a beta wolf in the Sullivan clan. He was ornery, obstructive, and loyal only to Lady Sullivan herself. He was also a good thirty years younger than Rosie Thorn. The dead pixie went up another notch in my estimation. Taste in men aside, she had certainly lived life to the fullest.

I took a few more details before leaving Mr Harris in peace and returning to the flat. Fred was in the living room, gazing out of the window. I cleared my throat and he jerked. 'Sorry, boss.' He pointed across the street. 'I was admiring the view.'

I followed his finger. From this vantage point, it was possible to see inside several of the flats opposite. Very few had their curtains drawn so the line of sight was unimpeded.

'If we can see into those flats,' Fred said, 'those residents can see inside here. They might be able to tell us when they last saw

Ms Thorn moving around. It could help us with the time of death.'

'We can knock on a few doors,' I agreed. Our success would depend on how nosy Rosie Thorn's neighbours were. I doubted there was anything suspicious about her death, however; there was nothing to suggest foul play, and she'd been an older lady. 'Is there anything else of note?'

'The milk in the fridge is three days out of date.' So she'd probably been dead at least that long.

I picked up a half-empty glass from the coffee table and took a cautious sniff. Gin and tonic. There were worse ways to die than in your own bed after a drink or two – I should know. Maybe Rosie had been aware on some level of what was coming and, in barely conscious preparation, poured herself a drink before retreating to her bed. Maybe we'd never know. Death – and dying – still held a lot of mystery, even for me. And I'd experienced both several times.

'Any sign of the paramedics to confirm the death?' I asked.

'They're backed up with urgent cases. Clearly Ms Thorn isn't going anywhere, so she's not a priority. I spoke to the local GP surgery and they confirmed she was registered there but she'd not made any appointments in the last two years. I guess she felt fit and healthy.'

That confirmed what Alan Harris had told me.

Fred continued, 'They're sending someone over to certify her death.'

I checked my watch. That could take a while, and word would get around fast. I should probably locate Robert Sullivan and Rosie's son before they heard the news via idle gossip. 'If you wait here until they arrive, I'll try and track down the family.'

Fred nodded, and I pretended not to notice his relief. Knocking on the Sullivan Clan's door wasn't a pleasant task at the best of times.

'Keep me updated,' I said as I headed out.

'You mean in case her body erupts in a ball of fire and she's resurrected in front of my eyes?'

I frowned.

'Stranger things have happened, boss.'

Yeah, yeah. I rolled my eyes and left.

THE SHINY, lacquered door swung open. 'Lady Sullivan isn't taking any callers,' Robert growled. He looked at me disdainfully. 'So fuck off before I put in a complaint to your superior. There are laws against police harassment, you know.'

I maintained a studiously blank expression. 'Actually, Mr Sullivan, I was hoping to talk to you.'

'I've not done anything.' His face darkened. 'And since when have you called me mister?'

'Can I come in?'

He folded his arms across his broad chest and glowered. Before he could argue further, I added, 'I'm afraid I have some bad news.'

His demeanour altered instantly: his skin paled and his jaw went slack. Performing a death knock is a truly horrible part of my job. It didn't help that I knew Robert had to do the same thing on behalf of his werewolf clan, so he knew why I was here. 'Who?' he demanded.

'If we could step inside—'

'Tell me.'

I wetted my lips. He was determined to hear it now, here on the doorstep. 'Rosie,' I said quietly.

Almost immediately Robert started to shake his head. 'No.'

'My sincerest condolences, Mr—'

'No. You've made a mistake.'

It was always possible but in this case I doubted it.

'How?' he demanded. 'How did she die?'

'We won't know for sure until a post-mortem is carried out, but it looks like she passed away in her sleep, in her own bed.'

'Natural causes?'

'Yes.'

'No.'

This wasn't the first time someone had refused to believe the tragic news I had to give them. 'I'm very sorry, Mr Sullivan.'

'It's not her.' He tossed back his head. Dark patches of fur were appearing across his cheekbones, which was quite some feat given that it was only two days since the last full moon and his lupine energy had to be massively depleted. 'I knew your incompetence would get the better of you one of these days, DC Bellamy.' He sniffed. 'I've been proven right.'

'Do you know how we can get hold of Rosie's son or granddaughter?' I asked. 'Or if there are any other family members we need to inform?'

Robert took a step forward so that his face loomed mere inches from mine. 'She's not dead, you vamp-loving freak!'

I opened my mouth but didn't get the chance to speak because his hand snapped out and encircled my throat. That was most definitely not how I'd anticipated our conversation would go.

His fingers tightened. This wasn't a warning shot, he genuinely wanted to kill me – even though we both knew I wouldn't stay dead.

I didn't want to hurt him but I wasn't about to let him strangle me, either. I launched a sharp kick, planted my foot on his shin, and followed it a second later with a knee to his stomach. It was far from a full-strength blow, but Robert released me with a grunt of surprised pain. He should have been pleased; I could have brought my crossbow with me. I'd have been well within legal – if not moral – bounds to use it against him, silver-tipped bolts or otherwise.

Unfortunately, he didn't know when he was beaten. He rushed me, head down and hands outstretched. His fingernails were already turning into misshapen claws, ready to rake the flesh from my bones.

I hissed with irritation and leapt sideways, out of his line of attack. Robert gave an inarticulate howl and wheeled round, now more wolf than man. There was a wild light in his yellow-tinged eyes. In the absence of any real culprit to blame for Rosie Thorn's death, he'd decided to blame me. He wouldn't back down, not now. Not unless I made him.

There were some supes I knew I wasn't strong enough to compel: Lukas, naturally; the werewolf clan leaders; the ghouls; one or two goblins, and a smattering of pixies. There were some supes whom I doubted I could compel and wouldn't try to dominate for fear of failing or losing face. There were also a considerable number of supes I couldn't bring to my will unless I used their real names.

I didn't know Robert's real name, but I knew my power was stronger than his, regardless of his position within the Sullivan Clan. I drew in a breath – and saw Lady Sullivan standing on the doorstep behind him. She shook her head.

I stared hard at her and then I stepped back.

'Come here, Robert,' she ordered. The air pulsated with her words.

Despite his emotional state, he was still her beta. He heard her command, and he was powerless to resist. His shoulders slumped, though his eyes were still sparking with fury. He bared his teeth at me, his lips drawn back over his pink gums. And then he trotted to her side.

'Good boy,' she said. She nudged him inside and closed the door, shutting him in. Her eyes met mine. 'Thank you, Emma.'

She knew as well as I did that I could have compelled Robert to calm down. It wouldn't have done him any favours, not in the long run, and it certainly wouldn't have helped the Sullivan clan's standing. They touted themselves as the strongest werewolf clan in the country, but they'd lose both pride and status if one of their betas was brought to his knees by a mere police detective.

Letting her take control wasn't a wholly selfless move on my part, however. If it became common knowledge that I'd grown in power enough to dominate a beta wolf, it would be dangerous for me, too.

'Under the circumstances,' I said, 'I'm prepared to forget what just happened. But this cannot be allowed to happen again.'

'Robert will understand,' she told me. 'I will make sure of it.'

'Not only him. All your wolves,' I warned.

The only sign she agreed was a slight nod. It would have to be enough.

'Grief is a powerful emotion, Lady Sullivan,' I continued. 'It can over-ride sense and reason. But there is information I need from Robert, and it would be helpful if I could have a proper conversation with him.'

'It might be best to wait a few days.'

'I need to locate Rosie Thorn's immediate family,' I said.

'I'll talk to him and let you know where they are before the day is out. When he's ready, Robert will come and speak to you. Right now he needs *us*, detective. Not you.'

'Very well.' I paused. 'I know it doesn't help him just now, but she was a good age for a pixie.'

Lady Sullivan's gaze didn't waver. 'As you said, detective, grief is a powerful emotion.'

Indeed it was. I sighed, then I turned on my heel and left.

CHAPTER TWO

DETECTIVE SERGEANT OWEN GRACE WAS EYEING ME FROM OVER the top of his computer screen. He seemed to think he was doing it surreptitiously, but it was hard to ignore the continual glances. Something was on his mind.

I focused on my paperwork. He'd speak up sooner or later. Where DS Grace was concerned, it was more fruitful to allow him time and space to formulate his thoughts.

Liza pushed back her chair and stood up. 'I'm nipping out to grab a sandwich. Does anyone want anything?'

'Cheese and tomato, please,' I said.

'Always the adventurous one,' she muttered. 'What about you, Fred? I suppose you'd like chips drowning in vinegar and smothered with cheese, all the better to clog up your arteries.'

He beamed and ignored her sour tone. 'Thanks, Liza.'

'What would you like, Honey Puff?' she asked Grace.

'I'll have the same as you, Sweet Cheeks,' he answered, with the special smile he reserved purely for her.

Fred rolled his eyes and pretended to stick his finger down his throat. Liza looked at him unsympathetically. 'You're feeling ill? Better avoid those greasy chips – I'll get you a salad.' She planted a kiss on Grace's cheek and swept out of the room.

Fred frowned. 'Do you think she's really going to bring back a salad?'

I grinned. 'Probably.'

He grabbed his helmet and stood up. 'I'd better go with her.' He sprinted after her.

I returned my attention to my screen. Only one more report to go. Hurrah.

From across the room, Grace drew in a breath. I glanced up expectantly. Here we go. 'Have you located Rosie Thorn's family yet?' he asked.

Hm. That wasn't what he really wanted to say, but I'd go with it for now. 'I tracked them down yesterday. Her son is laid up in hospital in Bahrain and can't travel, but I spoke to her grand-daughter who's been granted next-of-kin status.'

The phone number that Lady Sullivan had procured for me had gone straight to voice mail. It had taken several messages and four days before the granddaughter picked up her messages. 'She's been travelling across Europe, so it took a while to catch her. She's on her way back here now.'

He grunted. 'Good. What about Robert Sullivan? Has he been in?'

'Not yet.'

Grace's mouth flattened. 'The post-mortem indicates Rosie Thorn died of a heart attack?'

'Yep. It was the werewolves' own pathologist who carried it out, so Robert can't complain that we missed anything during the examination. He's probably stayed away because he's embarrassed. I'm sure he'll show up sooner or later.'

'He'd better,' Grave muttered. 'If we don't hear from him by the end of the day, I'll talk to Lady Sullivan again. His behaviour was unacceptable. Given what he did to you, it's best if I deal with him from now on.'

We'd already been through this. I nodded and waited as Grace fiddled with his cuffs. He ran his tongue round his lips, cleared his throat, then held up a sheet of paper. 'I've had a request from the Hackney station. They'd like someone from Supe Squad to advise them on a recent crime they're investigating.'

So that was what he'd been holding back on. I barely avoided rolling my eyes. Since the Summit the previous year, supes of all creeds had been experiencing a surge of popularity. Tourist numbers at Lisson Grove and Soho were up, and barely a week went by when Lukas wasn't asked to present himself at a television studio for an interview.

I'd even seen an advertising campaign for a popular brand of perfume that was using members of the McGuigan clan as models. *'Hate the smell of wet dog? Spritz yourself with this!'* That wasn't the actual tagline but it might well have been.

I was thrilled by the change in attitude – it was what we'd all wanted – but the turn of fortune occasionally had a whiff of the ridiculous. In my more pessimistic moments, I worried that being idolised wasn't much better than being vilified – it simply meant there was further to fall when the fuck-ups happened. I'd have preferred it if the supes were now treated in the same manner as humans, as neither evil beings nor snowflakes. Supes were both as good and bad as humans.

Not only the supes were getting attention; Supe Squad was receiving requests from all corners of London. It had been exciting initially, and it had felt as if we were finally being valued for our expertise and experience with all things supernatural. It didn't take long for the sheen to wear off. If I'd had a quid for every faked pentagram or random bump in the night that I'd been sent to check out, I'd be rich enough to buy a new car. Or at least get Tallulah a fresh coat of spray paint.

'Any details?' I asked.

Grace shook his head. 'Afraid not.'

It was possibly the Hackney team were being deliberately

taciturn because they knew the crime wasn't supernatural. Maybe they wanted an attending Supe Squad detective to make it appear that they'd pulled out all the stops. There were downsides to being popular. 'Fine,' I sighed.

'You'll do it?'

'Do I have a choice?'

Grace flashed me a grin. 'Not really.'

I rubbed the back of my neck and forced a smile. 'Then I can't wait.'

I PRESENTED myself at the front desk of the Hackney Police Station shortly after 3pm. The uniformed desk clerk did a double-take when he saw me. 'You ... you ... you're DC Bellamy!' he gasped.

I was tempted to perform an elaborate curtsey. 'That's me.'

'I'm a huge fan!'

I smiled politely. 'Thank you.' I consulted the paper Grace had given me. 'I'm looking for Detective Inspector Colquhoun. Is she in?'

'She certainly is.' He went on beaming at me.

I gazed at him. Finally, I said, 'Could you tell her I'm here?'

'Oh!' Flustered, he picked up the phone. 'If you wait a moment, I'm sure she'll be down shortly.'

I nodded and sat as far away from him as possible. Hopefully, he wouldn't ask for my autograph like the traffic warden who'd stopped to give Tallulah a ticket the other day. Neither of us needed to be embarrassed in that way.

I sat there for five minutes, then ten. When my wait stretched to fifteen minutes, and the desk clerk was starting to look distinctly red-faced and uncomfortable, I wondered if this was a measured show of power on DI Colquhoun's part. Maybe she wanted to make sure I knew my place. Popular or not, I was still a

Supe Squad detective, and I wasn't considered as useful as a typical police officer.

When the inner security door finally opened and I registered her tired features and drawn look, I realised that I was making the cardinal sin of thinking everything was about me. Colquhoun clearly had her own stresses and woes. From the look in her eyes, my presence was little more than an annoyance.

'DI Colquhoun,' she snapped. 'You're the DC? From Supe Squad?'

'Emma Bellamy,' I replied with a smile. She didn't bother returning it.

She looked me up and down. 'You're probably wasting your time, but thank you for your effort in coming across town.'

I appreciated the sentiment, and it was refreshing that she seemed to be saying exactly what she was thinking. 'Why do you think I'm wasting my time?' I asked.

'This isn't a supe crime, it's a psychopath crime. Last time I checked, those two things didn't go hand in hand.' She shrugged. 'But it's unusual enough for my boss to want to bring you in. Blame him, not me. I'm sure you have better things to do.' Under her breath she added, 'I know I certainly have.'

'In that case, show me the files and I'll give you my opinion. Then you can get back to whatever you were doing as quickly as possible.'

DS Colquhoun sent me a sharp look. When she realised I was being genuine, she smiled. 'You're not what I was expecting.'

I decided I didn't want to know what she'd been expecting.

'Anyway, it's not just the files I'm supposed to show you,' she said, 'I've been ordered to take you to the scene. Don't worry.' She patted the bag by her side. 'I've got forensic suits here so your clothes won't be ruined.'

Forensic suits? I frowned at her. 'Why would they be ruined? What is the crime you're investigating?'

She stared at me. 'Didn't they tell you?' She let out a bark of a laugh. 'It's lucky I know who your boyfriend is. You're less likely to get squeamish. It's a doozy.'

So it wasn't a fake pentagram or a random noise in the middle of the night. A shiver ran down my spine. I had the sudden feeling I'd have preferred dealing with those after all.

COLQUHOUN TOOK me to a large first-floor flat in what had once been a grand Victorian villa less than a mile from the police station. 'It was called in late last night by one of the neighbours,' she told me. 'The scene is still fresh.'

I took the forensic suit and pulled it on over my clothes, swathing myself in white so that only my face remained visible. Then I pulled on gloves, a mask and completed the look with blue booties. Colquhoun did the same, tucking her brown curls underneath the white hood of her suit. 'If you think you're going to vomit—' she started.

'I won't.'

She gave me a hard look. 'Okay.' She lifted the blue crime-scene tape. 'It's through here.'

I stepped across the threshold. I could already smell the blood from the ground-floor entrance.

'Best guess so far,' she told me, 'is that the killer gained access through the communal garden.' She pointed down the hallway. 'See the smashed window?'

Two fingerprint technicians were dusting the frame for prints, and I watched them for a moment or two. There was something odd about the scene. Finally realising what it was, I asked, 'Have you already cleared up the glass shards?'

'There was no glass to clear up,' Colquhoun replied. 'The killer cleared it up himself. Maybe he's a neat freak, or maybe he was trying to delay detection.'

I chewed on my bottom lip. If there was no broken glass,

anyone passing by, especially at night, would be more likely to think the window was open rather than smashed in. It spoke of a meticulous perpetrator. To my mind, it also spoke of something else. 'Overkill,' I said aloud.

Colquhoun snorted. 'Mate,' she said. 'You ain't seen nothing yet.'

Grim anticipation tightened my stomach. I swallowed. Colquhoun had been correct. I wasn't squeamish, not by a long shot, but that didn't mean I enjoyed this sort of thing.

I trailed after her to an open door marked as Flat 1A. My brow furrowed. 'I thought you said the crime occurred on the first floor.'

'It did, Miss Pedantic.' Colquhoun looked slightly amused. 'But this ground-floor flat is relevant because the occupants were the first to report in to the police.'

My frown deepened. 'They heard a scuffle?'

'Oh no. They didn't hear a thing – but they did see something. And they felt it, too.'

I was even more baffled. Colquhoun swept an arm in front of me. 'Go on,' she said. 'Take a look.'

I edged deeper into the flat. It was empty, although there was evidence of the crime-scene techs. I glanced into the large airy kitchen and one of the bedrooms. Nothing there. Then I peered into the living room; instantly, I drew back with a hiss.

Colquhoun was watching. 'Oh yeah,' she said drily. 'It's what you think. The couple who live here were snuggling up on the sofa watching a romantic film. He was nuzzling her neck; she was caressing his leg. The candles were lit, the wine was poured. It was the perfect scene.' She pursed her lips. 'It's hard to believe that people actually manage to live like that in real life. Where do they find the time?'

At my look, she shook herself. 'It's been a long week and I live alone with my cat. What can I say? Still, at least when I've gotten lucky off Tinder and I feel something wet on my face, I can be reasonably certain that it's not blood dripping from the flat above me.'

I clenched my teeth and looked at the scene again. There was a dark patch across the ceiling. As far as I could tell blood had dripped through the light fitting and dribbled onto the couple sitting on the sofa. No wonder they'd called it in. I gazed upwards. There had to be a lot of blood for it to soak through the floor and leak into the flat below.

'Wait until you see upstairs,' Colquhoun told me. 'It's a fucking bloodbath.'

CHAPTER THREE

BACK AT THE HACKNEY STATION, I SIPPED ON OVERLY SWEET TEA and tried not think too hard about how much blood there had been at the flat. Even knowing what I did about the capacity of the human body, it seemed astonishing that so much could come out of one person. The entire floor of the first-floor living room had been drenched, as if an interior decorator had popped in and decided that O positive was this season's most promising colour for wall-to-wall carpets.

'No footprints,' I said aloud. In fact, there was nothing to suggest anyone had been in the room apart from the victim. I could see why Colquhoun's boss believed there might be a supernatural connection.

Colquhoun slid a photo across the desk. 'A member of the public found that beside a bin a few streets away from the scene and reported it in. We're checking the rest of the area, but nothing has turned up so far.' She pointed to it. 'It's coated in blood. The test results haven't come through yet, but I think it'll be a match.'

'I don't suppose...'

'It's an ordinary bucket. You can buy them anywhere. There are probably millions produced every year.'

That figured. 'So the killer collected the victim's blood in a bucket and then,' I grimaced, 'painted the floor with it?'

Colquhoun nodded. 'Hence the lack of bloody footprints. Judging by the marks, it looks like he used a paintbrush to cover all the areas, but we've not found it yet. In any case, he took care not to paint himself into a corner.'

I shot her a look at the grim joke, but she wasn't smiling. I didn't bother commenting on her use of a masculine pronoun. It was a reasonable assumption when ninety-three percent of killers in this country were male. Not that I hadn't come across my fair share of female murderers.

I thought about the room. There had been no arterial spray on the walls; in fact, they'd been pristine without a single smudge or splatter. 'The victim must have been killed elsewhere,' I said.

Colquhoun shook her head. 'We'll know more when the post-mortem results come in, but the initial crime-scene techs think he was murdered on site.'

Huh. Exsanguination is a messy business but, apart from the floor which had been covered in blood, this had been a tidy killing. 'A medical professional? Someone who would know how to tap a vein and extract as much blood as possible?'

'That's what Don Murray, the Senior Investigating Officer thinks.' She pulled a face, although whether at the mention of the investigation's lead detective or the theory itself, I couldn't tell. 'But YouTube provides how-to videos on just about everything these days. It could be an amateur. Could a vampire have done this?'

The doubt in her voice mirrored my own. 'Even the strongest-willed vamp would struggle to be surrounded by that much blood. Besides, a vampire bite includes vampire saliva, which automatically works to heal wounds. Almost as soon as their fangs are withdrawn, the victim's blood ceases to flow. In theory, a vamp could drink that much blood if they were truly starving, but this blood was drained not drunk.' I met her eyes. 'Were there any bites on his body?'

'No.' She smiled slightly and I knew that she'd been testing me with the vamp question. I chose not to take offence; after all, we *were* strangers to each other.

'There's no sign of a struggle,' I said instead.

'No,' she agreed. 'And there aren't any defensive wounds on the body. But he was incapacitated somehow before his blood was taken. The post-mortem will tell us more.'

Fair enough. I chewed the inside of my cheek and considered. 'What can you tell me about the victim?'

'He wasn't a supe.' Colquhoun slid across another photo. 'Peter Pickover, forty-two years old.'

I gazed at the photograph. Pickover was seated behind a desk, pen poised in one hand and an affected frown on his face for the camera. He was wearing a suit and tie, and sporting a neatly trimmed beard and carefully combed hair that was only slightly balding. The Hackney police must have pulled the photo from LinkedIn or his company website. 'Lawyer?' I guessed.

'Civil servant. He worked with the Department for Transport. He didn't smoke, hardly ever drank, has less than fifty friends on Facebook and no apparent hobbies. Divorced with no children. It looks as if Peter Pickover went to work, came home, slept and then repeated the same routine every day. It wasn't much of a life.'

I looked up at Colquhoun.

'Yeah,' she said, 'I don't buy it either. That's a nice flat for someone on a civil servant's salary. And no social life to speak of?' She shook her head. 'He was hiding something. Whether that something is related to his murder or not is another question.'

She waved a hand at her colleagues who were bent over computer screens. 'They're on it. If there's anything to uncover about Pickover, that lot will find it.'

There is little dignity in death, and there are certainly few secrets when your entire life goes under police scrutiny. Not that it would matter to Peter Pickover any more.

'Can I see the photos of the scene before his body was removed?' I asked.

'Knock yourself out.' Colquhoun passed me a file. I flipped it open and started to skim through the various shots. Pickover had been found on a chair, naked apart from a pair of underpants. His head was slumped forward, his baldness more visible now that his hair wasn't preened for a professional photo shoot. I glanced at the marks on his arms and legs; they looked like needle pricks. Either he was a copious drug user, a diabetic or these marks indicated how his blood had been drained.

'You'll probably want to see this, too.' Colquhoun pulled out a photo of Pickover's face.

I drew in a breath. It had been as carefully painted with blood like the floor. I shuddered. 'What's that on his cheek?' I asked.

'Nothing.'

I frowned at her. There was a patch on Pickover's left cheek that hadn't been covered in blood.

'There's no blood on that spot – there's nothing there at all. Judging by the rest of his face, it seems to have been left clear deliberately.'

I held the photo away from my face to get a different view and tilted my head. 'It's a kiss,' I said suddenly. 'Like a lipstick mark without the lipstick.'

Colquhoun moved behind me and looked at the photo again. 'Nah. I'm not convinced.'

I traced the shape with my finger. 'It's definitely a kiss.'

She grimaced. 'Well, that's weird as fuck.'

I couldn't argue. 'Maybe you ought to look a little closer at the ex-wife,' I suggested

Colquhoun's mouth turned down. 'I've worked a lot of creepy

cases and seen a lot of shit, but I have a really bad feeling about this one. Really bad.'

She looked as if she needed a hug, but I knew better than to offer. 'Whoever did this is a sick bastard,' I agreed. 'But there's nothing to suggest supe.'

Colquhoun didn't appear surprised. 'I'd appreciate a written report all the same. Gotta cross those Ts.'

I smiled faintly. 'Gotta love those written reports.'

We exchanged glances of mutual despair and I stood up. I'd taken up enough of her time and I had little of use to offer. 'I'll email it over as soon as I get back to Supe Squad.'

'Thanks.'

I paused. 'There is one thing that doesn't add up.'

'Go on.'

'Whoever murdered Pickover cleaned up the shattered glass from the point of entry. They made sure not splatter blood anywhere except the floor. They took whatever needles and equipment they used in the murder away with them and left no trace of themselves behind.'

'Uh-huh.'

'Except for the bucket,' I said. 'The only thing they dumped is that bucket. Nothing else.'

'We checked for CCTV,' Colquhoun said. 'We've been up and down that street looking for private cameras, council cameras, any damned sort of camera. There's nothing. It's a total blind spot, probably one of the few in the city. It's as if the killer knew he wouldn't be filmed there.'

'Maybe he *did* know,' I said quietly.

I PARKED Tallulah in front of the Supe Squad building and called Lukas. 'Hey, you,' I said.

'D'Artagnan,' he purred. 'Are you having a good day?' When I didn't answer immediately, his voice sharpened. 'Are you okay?'

'Yeah, yeah, I'm fine. It's just … been a bit grim today. And bloody.'

Lukas's concern heightened. 'Literally bloody? Are supes involved?'

'No, it seems to be a human thing. It wasn't pleasant, though. I'll be a bit late tonight because I have to write up a report.'

'I'll be at the club. Come find me when you're finished.'

'I will.' Merely hearing his voice made me feel better. Then I caught sight of the hulking figure striding down the street towards me and the warmth inside me vanished.

'You know I can always send someone to help with any blood matters,' Lukas was saying. 'I reckon I can still surprise you with what a vampire can discover about haemoglobin.'

'I appreciate that.' The figure was drawing closer. 'I have to go. I'll see you later.'

'I love you.'

I smiled softly. 'I love you too.'

I hung up and reached for my crossbow before stepping out of the car. I thumbed off the safety and aimed it.

Robert Sullivan stopped and put up his hands. 'I won't attack you again, DC Bellamy.'

'Stay where you are.'

Max the bellman peered out from the doorway of the hotel next door. 'Do you need some help?' he asked anxiously. 'Should I call someone?'

I didn't take my eyes off Robert. 'No, I've got this. Thanks, Max.' I lowered the crossbow an inch. 'You don't look very well,' I observed to the werewolf. Frankly, that was an understatement: his clothes were rumpled, as if he'd slept in them for days, and he had a scruffy beard and dark circles beneath his eyes.

'I apologise for my behaviour a few days ago,' he said stiffly. 'I should not have acted as I did. I was wrong.'

I blinked. I'd been expecting an apology sooner or later because Lady Sullivan would have demanded it of him, but I'd expected it to be more grudging than this. I inclined my head. 'Apology accepted. You were under a great deal of stress and, surprising as it may seem, I do understand. Let's say no more about it.'

I let the crossbow tip fall and turned for the Supe Squad door.

'But I have to say more about it.' There was a ragged edge of desperation in his voice.

I glanced at him. 'You've apologised. That's enough.'

'I need you to look into Rosie's death!' he burst out. 'I need you to investigate it!'

I felt a sudden wave of sympathy for him. 'She died of natural causes. She was almost eighty years old, Robert. It was a heart attack – your own pathologist confirmed it. I'm very sorry for your loss, but there's nothing more I can do.'

He shook his head vigorously. 'She didn't die of natural causes.'

'Robert—'

'Hear me out. Please.' His head drooped. 'Nobody else will.'

Damn it. I sighed; I was a fool for doing this. 'Fine. Let's go inside.'

The grizzled werewolf didn't smile, but he did shudder with relief. Poor bloke. I hoped I wasn't going to prolong his pain by pandering to his wishes. I gestured for him to go through the door first; I didn't think this was a sneaky way to get in another attack, but you could never be too sure. When he passed me and I caught a whiff of unwashed body odour, my sympathy only increased.

I took him straight to the interview room. Owen Grace popped his head out of the office, his eyes widening in alarm when he saw Sullivan. 'DC Bellamy,' he said in warning.

I waved at him. 'It's fine.'

'I told you I would deal with Mr Sullivan when he arrived.'

That remained the most sensible option but the old were-wolf had come to me. 'Why don't we take him together?' I suggested. 'He's already apologised. Now he's asking for our help.'

Grace stiffened. '*Now* he wants our help?'

'I think we should at least listen to him.'

He clicked his tongue but followed me into the room. He sat down, folding his arms and glaring. I took the chair next to him.

'Well?' Grace enquired.

Robert didn't waste any time on a preamble. 'Rosie didn't die naturally. Someone killed her.'

'What makes you think that?'

'I've known her for a long time. We used to be married.'

Grace leaned forward. 'May I ask why you split up?'

A spasm of pain crossed Robert's face. 'She instigated the divorce. She said she was no longer in love with me.'

'You didn't feel the same?' I asked.

'I love her,' he said, not realising that he was still speaking about her in the present tense. 'I've always loved her. But she's a free spirit, and she could never be tied down for too long.' His voice took on a wistful edge. 'I was hers for two glorious years, and then she got bored. I didn't really bother about my position in the clan when we were together, but after she left I threw myself into my work. She always said that I'd never have become beta if she'd not left me.'

'You stayed on good terms after the divorce?'

Robert nodded. 'Wishful thinking on my part. I thought that if I stayed in touch with her, maybe she'd realise her mistake and see that we belonged together.' His mouth drooped. 'She never did.'

Grace unfolded his arms and leaned forward. It was clear that Robert's manner had changed his feelings. 'I'm very sorry for your loss,' he said, sounding as if he meant it. 'What makes you think her death wasn't a natural one? Ms Thorn's age—'

Robert interrupted. 'Her age means nothing! Rosie was as strong as an ox. Her heart was in perfect condition.'

Except according to what her own GP surgery and her next-door neighbour had told us, Rosie Thorn had avoided visiting her doctor for years so how would he know that?

'Sooner or later our bodies give out.' I spoke as gently as I could. 'You know that, Robert.'

'There's more!' His expression was becoming even more desperate. 'I saw her body when it was brought to the morgue. The lipstick she was wearing...' He shook his head, 'Rosie would never have worn lipstick. She didn't need to – her lips were the perfect shade of peony pink. She would never had put on *purple* lipstick!' It sounded like he'd spent some time since his divorce thinking about the exact shade of Rose Thorn's lips.

'When did you split up?' I asked.

'Eighteen years ago.'

That was a long time to hold a candle for someone. 'Perhaps her tastes changed?'

'I told you,' he said through gritted teeth, 'we were still friends, and I know she would never have worn lipstick, let alone such a garish colour.'

Both Grace and I knew it wasn't exactly evidence of murder. I reckoned that, deep down, Robert knew it too, but we couldn't ignore his suspicions. There was always a chance that he was right. Rosie deserved our full attention, and so did Robert Sullivan.

'When Thistle gets here, she'll tell you the same thing,' he said. 'She hadn't spoken to her much in recent years but she knows what Rosie was like. She'll tell you.'

'Thistle is her granddaughter?' Grace asked.

Robert nodded.

'We'll talk to her and see what she says. But you have to understand that there's not much to go on. Everything suggests Rosie died naturally.'

Robert's hands twisted in his lap. 'I know I have no rights here. All I'm asking is that you look into my Rosie's death a little more. Please.'

'*I'll* look into it,' Grace said firmly. 'Given your attack on DC Bellamy, it's better if I do this.'

Robert Sullivan looked truly contrite. 'I'm really very sorry about that.'

'All the same—'

'It won't happen again! I promise.'

Grace's expression didn't change. 'All the same,' he repeated, 'DC Bellamy will not be involved. I'll poke around and see what comes up. However,' he added sternly, 'you need to manage your expectations, Mr Sullivan. It's likely that there's nothing to find.'

Robert looked from me to Grace and back again. It was the best he was going to get and he knew it. 'Alright,' he mumbled finally. 'Thank you.'

'I'll let you know if I find anything.' With that, Detective Sergeant Owen Grace stood up and showed Robert the door.

CHAPTER FOUR

LUKAS WAS AT THE END OF THE BAR, SURROUNDED BY SEVERAL scantily clad women. As far as I could tell, they were enjoying his company as much as he was enjoying theirs. I grinned and ordered a drink from the bartender before heading up to the mezzanine level. Once there, I plonked myself down on Lukas's golden throne.

I started to count. It took him eight seconds.

'You're sitting in my chair, D'Artagnan,' he murmured.

'You weren't using it. In fact, you looked rather busy.'

'Jealous?'

Maybe a little. 'Nope.'

'Liar.' He leaned down and gave me a long, lingering kiss. My stomach flip-flopped. 'There,' he said. 'That will remove any doubt that I'm spoken for.'

I reached up and brushed away an inky-black curl from his face and wondered if Rosie and Robert had shared similar moments of closeness during their relationship. 'If we split up,' I asked suddenly, 'do you think we'd remain friends afterwards?'

Lukas's eyes darkened. 'Split up?'

'Hypothetically speaking.'

A deep growl emitted from his chest. 'No,' he said shortly. 'We would not be friends. There is no way that I could see you regularly if you weren't mine. The pain would be far too great.' He stared hard at me. 'What's going on?'

'It's nothing.' At his look, I waved him off. 'Honestly. It's just a case I'm working.'

He relaxed slightly. 'You're talking about Robert Sullivan and Rosie Thorn.'

'You know about them?' I asked, surprised.

'Of course. I make it my business to know such things. He was always smitten by her. When they got together, it provided considerable gossip. Pixies and werewolves don't usually make successful partners, but Rosie was a special case. I'm surprised she died. I'd always thought of her as one of those people who would go on forever.'

Hmm. 'You're not alone in that,' I said.

Lukas reached for my hands and entwined his fingers with mine. 'Let's go home. You look exhausted. I'll cook us something nice, and you can have a hot bath and stop worrying about hypothetical situations that will never happen.'

That sounded great. 'Don't you have work to do here?'

'The others can keep an eye on this place. Everything else will keep.'

'Your groupies will be disappointed.'

He laughed. 'They'll get over it.'

Lukas extended a hand to help me up, and we strolled back down to the ground floor of the club. The crowd parted to allow us to pass. Even now, after all this time with him, there was something about the deference the other supes offered him that made me feel uncomfortable. It made him less like cuddly boyfriend and more scary Mafia boss. I shook off the feeling. That was his public façade, not his private reality.

We were almost at the door when we heard the scuffle. An

ear-piercing shriek rose above the beat of the music and several suited vamps rushed past us.

'Let me past! Let me fucking past!'

I craned my neck round to see a petite woman, dressed in a powder-pink power suit with enormous shoulder pads that wouldn't have looked out of place in the eighties, shake her fists at the group of vampires.

'Not tonight, love,' one of the vamps said. I recognised him as one of Lukas's up-and-coming foot soldiers, Christopher-something. 'You should go home. You've had too much to drink.'

'I'm completely sober,' the woman sniffed. 'And you're the one who should watch what you drink. Otherwise who knows what might happen?'

Christopher frowned with confusion. 'What? Is that a threat? Listen, lady…'

Lukas immediately stepped in. 'Good evening, ma'am.' He was all smiles and cheery reassurance to defuse the situation. 'Thank you for coming to my club tonight. Let's step outside where we can hear each other properly and discuss the problem.'

'There is no problem,' she snapped. 'I'm perfectly fine, despite this toothless idiot's attempts to bar my way. I only need to see Horvath. Once I've spoken to him, I'll be out of your way.'

'I'm Lukas Horvath.'

She frowned at him. 'Are you?' She looked him up and down then reached out to poke him with her index finger. 'Oh. So you are. Where's your girlfriend? The fiery one?' She tutted to herself. 'I can't see a damned thing without my glasses!'

Lukas gently steered the woman towards the door. 'When did you last see them?'

'See what?'

'Your glasses.'

'If I knew that, I'd still have them with me, wouldn't I?'

I pressed my lips together, tried not to laugh and followed them into the street. The two bouncers at the door took several steps backwards, their expressions fearful. I tilted my head and looked at the woman again. She seemed rather … colourful … but she wasn't scary. I couldn't imagine why she would frighten two tough, muscular vamps; they were used to dealing with far more trouble than a mere woman on her own.

The nearest bouncer coughed loudly. 'She's a Cassandra, my Lord.'

Lukas flinched. I stared at the woman. A Cassandra? Did that mean—?

'Yes, yes,' she said. 'I'm a Cassandra. Blah-blah-blah. Call me Zara – I don't answer to Cassandra. That's *what* I am, not who I am. Now,' she said, barely pausing to draw breath, 'where is she? Where's your girlfriend?'

'You should leave,' Lukas told her, his tone far colder than a moment earlier.

At the same time, I spoke up. 'I'm here.'

Zara twisted round and squinted. 'Ah. Good. I knew you'd be here. I'm glad I caught you before you went home for a hot bath.'

'Emma.' Lukas's voice was low and filled with warning.

I gave him a reassuring smile before focusing on Zara. 'What can I do for you?'

She extended her arms, twisting her wrists first one way and then another as if she were about to perform some elaborate dance. 'It's not what *you* can do for *me*, Musketeer, it's what *I* can do for *you*.' She winked. 'One for all, and all for one.'

By my side, Lukas stiffened.

Zara raised her eyes heavenward and started to chant. 'Peter Piper picked a peck of pickled peppers. A peck of pickled peppers Peter Piper picked.'

Uh…

'Let's go, Emma,' Lukas ordered.

Maybe he was right. I had better things to do than stand in a cold dark street listening to tongue twisters.

'If Peter Piper picked a peck of pickled peppers,' Zara trilled, 'then where's the peck of pickled peppers Peter Pickover picked?'

I froze. 'What did you say?'

A slow smile spread across her face. 'You heard,' she said slyly.

DS Colquhoun had told me that Pickover's name wouldn't be released until tomorrow afternoon at the earliest. They were still trying to track down some of his more distant family members.

'What do you know about him?' I demanded.

'His business is a bloody one.'

I stepped forward. 'I need you to come with me to the Supe Squad station to answer a few questions.'

She blinked at me innocently. 'Are you arresting me?'

'No, but—'

'Then I'm not going to Supe Squad.' She lowered her voice conspiratorially. 'Too much love and romance there. It makes me feel queasy.'

My eyes narrowed. Considering the relationship between Liza and Grace, this woman seemed to know a great deal about what was going on at Supe Squad. 'Who exactly are you?'

'I've already told you. I'm Zara.' Her smile vanished. 'Look for the goblin, Musketeer. He has what you need.'

My brow creased. 'What goblin?'

'Look for him!' She danced away. 'He has the peck of pickled peppers that Peter picked.'

I started after her, but Lukas caught my arm. 'Don't,' he said. 'She's done enough harm already.'

I caught a movement out of the side of my eye: the heavier of the two vamp bouncers was crossing himself. I knew for a fact that he wasn't Catholic. Or religious.

'You said she's a Cassandra. She can see the future?'

The bouncer crossed himself again. 'She's a freak,' he muttered.

'We don't use that word any more,' I reminded him.

Christopher nodded agreement while Lukas avoided my eyes. 'He's not wrong.'

I crossed my arms, unimpressed. 'Explain it to me.'

His reluctance was obvious but, even so, he drew in a breath and started to explain. 'There are very few true Cassandras in existence. I knew one slightly back in the sixties, but she killed herself before she turned thirty.'

He grimaced. 'It's not an easy life. Stupid people sometimes think they could find out the lottery numbers in advance, that kind of thing.' He shook his head. 'That's not what it's like. Cassandras can't control what comes out of their mouths or what they see. Try and befriend one and before too long you'll know the date of your death, the ways your friends and family will betray you, the lies you'll be told and the disasters that will befall you.'

'It's all bad news? Cassandras don't foretell anything good?'

Lukas met my eyes. 'A year or two ago, Cassandra might have told me that I'd soon meet the love of my life and then be forced to watch her die.'

Yeah, okay.

'And who really wants to know scraps of their own future? Surely the joy of life is *not* knowing what's around the corner. I want to make my own future, I don't need someone telling me what it should be. If they did, I'd either use all my energy to avoid impending darkness or do nothing because I believed I had glorious times ahead. Knowing the future *affects* the future.'

'That's fair enough,' I said. 'But it doesn't explain why you reacted so negatively to Zara. If she really is a Cassandra, it's not her fault.'

'As I said,' Lukas told me, 'there are very few true Cassandras. There are some fakes who can cause as much – if not more – damage as the real ones. They can manipulate people, blackmail them, or make up shit and scam them. There are some who only have a smattering of the foretelling, and you never know whether what they're saying is real or fake. Most of the time they don't know themselves.'

The heavy vamp who'd crossed himself piped up. 'It's true, my lady. My cousin met a Cassandra once. He told her that if she got pregnant, her child would grow up to be a thing of evil. She had a hysterectomy then found out that particular Cassandra had only ever made three true predictions. Nothing else he said ever came true.'

Shit. 'Cassandras can be male as well as female?'

'Sure,' Lukas said. 'The name is based on Greek mythology and a woman called Cassandra who was cursed with telling the future, but real Cassandras can be either sex.'

I nodded slowly. 'She spoke of Peter Pickover. That's the name of the murder victim at the crime scene I attended this morning. She couldn't have known that unless she had some sort of power.'

From the doorway, Christopher held up his phone. 'Seen this?' he asked. 'It's a local Facebook page.'

I glanced at the screen and read the post. My stomach tightened. Damn it.

'*Peter Pickover was murdered last night. The police called in a Supe Squad detective to investigate, so it must have been a vamp or a werewolf who killed him,*' Christopher read aloud. So much for not releasing his name before tomorrow.

'That's how scammers operate,' Lukas said. 'They find a bit of information and use it to make you think they're telling the truth. Zara was probably lying through her teeth. It doesn't mean that she's not dangerous,' he added darkly.

'She called me Musketeer,' I pointed out.

'Everyone knows your nickname is D'Artagnan. That's hardly a secret.'

'In Greek mythology wasn't Cassandra's real curse that nobody believed her prophecies?'

'Then it's lucky that we're not living in a myth,' he replied. 'If she's a real Cassandra, that's all the more reason to avoid speaking to her. What you choose to do is up to you, but I wouldn't believe a word that came out of her mouth.'

He turned to the bouncers. 'She's barred from the club. If she comes by again, let me know and I'll deal with her. We don't want her around here.'

My stomach twisted uneasily. Lukas's easy dismissal of her, not to mention his distaste, bothered me deeply. And I still didn't feel that I could discount what she'd said. First thing tomorrow, I decided, I'd get in touch with the goblin community. Just in case.

CHAPTER FIVE

THE DE FACTO HEAD OF THE GOBLIN COMMUNITY WAS MOSBURN Pralk, the manager of the Talismanic Bank. It was fortunate that he liked me because most people wouldn't take too kindly to a phone call first thing in the morning about something a strange woman had said late at night in the middle of a street.

'You think a goblin had something to do with the murder of a random human in Hackney?' Pralk enquired.

'No.' I scratched my head. I didn't really know what to think. 'But maybe some goblin somewhere knew him? Or had dealings with him?'

'It all seems very unlikely, detective.'

I sighed. 'I know, but I have to check it out. It might be nothing but I want to be sure.'

'I'll ask around. Don't get your hopes up.' He paused. 'Now, while I have you, have I told you about the excellent interest rates we're offering on credit cards at the moment?'

When I finally hung up twenty minutes later, Fred placed a cup of coffee on my desk. 'Everything okay?'

'I think I've just signed away my firstborn.'

'You're pregnant?' he gasped.

Liza took that moment to walk into the office. 'You're having that vampire's baby?' she shrieked. 'Are you crazy?'

'No.'

Her eyes widened. 'You're having someone else's baby? Did you cheat on Horvath?'

I glared at them both. 'Don't be ridiculous. I'm not pregnant. It was a joke. Clearly not a very good one.'

Fred and Liza exchanged knowing looks and I sighed. 'I'm really not pregnant.' But I suddenly realised I wouldn't hate the idea if I were. Lukas would be a good dad. I blinked. Sometimes I surprised even myself.

Liza glanced at my feet. 'What are you doing?' I asked.

'Checking for swollen ankles,' she said.

Fred grabbed a cushion from the sofa and thrust it in my direction. 'Here,' he said. 'For your back. I can pop out later and get you some pickled gherkins, if you like.'

'Ha-ha. I could kill both of you, you know. It'd be a justifiable homicide.' They started to snicker in unison.

Fortunately for my untrustworthy colleagues, someone took that moment to ring the doorbell. 'You two are very lucky indeed,' I said, stomping out to answer it.

Their laughter grew louder. I smoothed my expression and opened the door. 'Good morning. I'm Detective Constable Emma Bellamy. How may I help you today?'

The tired-looking pixie on the doorstep hefted her large, faded backpack and ran a hand through her cloud of pink hair. 'I'm Thistle Thorn,' she said. 'We spoke on the phone a few days ago. I'm here about my grandmother.'

My eyes widened slightly. She must have come straight from the airport. 'Thank you so much for coming by,' I said. 'My deepest condolences.'

She gave a distracted nod. I stepped back and gestured her inside. 'Would you like me to take your bag?'

'I can manage.'

'Okay. Come through,' I said. 'I'll put the kettle on and you sit down.' I led her to our new visitors' room, which Grace had insisted we create. Grudgingly, I had to admit the expense had been worth it.

Thistle sat down heavily on the nearest chair. 'Wait here,' I said. 'I won't be a moment.' I turned around and almost collided with Fred. 'Can you keep Ms Thorn company?' I asked.

'Sure thing, boss.' He smiled at Thistle. 'I'm very sorry about your grandmother,' he said formally, seating himself at a distance from her.

'Thank you,' she said softly. 'We weren't close, but her death was unexpected.' She hesitated. 'What's your name?'

'PC Frederick Hackert.'

'Nice to meet you, PC Frederick Hackert. Did you know her? My grandmother, I mean?'

'I'm sorry to say I didn't.'

I left the room and headed for the office. Liza already had the kettle on. 'Rosie Thorn's granddaughter?' she asked.

I nodded and grabbed some cups and a tray.

'I'll bring these through,' Liza said. 'Owen's been out talking to some of Rosie's neighbours, but he's on his way back.'

'Thanks.' I smiled at her and returned to the visitors' room. Neither Fred nor Thistle had moved, but they were engaged in animated conversation.

'Samarkand sounds amazing,' Fred said.

Thistle nodded. 'It really is. The architecture is extraordinary. The whole city is steeped in history.'

'It was once part of the Silk Road, right?'

'Yep.' She smiled. 'Apparently, in its heyday there used to be a djinn on every corner.'

'No!'

'It's true.'

'Did you see any djinn when you were there?'

'There aren't many of them around now. I was tracking one down when I got the message about my nan.'

Fred's twisted his hands together in his lap. 'I'm really sorry you had to find out that way.'

'It's fine.' She met his eyes. 'Honestly. The last time I spoke to her, she seemed very healthy and happy. She was almost never ill, and her mind was sharper than mine.' She gazed at him. 'Better to go out while you're at the top of your game than to go through a long, painful decline, right?'

Fred offered her a tentative smile.

I cleared my throat. 'The tea is on its way,' I said. 'And so is Detective Sergeant Grace. He will chat to you about your nan. There are a few details to sort out.'

Thistle looked confused. 'Details? What sort of details?'

'Well,' I demurred, unsure how much to tell her, 'we have a few questions.'

'Indeed,' Grace interrupted, appearing in the doorway. 'There are a few things we still need to look into.' He smiled at Thistle. 'Thank you so much for coming.' He glanced at me. 'I'll take things from here. PC Hackert, you should stay.'

Fred nodded and I left them to it. The last thing Thistle Thorn needed right now was to be crowded by police officers. Fred had established a rapport with the bereaved pixie and DS Grace was taking over the case. I had other avenues to pursue.

GRACE AND FRED remained closeted with Thistle when Pralk called me back. 'Okay, DC Bellamy,' he said cheerfully, 'I've got three names for you. Only one is a bank employee, but they all have some connection to Hackney. I seriously doubt that any of them are involved in your murder, but I understand that you want to leave no stone unturned.'

Bless him. 'I really appreciate this. You worked fast to get those names.'

'We're a small community.' He paused. 'And the last time a goblin was on the wrong side of the law was more than a hundred years ago, when a gentleman by the name of Addicus Jones walked out of a shop without paying for his newspaper.'

Point taken. 'None of them are suspects, Mr Pralk. I'm merely following up possible leads.'

'As you wish,' he said mildly. 'I've emailed you their details.'

I thanked him again and hung up, then printed out Pralk's information and headed for the door.

'Should I inform the Hackney team what you're doing?' Liza enquired.

Not a chance. 'This is a wild goose chase, but at the moment I've nothing more important to do. They don't need to know unless I turn anything up.' And, regardless of any strange prophecies, the chances of that were remote indeed.

I flashed her a quick smile. The first address was practically round the corner. I'd be back in time for lunch.

As ROBERT SULLIVAN HAD PROVED, people react in very different ways to the police showing up at their door. Most are fearful, worried that we're going to impart some terrible news. A surprising number appear guilty, hands shaking and nervous sweat breaking out on their brow, as if they believe their crimes have finally caught up with them. In those circumstances, they've often done nothing illegal – it's down to a genuine fear of the police which, I have to admit, is sometimes depressingly justified. There's even a word for it: capiophobia.

Some people are filled with bluff and bluster, squaring off in a show of defiance; others – often the saddest cases – are happy to see us. And then there are those like the golden-skinned Felicious

Wort who are merely irritated. I couldn't entirely blame him. It looked as if my knock had woken him up.

'Whadda ya want?' he snapped.

I introduced myself, although it was clear from his manner that he knew who I was. 'I have a few questions for you, Mr Wort,' I said. 'But if you're busy, I can come back later or you can pop down to Supe Squad within the next day or two when you're free. It's not urgent. I won't take up much of your time.'

He adjusted his pyjama trousers and glared. 'Ask now. Whatever this is, let's get it over and done with.' He sniffed loudly. 'I ain't done nothing.'

I kept my smile professional, relieved that I could tick him off my list so quickly. 'I believe your girlfriend lives in Hackney?'

Wort's eyebrows snapped together. 'How'd you know that?'

I didn't answer.

A rumble sounded in his chest and he bared his teeth. 'Fine,' he said. 'Yeah, she lives there. She's human. So what?'

'When did you last visit her there?'

'The weekend.' He rubbed his eyes. The longer we spoke, the more alert he was becoming. And the more annoyed. Then something seemed to occur to him and his eyes widened. 'Wait,' he said. 'Wait. Is she—?'

I hastily interrupted him. 'This isn't about her. I have no reason to believe she's not there now.'

Wort's body sagged with relief and I castigated myself for not being clearer from the start. He pulled away from the door but left it wide open. He hadn't invited me in, so I stayed where I was, wondering where he'd disappeared to.

A moment later he returned with his phone to his ear. 'You're sure you're alright?' he said into the handset. I heard a tinny voice reply. 'Alright, alright. Jus' checking. Talk to you later, babe.' He disconnected and glowered at me again.

'My apologies, Mr Wort. I didn't mean to alarm you. I have one more question for you.'

His lip curled. 'Go on then.'

'Where were you two nights ago?' I asked.

'Working,' he said. 'Night shift.' He yawned. 'Like last night when I was called in at the last minute because the other guy didn't show.' He looked at me pointedly. 'Your day is my night, detective.'

'I'll be out your way in a moment. Can your employer verify you were there?'

'Yes,' he bit out. 'I work at a warehouse as a security guard. A few of us do.' He tilted his head. 'Or did you think every goblin works in finance?' he sneered. 'We're not all with the Talismanic bank, you know. My firm often hires goblins. We look good and we're trustworthy.'

I smiled politely. 'What's the name of the firm?'

Wort sighed at the continuing imposition. 'Wait here.' He disappeared again, this time returning with a business card. 'Here,' he said, thrusting it towards me. 'All their details are there. I clocked in at 10pm and clocked out at eight in the morning.'

'Thank you. I appreciate your time and your help.'

'What am I supposed to have done?'

'Nothing, Mr Wort. Nothing at all.'

He grunted and closed the door. I turned and started to walk away, then I halted in the middle of the path. Wait a minute. I knocked on Wort's door again. He flung it open with some force. 'What now?' he snapped.

'The person who didn't show up for their shift last night,' I said. 'Was it a goblin too?'

Wort's eyes narrowed. 'What if it was?'

'Who was it?' I asked.

He stared at me. 'Gilchrist Boast.'

'Does Mr Boast regularly miss his shifts?'

'Not as a rule.' He folded his arms. 'Thought you were asking about two nights ago. Not last night.'

I chose not to respond to that. 'Do you happen to know where Mr Boast lives?'

There was a dark cloud of suspicion on Wort's face. 'Plant Lane. Dunno what number, but it's the house with the blue door next to the pub.'

'Thank you, Mr Wort.'

'What's this about?'

I was already walking away. I wasn't sure I could explain, even if I tried. 'Thanks for your time. I won't bother you again,' I called over my shoulder. 'Sleep well.'

CHAPTER SIX

PLANT LANE WAS AN INTERESTING STREET. FOR ONE THING, IT WAS remarkably short. And narrow. Old cobblestones, often cracked in places, lined the road.

Nothing beyond a Smart car could have driven down it – even Tallulah would have struggled. On the one hand, it meant that the residents enjoyed a quiet, traffic-free zone; on the other hand, they'd have the daily nightmare of finding somewhere nearby to park. It wasn't the place to live if you were a petrolhead.

I found the pub quickly enough because it was the only business on the street. It was firmly closed to customers. I peered in through the grimy windows but saw no signs of life. A sign on the door indicated that it would open at four o'clock, hours away.

I located the house with the blue door which was, as Felicious Wort had said, right next to the pub. It possessed neither number nor name, but that didn't seem to stop the postman who'd stuffed a bunch of letters and junk mail into the letterbox.

I rapped sharply but, although I waited for several moments and knocked loudly again, nobody answered.

I abandoned the door and headed for the ground-floor

windows. In the nearest window, a closed blind obscured whatever lay beyond. I traipsed round the corner and found a smaller window with frosted glass, probably for the bathroom. Fortunately, it had been propped open; unfortunately, it was too high to be an easy vantage point.

I jumped up and tried to peer through the gap. Bath – check. Toilet – check. I jumped again. Red towel hanging on the back of the door. Toothbrush and toothpaste in a slim container on the side of the sink. I tried to call through the gap. 'Hello? Mr Boast? It's the police. I'm from Supe Squad. My name's Emma Bellamy and I'm here to check on your welfare.'

No answer. Maybe he'd not shown up for work last night because he'd taken an impromptu holiday, or there was a family emergency and he'd been called away. I jumped up for a third time and glanced through the bathroom door to the hallway beyond.

That looked like a pair of feet lying awkwardly on the grey carpet. Shit. He wasn't on holiday.

Returning to the front door, I glanced around. It was possible that Boast left a spare key with one of his neighbours. It was also possible that he was still alive in there and had merely collapsed. Time could be a factor in his continued existence and I couldn't delay. I called for an ambulance, then I splintered the Yale lock with one blow and broke down the door.

It didn't take long to discover that I was already too late.

Boast was lying on his back, his arms and legs spreadeagled. His eyes were wide and staring and, when I knelt down to check for a pulse, I felt nothing but cold skin. He'd been dead for hours. I hissed under my breath.

I couldn't see any wounds or obvious reason for his sudden death, but there was no way he'd died of natural causes. The mark on his cheek meant that he must have been murdered. I didn't need to squint to know what it was: blood in the form of a lipstick mark, in the exact spot where Peter Pickover's cheek had been left bare. The deaths were connected; they had to be.

I rocked back on my heels and briefly closed my eyes. Nothing about this made any sense and I had a sickening sensation in the pit of my stomach. It was going to get a lot worse before it got better.

I swallowed hard and opened my eyes again. Was the bloodied kiss the only mark or was there something else to find here? I couldn't move Boast's body to check for wounds without disturbing the scene, so I only had my eyes to rely on for now.

I glanced up and saw the arcing spray of dark blood on the nearby wall, then surveyed Boast's body. He was fully clothed in his security guard's uniform. Whatever had happened here must have started just before he was going to leave for work. The warehouse was at least twenty minutes' drive, which meant it had begun before 9.40pm.

I clenched my jaw. Could I have prevented his death if I'd acted upon Zara's information? There would be time for personal recriminations later.

Boast's hands were clenched, but the index finger on his right hand was unfurled. I checked his left hand and swallowed; the index finger was missing. There was very little blood, suggesting it had been removed post-mortem. It had been done for a reason.

With no sign of Boast's severed finger, I turned my attention back to the digit that remained attached. It appeared to be pointing at something. I looked up; there was a room directly in line with the fingertip.

I stood up shakily and peered inside. I didn't register anything out of the ordinary, and before I could investigate further I heard a shout from the front door.

The paramedics had arrived. Like me, they were far, far too late.

Detective Chief Inspector Donald Murray ran a hand through his thick mane of chestnut-brown hair. 'Run through it for me one more time,' he said.

There were only so many ways I could tell the same story. 'A woman tried to gain access to Heart.'

'That's the club that belongs to your boyfriend.' He paused before adding importantly, '*The* Lord Horvath.'

'Uh, yes. She said she wanted to speak to him – and me. We met her at the entrance and she was escorted outside.'

'That's when she told you to look for a goblin? A goblin who had Peter Pickover's peck of pickled peppers?' Murray's brow creased as he attempted to make sense of it.

'He does have a peck, sir,' DI Colquhoun said grimly. 'He's got a peck on his cheek.'

I grimaced. DCI Murray, however, lost his frown and now appeared remarkably enthusiastic. 'Excellent stuff. Excellent stuff.' He rubbed his hands together. 'All you know about this woman is that her name's Zara?'

'I'm afraid so. And that she says she's a Cassandra.'

He tapped his mouth. 'Well, pretending you can tell the future is one way to try and get out a double-murder charge.'

I shook my head. 'I don't think she's the killer, sir.'

'Why not?'

'I was late. I didn't arrive at Heart until after nine o'clock, and I left with Lukas less than twenty minutes later. How could she have got from the scene of the murder to the club in that time? Gilchrist Boast would have left for work before she arrived.'

'Unless she turned into a bat and flew here.' He stared at me. 'Is that not a thing?'

I had no idea whether his question was serious or not. 'Um. No.'

He shrugged. 'Shame. Well, we still have to trace her to find out what else she knows.'

I couldn't argue with that.

'I'll set up a meeting with one of our artists,' Murray went on. 'If we can get a description of her and turn it into an e-fit, maybe we can track her down.'

I nodded. Whatever Zara's involvement was, we did need to talk to her again.

'Two linked murders,' Murray breathed. 'One more, and we'll have a serial killer on our hands.' From the way he spoke, it appeared that was what he was hoping for. By contrast, Colquhoun was studying the floor.

One of the uniformed officers appeared in the doorway. 'The, er, blood expert is here.'

If anything, Murray's excitement increased and he beamed. 'Show him in!' Then he seemed to think of something. 'Wait. No, don't show him in. I'll meet him outside. Have him wait at the cordon and I'll greet him there.'

He licked his palms, smoothed back his hair and adjusted his tie. Then he drew back his lips and thrust his mouth in Colquhoun's direction so she could tell him if there was any trapped food between his molars. She nodded; all I could do was blink.

I hadn't expected the SIO to be so keen to take up my suggestion of involving a vampire in the investigation, and I certainly hadn't expected him to worry about his appearance before meeting that vampire. Maybe attitudes towards supes had altered more than I'd realised.

As soon as Murray had turned his back on Colquhoun and marched out of the room, she rolled her eyes.

'DCI Murray,' I started. 'Is he—?'

She shook her head. 'Don't,' she said. She sighed heavily. 'Just don't.'

Her lack of an answer didn't diminish my curiosity.

As I left, I watched Murray stride down Plant Lane towards the cordon holding back the press and public. Lukas was waiting there, his arms folded and his expression blank. I wasn't surprised that he'd come after I'd called and requested the help of a vampire; after all, he was the one who'd suggested a vamp could help with any blood-related matters.

Now that a member of the supe community had been killed, Lukas would have put everything else on hold to get involved. It probably wouldn't be long before the werewolf clans would also jump forward to help. I wondered if DCI Murray would welcome them with open arms and slicked-back hair, too.

He marched straight up to Lukas. They shook hands, with Murray pumping vigorously before clapping Lukas on the back like they were old friends. Several camera flashes exploded, and the crowd of reporters yelled questions. Murray didn't answer any of them, but I noticed that he angled himself towards the journalists with the sort of wide-legged stance that politicians often adopt to appear powerful. Ah. Murray hadn't been adjusting his appearance for Lukas, he'd been making himself look good for the cameras. Suddenly, several things started to make sense.

I went back inside. I had no desire to be in the next day's newspapers.

Lukas flashed me a crooked grin when he finally entered behind Murray.

'Here,' DCI Murray declared with a flourish, 'is the dead body.'

Lukas brushed past him and knelt beside Gilchrist Boast's corpse. His jaw was tight as he examined the goblin. 'Do you have the blood sample?' he asked.

Murray nodded at one of the uniformed officers, who darted forward with a small, sealed, plastic container. Lukas unscrewed the lid and sniffed the sample of Peter Pickover's blood, then drew closer to the bloody mark on Boast's cheek.

I wasn't the only person in the narrow hallway who leaned forward, anticipating what Lukas was going to say. Even DI

Colquhoun held her breath. It didn't take him long. 'Yes,' he said darkly. 'They're a match.'

Only DCI Murray smiled. 'Fabulous!'

Lukas glanced at me. I did my best not to react.

'You know,' Murray remarked to nobody in particular, 'every SIO should have a vampire on the team. It's much faster than using a laboratory. Instant results. That's my kind of thing!'

Lukas inclined his head. 'I'm glad to be of help.'

'And I thank you for that help,' Murray said pompously. 'DI Colquhoun will show you back to the cordon.'

Lukas didn't move. 'There's more.'

'More what?'

Lukas glanced my way again. 'More blood. It's faint, but I can smell it lingering somewhere else in this house.'

My eyes darted to the living room. Lukas stood up and walked over, hovering in the doorway and scanning every inch of the room. 'There,' he said. 'In that frame on the sideboard. That's blood – the same blood.'

I moved over to look, and so did Murray and Colquhoun. All three of us stared at the small, framed picture. It was crudely done. 'That's a double decker-bus, right?' I said.

Colquhoun nodded. 'Painted in blood.'

'There at the bottom,' Murray said. ' Where the … artist's signature should be. Is that—?'

'Gilchrist Boast's finger? Yeah, it looks like it.' I said. The severed finger had been clumsily taped to the picture with Sellotape.

'Not just painted in blood, finger-painted in blood.' Colquhoun turned to me. 'What the fuck is going on?'

I couldn't answer. I had no earthly idea.

CHAPTER SEVEN

AT THAT MOMENT, THE ONLY PERSON WHO BELIEVED A PRESS conference was a good idea was the man at the makeshift podium – the Senior Investigating Officer. It was his show.

'Murray's not a bad detective,' Colquhoun murmured. 'And he's not a bad SIO.'

I didn't say anything. I was waiting for the 'but'.

'But he's ambitious,' she continued. 'He wants to be one of the Met bigwigs.'

I had no issue with ambition, but I did have an issue with ambition that got in the way of results or compromised safety. The fastest way to make a name for yourself is to get yourself into the public eye, and that was why DCI Murray was standing in front of a gaggle of journalists. But we didn't have any answers and our only lead was Zara – and there was no sign of her. Releasing information to the press might encourage the killer to murder again. Murray hadn't taken time to consider the implications of what he was about to do.

He tapped the microphone and it whined in response. 'Ladies and gentlemen,' he intoned. The microphone whined again. An irritated scowl crossed his face and he turned it off. He raised his voice so that he could be heard. 'I have a brief statement to make and then I will accept questions,' he shouted.

The journalists stirred eagerly, arms outstretched and phones pressed to record.

'Two nights ago, the body of a man in his forties was found at a house on Hanover Street in Hackney. We have identified the victim as a human male named Peter Pickover. His murder was particularly gruesome and, as a result, I immediately felt there were supernatural elements to consider. For that reason, I called in Supernatural Squad to advise.' He pointed at me.

I did my best not to cringe and cursed him for ordering my presence at the conference. The sole reason I was there was to make him look good.

'This morning a second victim, a male goblin, was found murdered at an address close by, together with blood from the victim in Hackney. In order to fast track our investigation, I called in London's leading vampire, Lord Horvath, to help. We have two victims, one human and one supe. As a result of Lord Horvath's help, we believe we have one killer.'

While my skin prickled uncomfortably, DCI Murray paused for effect. 'We are calling him the Cupid Killer.'

I looked up. Were we?

'If any members of the public have information, we want to hear it. Our enquiries will be extensive, and I would like to take this opportunity to reassure the public that no stone will be left unturned. I would also like to tell the Cupid Killer that his murdering days are numbered. I will not stand for such terrible acts occurring in my glorious city.'

Colquhoun snorted. 'I'm sure the *Cupid Killer* is quaking in his boots,' she muttered under her breath.

I absolutely refused to call him the Cupid Killer.

Murray gave a grandiose flick of his head. 'I will now take questions.'

'Why have you given him the name of Cupid Killer?' the first journalist asked.

Murray looked delighted that she'd asked. Apparently he couldn't wait to reveal the gory detail. 'Both victims were found with kiss marks on their cheeks.' He pointed helpfully to his own cheek in case the journalists weren't familiar with that part of a person's anatomy.

'So you have DNA samples? Saliva?'

'The kiss marks were created,' Murray paused for effect, 'with blood.'

That caught everyone's interest. I guessed I should be grateful that we'd managed to persuade Murray to avoid mentioning the painting. There are good reasons why every single detail of an investigation is not released to the public.

'Is there any connection between the two victims?'

'We're looking into that,' Murray said.

'Is the killer a supe or a human?'

'We're looking into that.'

'What do you think the motives are for these murders?'

'We're looking into that.'

I sighed. Instead of looking like we were on top of the crimes, this press conference was making us look like idiots who knew nothing. I pursed my lips. Actually, that part was true.

'Will there be more murders? Should people be afraid?'

Murray sidestepped giving an answer. 'I will do everything I can to find the person responsible for these reprehensible crimes.' He nodded gravely. 'Thank you for your time.'

The journalists yelled a further barrage of questions as Murray stepped down from the podium. He twitched his finger to indicate that Colquhoun and I should follow him into the waiting police van.

'It's a shame it's not February,' he remarked, once the van doors were closed. He looked at us both expectantly.

I supposed I had to bite. 'Why is that, sir?' I asked politely.

'Well, then we could have called him the Valentine Killer. It's more menacing.'

Uh-huh. 'I think, sir, that the fact we're dealing with two murders is menacing enough,' I said. 'And perhaps we ought to consider the differences between both scenes. I know the blood links them and Zara led us here, but—'

Murray's eyes narrowed. 'Let's not over-complicate matters. Do not think for one second, Bellamy, that I am making light of these terrible crimes. There's a killer on the streets and the public need to know what's going on so they can take appropriate action. They need to protect themselves and inform us of anything that will lead to the bastard's arrest. And public aware-ness will help me to request more manpower and funding. I am SIO here – you are a DC who is only along for the ride.'

He sniffed. 'I had planned to send you to find this Zara woman and bring her in for questioning after you've spoken to the e-fit artist. It's what you should have done when she first approached you. But DI Colquhoun can do that. You can man the phones to see what information *my* press conference turns up.'

Bugger. Perhaps I ought to have tempered my tone.

DI Colquhoun intervened. 'With all due respect, sir, if Zara's skills are real then she's part of the supe community. She's more likely to speak to a member of Supe Squad than to me.'

'She's a person of interest and you're a police detective, ' he snapped. 'Find her and get her to talk. Do your job.'

'What about Lord Horvath?' I asked.

'Your boyfriend has done what we needed him to do. He's not a part of this investigation.' He glared at me. 'Now go. You have your orders.'

LUKAS HANDED me a cup of takeaway coffee. 'Remind me again why you wanted to be in the police,' he said mildly,

I sent him a sideways look but didn't bother answering. He looped an arm round my shoulders. 'Any thoughts on suspects?'

'Nothing useful.' I sighed. 'Just…' My voice trailed off.

'What?'

I wrinkled my nose. 'Peter Pickover's house was gruesome – beyond gruesome. There was so much blood that it leaked into the flat below, but it wasn't a messy scene. Boast's murder was careless, with far less attention to detail. I'm not denying the kiss link with Gilchrist Boast, but they are two very different murder scenes. It's also highly unusual for someone to kill both supes and humans without good reason.'

'You think there might be two killers working together?'

'It's possible. More often than not, serial killers choose a particular type of victim. Boast and Pickover were single males, but that's the only real similarity between them.'

Lukas frowned. 'Are we talking serial killers?'

'Terrible as they are, two murders don't make a series.' I nibbled my bottom lip and mused aloud. 'Whether there's one murderer or two, they came from somewhere. You don't leap straight from the starting blocks into exsanguinating a living, breathing person or dismembering a corpse. Both scenes were contrived in their own separate ways. It feels like there's more going on here.'

Lukas didn't disagree. 'So what's the plan? Where will you start?'

'The phones.' I cursed under my breath. 'It's my punishment for saying the first thing that came into my head. I have to spend the rest of the day listening to tips from the public.'

'You don't think you'll get anything useful?'

'Murray has set up an anonymous tip line. Even if someone has something useful to tell us, there's a good chance it will get lost amongst the hundreds of kooks, cranks and time wasters.'

'Can I help?'

I glanced up at him. 'The Metropolitan Police thanks you for your support and no longer requires your services.'

'Mm.' He gave me an arch look and repeated his question. 'Can I help?'

'Find out everything you can about Gilchrist Boast. We need to know if there's any link between him and Pickover.'

Lukas smiled. 'Consider it done.'

The police van door opened and DCI Murray stepped out. He squinted into the sunlight then spotted Lukas and me. He pulled back his shoulders and looked as if he were about to storm over. I didn't need to give him more reason to be pissed off with me. 'Thanks for the drink, Lukas.'

'My pleasure, D'Artagnan.' He kissed my lips. 'Keep in touch.'

I nodded, drained my cup, and headed off to play my part as a call-centre operator.

'I MURDERED THAT MAN IN HACKNEY.'

I leaned back in my chair. Why were standard-issue headsets always so uncomfortable?

'And then I murdered that goblin.'

'What's your name, sir?' I asked.

'Kill-A-Lot. Sir Kill-A-Lot.'

'Are you aware, Sir Kill-A-Lot, that lying and wasting police time is an offence punishable by up to six months in prison?'

'I'm not lying. I killed them both.'

I eyed the half-empty packet of biscuits. A serving size was two biscuits and I'd eaten ten. It made sense to go ahead and finish the rest. 'Why did you shoot them?'

'Cos I felt like it! I took my gun and pow-pow-pow!' He started laughing. 'I'm a mean murdering machine!'

It was the glee in his voice that truly depressed me. I logged the details, including that he'd managed to get the basic facts of both murders wrong, then I pressed the answer button again. Call number forty-one. Whoop-dee-fucking-whoop.

'My neighbour came home at 3am on Thursday – 3.02, to be precise. I made a note of the time.'

'I see,' I said. 'And is there anything else that makes you think your neighbour is linked to the murders?'

'He's dodgy. I know he is. He's been carrying on with Mrs Belfry at number twenty-six. He's always slipping out to her house. He sneaks into her garden at night and they canoodle in her garden shed. And,' the man said importantly, 'he votes for the Green Party.'

I passed a hand across my forehead. 'Is that relevant?'

'Those naturists are all crazy.'

'Do you mean naturalists?'

'That's what I said. Anyway, you should check him out. Send a squad car round. And while you're at it, tell him that he has to cut back the tree at the bottom of his garden. It's encroaching on our space.'

'Is it possible that your neighbour was visiting Mrs Belfry on Thursday night? Or do you think he was elsewhere?'

Silence filled the line, and a moment later the caller hung up. I reached for yet another biscuit and made some notes. Did I think this neighbour was a brutal murderer? No, but everything had to be written down so it could be followed up if necessary.

I pinched off a headache and glanced round the room. Half a dozen police officers were manning the phones; from their expressions, none of them was having any more luck than I was.

A shadow fell across the desk. I glanced up at DI Colquhoun. 'Any joy?' she enquired.

I sighed. 'Nope.'

'Me neither. Without a surname, it's nigh on impossible to find your Zara. Even the e-fit picture, good as it is, hasn't helped. I toured Soho and Lisson Grove and spoke to several supes, but they shut me down whenever I mentioned I was looking for a

Cassandra. We're chasing whispers when we need something concrete. Meanwhile, the internet is filled with Cupid Killer conspiracy theories,' she added grimly.

DCI Murray's wish for publicity had been fulfilled, but with publicity came pressure. We needed to get some results soon because the public's patience would grow very thin very quickly. I hoped that no corners would be cut in the process – and no more lives would be lost.

'Two murders within twenty-four hours of each other, and not even a hint of evidence or a witness.' I shook my head. Colquhoun's frustration mirrored my own. 'We've got nothing.'

My phone buzzed. I glanced down at the screen then showed it to Colquhoun. 'What do you think?' I asked. 'Can I sneak away for an hour or two?'

She smiled. 'Sure. I've got your back.' She nodded at the phone. 'Let's hope she's got something useful to share.'

I grabbed my bag and stood up. 'Oh, believe me,' I said, 'she usually does.'

CHAPTER EIGHT

Dr Laura Hawes was elbow-deep in a corpse when I arrived. I knocked on the window to let her know I was there, then waited while she finished up. When she left the morgue room, she was beaming. It was hard to believe she'd spent the last hour digging around inside a dead body. 'Good to see you!'

I grinned back at her. 'You too!' As the first person to register my ability to rise from the dead, Laura had always held a special place in my heart, though I couldn't say that aloud. It sounded too damned weird.

'Thanks for coming down,' she said. 'I heard you were in Hackney and I know it's a trek from there. I hope I didn't pull you away from anything important. I could have sent you my report by email or called it through.'

I doubted that Sir Kill-A-Lot and copulating neighbours counted as important, not in this investigation. 'Honestly, Laura, it's a pleasure to be here, despite the circumstances.'

Her smile dimmed. 'Hmm, yes. Gilchrist Boast. His body is in the next examination room. Poor man.' She sighed. 'I doubt he even knew what hit him.'

She led me next door. Boast was lying on a steel gurney. She

58

pulled back the sheet that was covering him. 'It was a reasonably straightforward post-mortem. He was struck from behind with a heavy implement.' She pointed at his head. 'Three separate blows, each one with considerable force. From the angle, I suspect you're looking at someone about the same height as Mr Boast.'

I estimated that Boast had been about six foot tall, which was short for a goblin, but not for anyone else. Laura's theory hardly narrowed down the pool of potential suspects.

She continued. 'The first blow probably killed him, while the subsequent hits were unrelated to his death. The forensic techs found a cast-iron pan in the kitchen sink – it's stained with blood and appears to be the murder weapon. We'll know more when all the tests are done, but it fits with the wounds to his skull.'

'I was first on the scene,' I said. 'He was lying on his back, not his front.'

She nodded. 'It appears that he was moved after he died. I don't usually speculate about motive but I imagine it was so that the mark could be placed on his cheek. It was obviously done deliberately.' Her mouth flattened. 'His death was sealed with a bloody kiss.'

Indeed. It somehow made his murder far more gruesome – and that was probably the point. I sighed. Three full-handed blows meant that the killer wasn't taking any chances: he'd wanted Gilchrist Boast to die. His death had been brutal, fast and indelicate. That was quite at odds with the slow bloodletting that Peter Pickover had experienced.

I thought again about the spray of blood on the wall at Boast's house – and the lack of any similar marks at Pickover's flat. That had been done deliberately, but the marks on Boast's wall had not.

'The pan,' I said, changing tack. 'Do you know where it came from?'

'I thought you might ask that. The CSIs said it matched a set in Gilchrist Boast's kitchen, so it doesn't appear it was brought to the scene by the killer.'

I nodded slowly. So the killer hefted all their implements of death to Pickover's home, yet only used what was to hand at Boast's place. I pointed at his hand. 'What about the finger?'

Laura held up a baggie. 'The one found in the picture frame is definitely Boast's. It was removed soon after his death.'

I peered at it. It wasn't a clean cut: the edges of the flesh were ragged. Laura caught my thought. 'Whoever sliced his finger off found it hard. I don't think the techs have found the blade that was used, but it wasn't particularly sharp and there was consider-able ... sawing.'

I felt queasy. It didn't sound as if someone with medical expe-rience had done this – also unlike the Pickover scene. 'And the kiss mark on his cheek?'

'Again, I can't be sure until all the test results come back but it looks to have been daubed on with the tip of his own finger, like the painting of the bus was.'

Grim. I shuddered then focused on other things. Boast's killer must have come from behind him, from the kitchen where the murder weapon was located rather than from the front door. There had been no sign of forced entry and no broken windows. The murderer could have sneaked in through the open bathroom window, gone to the kitchen to grab the pan and waited for the right moment. Or Gilchrist Boast could have let them in.

'You've heard about the other murder?' I asked.

Laura nodded. 'I heard what your Lord Horvath said, and I had a copy of the initial post-mortem report sent over. Peter Pickover appears to have been injected with a considerable amount of atropine prior to his blood loss.'

'Atropine?'

'One of Agatha Christie's favourite poisons. It breaks down in the human body quickly, so it's not always detectable unless you test for it early. It's also common because it's used in many routine medical procedures – eye drops, for example. In the right quantities it's a life saver, but in the wrong hands…'

She pulled a face. 'It would have made it easier to overwhelm Peter Pickover. He was probably already unconscious by the time his blood was being drained. And yes,' she said before I could ask, 'I've already sent a sample of Gilchrist Boast's blood for atropine testing. I'll let you know as soon as I've got the results. What I can confirm is that Horvath was correct: the kiss mark on Boast's cheek is a match for Pickover's blood.'

Talking to Laura and learning what she'd uncovered usually calmed me and answered at least some of my questions. This time, however, my sense of foreboding only increased. There was a bigger picture here, but somehow I wasn't seeing it. Yet.

I met Laura's eyes. I didn't want to put words into her mouth, or plant ideas in her head, but I really needed to know what she was thinking. 'These two murders,' I started.

Thankfully, she interrupted. 'If it weren't for the obvious blood link, I'd have said they were committed by different people.'

Should I be pleased that her assessment matched mine, or dismayed that we thought there might be two murderers? 'Thank you,' I said. 'I appreciate your candour.'

'Always.' She smiled. 'In other news, I should tell you that I was approached by a werewolf yesterday. He wants a second opinion on a recent pixie post-mortem.'

Oh. My shoulders sagged further. 'A Sullivan werewolf?'

'Yep. Since my work with you, I've been getting a lot of supe-related jobs. As you can see.' She nodded at Gilchrist Boast's body. 'But I've never had a request from a werewolf. Usually they carry out their post-mortems in house. From what the wolf said, that happened with the pixie. I can't imagine why he doesn't trust his own people's work.'

'Let's just say he's a wolf on a mission. Are you going to do it?'

'It depends on the next of kin. I hear there's a granddaughter?'

I nodded. I didn't know what Thistle Thorn would want, and I was suddenly glad it wasn't my case. I dreaded to think how Robert Sullivan would react if Thistle refused to allow a second examination. 'Sometimes,' I said softly, 'the world seems so very fucked up.'

Laura's face lit with concern. 'Are you okay, Emma?'

'I'm fine. It's a been a long day, that's all.' I smiled at her.

'I'm always here if you need to blow off steam. I'm a good listener.'

'Honestly, I'm fine.' I broadened my smile. 'I'd better go. I've got at least one killer to catch.'

Laura grinned, but I felt her eyes on my back as I left.

I FOUND DCI Murray in his office, standing with his arms folded as he watched the clips of his press conference on the news. I wondered how many times he'd already watched them, then shook my head. His preoccupation with his public image wasn't my concern. 'Sir?' I prompted.

He turned and frowned when he saw me. 'What is it, Emma?'

'I think we need to give more credence to the idea that there are two killers, not one. I've been speaking to the pathologist who completed Gilchrist Boast's post-mortem—'

'You were supposed to be on the phones.'

I drew in a deep breath. 'Sir, she thinks there are distinct differences between the MOs at both scenes. So do I. The victims were killed in completely different ways—'

'They're linked by the blood. Your own damned boyfriend confirmed that.'

'The blood doesn't mean there aren't two separate killers working together.'

'Did Hannibal Lecter work with someone else? Did Norman Bates?'

This probably wasn't a good time to mention that they were both fictional characters. 'Sir—'

A uniformed officer popped his head into the door. 'We've got something,' he said breathlessly. 'It came through on the tip line.'

Murray immediately brightened. 'The tip line? *My* tip line?' He looked at me triumphantly. 'Well, what do you know? To think, Emma, if you'd done as I told you, you might have received the call.' He turned back to the officer. 'So what is it, constable? Information? A witness?'

The constable smiled. 'It's a video.'

Murray pumped the air with his fist. 'Yahtzee.'

I couldn't disagree.

THE CONFERENCE ROOM WAS PACKED. DCI Murray positioned himself at the front beside the large screen with the remote control in his hand.

'Dashcam footage,' he said proudly. He thumped his fist against his hand, making a loud slapping noise that echoed round the room. 'Dashcam footage that we wouldn't have if I hadn't insisted we go public. The upstanding member of the public who sent it in checked what they had after seeing my press conference on television.'

He beamed proudly. 'This could prove vital. It was captured early on Friday morning on Belldown Avenue. For those of you who weren't paying attention, that's where the bucket containing Peter Pickover's blood was found.' He raised the remote control and, with a flourish, pressed play.

Although the video had been taken at night, the street lighting and quality of the camera meant the footage was crisp and clear. The time stamp confirmed the date and stated it was past 2am. Even though I'd already watched it several times, I leaned forward with everyone else and stared at it again.

The useful part was only a few seconds long, but it provided a wealth of information. I had to admit reluctantly that the tip line had done its job. We didn't have a smoking gun – far from it – but I was woman enough to agree that this video could be invaluable.

The car passed right by the rubbish bin where the bloodied bucket had been left, and the bucket was visible on the approach. What was of far greater interest was the cyclist who'd stopped and was leaning over it with something in his hand.

The mutter rose and fell across the room. 'Is that him?' someone asked. 'Is that the Cupid Killer?'

Murray shook his head. 'I don't believe so. We know from the post-mortem and the 999 call from the couple in the flat below Pickover's that his murder must have taken place closer to eleven. The cyclist is seen here three hours later. He's unlikely to have hung around the area for that long. It would have been too risky.'

'So is he a random passer-by who noticed the bucket?'

'Possibly,' Murray said. 'But I have formulated another theory.' He pressed the remote again and zoomed in on the cyclist's hand. The heads of everyone in the room tilted as they squinted.

'Is that—?'

Murray smiled. 'A vacutainer? Yes. Known as a blood-collection tube to you and me.' He glanced at me for the merest flicker of a second before continuing.

'There are differences between the crime scenes. Although blood from Peter Pickover was found on Boast's body and the Cassandra linked them, we have nothing else to suggest that both men were killed by the same person. The style of death is different. The crime scenes are different. We have to consider whether one killer dealt with Pickover, then left some of his blood on Belldown Avenue to be picked up by a second killer, who took a sample of it to use on Gilchrist Boast.'

He put down the remote control and linked his fingers. 'People,' he said gravely, 'we need to expand our search. It's highly probably we are looking for two killers, not one.'

There was a moment of silence, then the room exploded in a chorus of mutters, gasps and curses. DCI Murray rocked back on his heels and watched the commotion for a few moments before bringing everyone back to order.

'Bertrand,' he said, pointing to a sombre detective with a lined face and rumpled shirt, 'your team have been looking at relevant convictions from recent years. You can narrow that down by focusing on violent criminals who were in jail at the same time. Who shared a cell? Can we come up with any suspects that way?'

He nodded at another detective. 'Focus on the cyclist. What make of bike is that? What about the helmet? Can we track those purchases and find our man? Is there more CCTV footage from either location with our second Cupid Killer?'

He paused. 'To differentiate, let's call him the Stupid Killer. After all, he's the one who got caught on camera.' He smiled happily. 'Cupid and Stupid. Find Stupid.'

Murray dealt out more tasks and I waited patiently, although I reckoned I knew what was coming. 'Colquhoun, stay on that bloody Cassandra woman. And Bellamy!' he barked. 'Tomorrow you're on the phones again.' He glared at me. 'This time I don't want to hear that you think such an assignment is beneath you. Our only real lead has come from the tip line.'

Everyone was looking at me – and judging. I wanted to protest that I didn't think answering phones was beneath me but I had skills and connections that could be put to better use, but It wouldn't do me any good.

I knew why Murray had publicly called me out: he didn't understand that there was no need to put me in my place and I didn't care that he'd taken credit for the two-killer theory. At the end of the day, we were on the same team and wanted the same thing – to find the bastards who'd done this.

'Finally,' Murray said, 'nobody is to talk to the press other than me. We'll keep any suggestion of a second killer quiet. The public don't need to worry any more than they already are. All press requests and questions come straight to me. Got that?'

We nodded.

DS Colquhoun sidled up to me. 'Betcha five quid it'll be on the news by tomorrow morning,' she whispered.

'I'm not taking that bet,' I replied. No chance.

She grinned.

'Well?' Murray demanded, his hands on his hips. 'If it's the end of your shift, go home and get some rest. I need you fresh tomorrow. If you're still working, stop dilly-dallying and get to it. Come on, people! Let's find Cupid and Stupid before the day is out!'

CHAPTER NINE

I parked Tallulah in the first available space, patted her bonnet and told her to be good, then walked the short distance to the pub where I'd arranged to meet Lukas.

As soon as I pushed open the door, I saw him sitting on a bar stool. He was chatting to the bartender as if he'd been frequenting this establishment all his life, even though I was fairly certain he never came to this part of London. I definitely didn't. It seemed like a nice area, but it was out of the way and, as far as I knew, there was nothing here of special interest.

Lukas did nothing by accident, however. I was sure we were meeting here for a reason.

The pub was crowded with all manner of drinkers either on their way home from work or popping in for a quick brew to round off their night. It didn't really matter how busy it was because I'd still have found Lukas in a flash. He has the kind of presence that draws you towards him, regardless of who else is in the vicinity.

I allowed myself a moment of quiet ogling. Lukas often preferred flouncy clothes, with frills and long cuffs and dramatic shades of velvet. Tonight, though, he was dressed in a simple pair of black trousers and a salmon-pink shirt that was open at the neck. The pink contrasted perfectly with his inky dark hair and was just tight enough to reveal the faintest glimpse of the tight muscles that lay beneath. His dark hair curled at the collar and his mouth was enough to make me weak at the knees. I even found the flash of his white fangs alluring. I was, I had to admit, a complete Lord Horvath groupie. There are worse things.

I was admiring the curve of his arse on the stool when he turned and grinned at me. Almost reluctantly, I sidled through the crowd to join him.

'I hope you enjoyed the view,' he murmured as I kissed him briefly.

'You knew I was there?'

'Of course. I sensed you the moment you walked in.' The corners of his mouth crooked up. 'But I thought I'd allow you the chance for a salacious gawk first. I like it when you do that. Perhaps I can return the favour later.'

His black eyes travelled the length of my body. I was tired, frustrated, covered in the grime and failures of the day, but Lukas still made me feel good. Something inside me gave way and I felt my muscles relax.

I hopped onto the stool next to him. 'Why are we meeting here?'

He shook his head slightly to indicate that he'd tell me later. 'Tough day?' he asked instead.

'You saw how it started.' I sighed. 'Nobody else has died, but it's not been fun. We've got one or two leads, but nothing great.'

A young man approached us, tilting his head in Lukas's direction so that his neck was exposed. 'Hi,' he purred. 'Would you like—?'

'No,' Lukas interrupted. There was enough dark menace in his tone to make the man back off immediately. At my raised eyebrows, he shrugged. 'I could have said much worse.' He glanced round me. 'Is your crossbow in Tallulah?'

I nodded.

'You're going to need it.'

'I don't think that kid deserves to be shot, Lukas.'

'Ha. Ha.' He gave me a little nudge. 'I'll pay my tab and meet you outside.'

I slipped out of the pub into the cool evening air and glanced up and down the road out of habit, as much as anything. A couple were walking hand in hand on the opposite side, there was an elderly woman trundling a shopping trolley along the pavement, and a group of teenagers cackling uproariously. So far so normal, but I wasn't about to gainsay Lukas's suggestion.

I scooted back to Tallulah to grab my trusty crossbow. Appearances could be deceptive. Maybe this wasn't the quiet leafy human suburb I assumed it was.

I pulled on the shoulder straps and secured the crossbow to my back, from where I could easily slide it out at a moment's notice. By the time I was done, Lukas was at my side. I gave him a quick smile and cut to the chase. 'So? What are we doing here, Lukas? Where are we going?'

He grimaced slightly. 'There's a … club here.'

'A club? What, like bowling? Stamp collecting? Book club?'

'Not that kind of club.' He sighed. 'The kind that would be considered illegal if the authorities knew about it.'

I gave him a pointed look. 'Hello,' I said. 'My name is Detective Constable Emma Bellamy and I'm with the Metropolitan Police.'

He chuckled, although his smile didn't reach his eyes. 'You know as well as I do that the Met ignore certain activities that fall outside the bounds of the law when it's in their best interests to do so. I persuaded the club owner that neither of us would make any moves against him. He took some convincing, but I made several assurances.'

I stepped back. So this wasn't date night. 'You have to give me more information than that, Lukas.'

He met my eyes. 'You asked me to look into a connection between Gilchrist Boast and Peter Pickover, so I spent the afternoon making a lot of loud enquiries. It seemed like the best way to find out information quickly. After a couple of hours of phone calls and questions, I was contacted by the club's owner. He says that both Boast and Pickover have visited it repeatedly in recent months. I spoke to several goblins who confirmed that Boast was hanging out there a lot.'

I sucked in a breath; so there *was* a connection between the victims. My blood thrummed with anticipation. 'That's brilliant. Good work.'

Lukas pulled a face. 'I don't deserve the credit. It could have taken days to establish they both visited Fetish without the owner's help – its client list is strictly guarded.'

Fetish? 'This is a sex club? That's not illegal.' Not usually, anyway.

'It's not sex. It's ... everything.'

'Lukas—'

'It's easier to see for yourself than for me to explain.' He gazed at me sombrely. 'If that's a problem for you, tell me now. I can go in alone and make enquiries on your behalf. Fetish isn't the only place like this in this city. I turn a blind eye to these clubs because people need ways to blow off steam that ordinary activities can't always provide.'

My eyes narrowed. 'By ordinary, you mean legal.'

'You've always known my relationship with the English legal system is turbulent, Emma.'

Disagreeing with the law was different to breaking it but, until I knew exactly what went on at Fetish, it felt like a pointless argument. 'Why do I need my crossbow?' I asked softly, trying to moderate my tone.

'Sometimes things can get a little rowdy. A lot of the patrons at Fetish bring their weapons.' If that was supposed to make me feel better, it didn't. 'Emma?' Lukas prompted.

Fine. 'This is about solving the murders,' I said. 'I'll ignore anything I see that isn't relevant.'

'Good. It's not my sort of place, and a few of my people have put in serious complaints about it, but it does cater for a specific market. In its own way, Fetish serves a useful purpose.'

I nodded distractedly. The oily slick of unease in the pit of my belly was growing. I knew why I was going to Fetish, even if I still didn't know what the place was, but I didn't have a good feeling about it.

ON THE SURFACE, it was the most unlikely place in London for an illegal club. It was a quiet suburban street, the sort of place that had family SUVs, pristine doorsteps and flowerpots that nobody ever stole or pissed in. There was even an active neighbourhood watch.

I wondered if the residents nearby knew what went on in the walled-off house on the corner and chose to ignore it, or if they fully embraced it and took part. I was about to find out.

Lukas pressed the buzzer next to the large iron gates. 'Lord Horvath and guest,' he said into the speaker.

There was no reply but the gates immediately slid open without so much as a judder or a creak. I noted the security cameras at strategic points, as well as the three men standing around the narrow garden who were making no attempt to hide the guns they were carrying. That wasn't something you typically saw except outside airports and embassies. I bit back the temptation to ask if they held permits for their weapons.

I followed Lukas up the stone steps and into the house. Inside there was a dark hallway – and more security men. With a jolt, I saw that one of them was a vampire.

Lukas had said he turned a blind eye to what went on, but if one of his people was working here with his tacit agreement that meant more than a blind eye. My stomach tightened with wary suspicion. As if sensing it, Lukas reached over and squeezed my hand.

The vamp hung back while a teenager appeared from a nearby doorway, munching on a packet of crisps. She looked us over, her face expressionless. 'Weapons?'

Lukas shook his head. 'Not me.'

'Fangs?'

'Naturally.'

The girl delved into her packet, tossed another handful of crisps into her mouth and crunched loudly. 'You?' she asked.

I cleared my throat. 'Crossbow.'

'Silver?'

'Yes.'

'Are you intending to use it?'

I stared at her. 'Not unless I have to.'

She couldn't have looked less interested. 'Anything else?' she asked.

'No.'

The security men watched her. Without a flicker, she nodded at them and disappeared through the same doorway from which she'd arrived. The nearest guard grunted. He didn't ask to see my crossbow or to take it, but he made a note on his tablet.

'ID?' he demanded.

I dug out my warrant card and presented it. The guard nodded and took down my details. I was surprised when Lukas presented his driver's licence and the guard did the same. It was unusual for someone in the supe world not to know who I was, but it was extraordinary that anyone, either supe or human, did not recognise Lukas. He used to stay out of the limelight but that had changed in recent months; these days, his face was all over the place.

The vamp caught me staring. 'Club policy, ma'am,' he said. 'Everyone has to present ID, and everyone's attendance is recorded. It's to keep us all safe. There are no exceptions. The Queen herself could stroll in and she'd have to show her ID.'

Did the Queen have ID? I supposed a £20 note with her face on it might suffice. Anyway, it wasn't a bad policy and the lack of preferential treatment made me relax slightly. 'Thanks for explaining.'

'You're welcome.' The vamp's eyes shone. 'You're going to love it here. It's amazing.'

I wasn't quite so sure but I nodded anyway.

The other guard smiled too, happy now that all the entrance protocols had been observed. 'Have a good evening,' he said. He stepped back, allowing us access to whatever lay beyond.

The vamp inclined his head. 'My Lord,' he said to Lukas in a deeper, more dramatic tone. 'And DC Bellamy. Welcome to Fetish.'

I glanced at Lukas's face. He wasn't smiling, but he acknowl-edged the vamp with a brief nod. Once we were out of earshot, I said, 'I don't understand.'

'The vampire?'

'Yep.'

'It's his day off. He moonlights here. He's been doing it for a few months.'

'And you're okay with that?'

Lukas considered the question. 'It doesn't interfere with his work for me, and he's been honest about it. He asked for permis-sion before he started. I trust my people, Emma, and they've got their freedom. They're not beholden to my every whim. Some vamps hate Fetish, some vamps love it. We're all different.'

Fair enough. 'Who hates it?'

'Christopher, for one. He's repeatedly complained about it. Scarlett isn't a fan, either, although she doesn't moan about it quite as much. Fetish tends to inspire strong opinions.' He paused. 'But I'll say one thing about this place – it's certainly not bland. Everyone who's been here has something to say about it.'

'What about the teenage girl? What was that all about?'

He wrinkled his nose. 'The kid is supposed to be a truth seeker. It's said she can tell whether you're lying or not.'

'Can she?' She could have a wonderful career in the police if that were true.

'Honestly? I have no idea – which is why it's wise not to lie to her.'

'So the bloke who runs this place doesn't care if I bring in a crossbow? He only cares if I lie about it?'

'You can control what's known. It's the unknown that tends to cause problems.'

Hmm. I passed a hand across my forehead. 'In the interests of resolving the unknown then,' I said, with more than an edge of snark, 'who does run this damned club?'

'An … interesting man,' Lukas said. I doubted he meant interesting in a good way. He leaned into my ear. 'It's better if you make up your own mind about him.'

'Lukas,' I started, 'what do you—?'

He shook his head before I could finish the question. 'You'll see for yourself.'

I stared at him. What the hell were we getting into?

'It's fine,' he said. 'There's nothing to worry about.'

That statement encouraged me to worry even more, but there was no time to say anything else. The door at the end of the hallway opened of its own accord, and I heard the thump of music and the roar of voices.

It was time to find out what Fetish really was.

CHAPTER TEN

THE ROOM WAS VAST, OCCUPYING MOST OF THE GROUND FLOOR. There was so much going on that I didn't know where to look first.

Immediately to our left, two people were perched on either side of a round table. They were surrounded by a small crowd gazing eagerly as the pair arm wrestled. Neither appeared to be giving way and, judging by their straining biceps and the sweat dripping down their faces, they'd been at it for some time.

There were booths along the far side of the room like you'd find in a traditional American diner. Several were occupied, mostly with couples. At least three of the couples were engaged in far more than necking. I blinked rapidly and tried not to stare. That was a little more skin-to-skin action than I was comfortable with seeing in public.

But there was far more to Fetish than sex.

A bowling lane ran down part of the room, there was a full-sized tennis court in the far corner and what appeared to be a plunge pool next to it. In one alcove I saw a boxing ring and in another a firepit. Smack bang in the centre of the room was a raised stage. Two women were standing on it yelling Shake-spearean insults at each other.

I scratched my head. After what little Lukas had told me, I hadn't known what to expect. Now I understood why he hadn't tried to explain it to me; words alone couldn't do this place justice.

More than a few heads turned in our direction, and I saw expressions of wariness and fear. At least two people, one a were-wolf and the other whom I was certain was a druid, looked on the verge of bolting. It wasn't Lukas they were worried about, it was me. I smiled benignly at them.

'Is there anywhere we can get a drink?' I asked Lukas.

His black eyes gleamed as he recognised my discomfort and my concerted effort to hide it. 'There's a bar over here. The espresso martini is to die for.'

I spotted faded bloodstains on the floor near my feet and hoped that Lukas didn't mean that literally.

We strolled over. I swallowed as we passed a pixie sharpening a set of knives on a whetstone. He was bare chested, and his skin was dripping with blood. A vampire was gazing at the droplets and drooling.

'You know,' I said faintly, 'this is the sort of place that supe phobics imagine when they think about what we do in our free time.'

'There are as many humans here as there are supes,' Lukas replied mildly.

That much was true. We'd passed dozens of them so far, including a man in a gimp suit, a woman in a fairy costume, and at least four who weren't wearing anything at all. Despite the weirdness of it all, I'd yet to see anything that I could class as ille-gal, however.

We reached the bar. I wanted to maintain a clear head so I ordered an orange juice. Lukas requested a double vodka. I gave him a questioning look. 'Honestly, sometimes it's easier to deal with places like this when you're drunk,' he said.

'That's not very reassuring.'

He pulled a face. 'Sorry, D'Artagnan.'

We took our drinks to a small table near the bar. As soon as I sat down, there was a roar from the small crowd watching the women on stage. One of them was dancing around in delight while the other looked defeated. Several members of their audience started handing over money with pained expressions. They must have been betting on the outcome, although how the winner had been decided was beyond me. Interesting, indeed.

I took a sip of my juice and twitched uncomfortably. I knew without Lukas telling me that grabbing hold of the nearest customers or staff members and peppering them with questions wouldn't yield any answers. It would only make everyone keen to avoid me. But I didn't like this place. I couldn't say what in particular put me on edge – its illegality, perhaps. Whatever it was, I certainly wasn't enjoying myself.

Lukas squeezed my fingers. 'Stop thinking so hard,' he murmured. 'If you start to relax, everyone else will too and then you might get some information.'

Before I could respond, a trumpet sounded. The noise filled the space and everyone immediately fell silent. A second later, the lights were turned off and the vast room was plunged into darkness. I stiffened. What was going on now?

A voice boomed over the tannoy. 'Ladies and gentlemen, supes and humans, Fetish is proud to present tonight's main entertainment!'

Cymbals crashed and a spotlight illuminated the stage. A man was standing there, his head bowed. He had flowing green hair, but he was far too tall and broad to be mistaken for a pixie. He was barefoot, wearing ankle-length white-linen trousers and a shirt that caught the light as if it were made of sequins. On his face was the most extraordinary amount of make-up. The glitter and pink slash were reminiscent of Ziggy Stardust – or a cartoon character. To top it all off, he was holding what looked like a staff. Whoever this guy was, he wasn't shy about standing out in a crowd.

I glanced at Lukas. He nodded tightly. So this was the owner of Fetish.

The man slowly raised his head and, as he did so, music started to pump. It was a slow hum to begin with, gradually growing into a crescendo of drums and drama. He started to spin, moving in time with the music. I looked down and gasped. His feet were no longer touching the stage – he was spinning in mid-air.

'What the fuck?' I muttered.

Lukas nudged me in warning and I clamped my mouth shut. The music was almost unbearably loud. I was reaching up to cover my ears with my hands when there was a sudden bang and it stopped. The spotlight flashed once, then, after a second of total darkness, the lights came on.

The green-haired man was no longer on the stage but had somehow moved to the opposite side of the room and was standing next to the wall. I felt faintly sick as I saw that there were manacles and chains drilled into it.

My hands twitched, and involuntarily I reached for my cross-bow. I'd barely touched it when a security guard appeared in front of me. He shook his head. 'Nothing that is about to happen is against anyone's free will, detective,' he said quietly.

They all knew who I was. Whether that was good or bad remained to be seen.

'There is no problem here,' Lukas replied.

Despite the guard, I slid out my crossbow. He stepped back, but he didn't take his eyes off me.

'I am MC Jonas,' the green-haired man intoned.

From nowhere, a giggle bubbled up from my chest. There was something ridiculous about the way he was presenting himself. I

78

looked around but nobody else was laughing; they weren't even smiling. In fact, most of the audience were gazing at Jonas with something akin to awe.

'Some nights at Fetish are about pleasure,' Jonas continued. 'Some nights are about pain.' He smiled slowly. 'Some nights are about both. Our main contender for this evening's entertainment is Mr William Moss. Take a bow, Mr Moss!'

A thin man pushed his way out of the crowd. I squinted: he looked entirely human to me. A cheer rose from the onlookers and he beamed broadly, bowing to his audience. He certainly didn't look as if he were being forced into anything.

'William Moss, do you participate freely and without compulsion?'

Moss raised his head and yelled to the ceiling, 'I do!' The crowd roared with delight.

Moss walked over to the manacles and allowed Jonas to chain his wrists and his ankles.

'The challenge is this,' Jonas said. 'William Moss cannot utter a sound between now and midnight. If he remains silent, he wins.' He raised a finger and pointed around the room. 'If any of you can make him speak, squeak or gasp, you will win. Dismemberment and broken bones are forbidden, but everything else is fair game. One hundred pounds to participate. Either Mr Moss takes the pot home at the end of the night, or one of you lucky people will.' He turned his finger to Moss. 'What happens to him is up to you!'

William Moss was still grinning.

'The challenge,' Jonas bellowed, 'starts now!'

Almost immediately three people jumped forward and thrust money towards Jonas. He shook his head and gestured at a young woman standing at the side holding a bucket. The first person dropped in the money then darted towards Moss. Without any warning, he slammed his knee into Moss's stomach. Moss doubled over. Jesus.

I sprang up, ignored Lukas's hissed warning and pushed past the security guard before marching through the crowd.

'Oi! You can't do that!' a werewolf yelled at me. 'I'm next! Just 'cos you're polis doesn't mean you can jump the queue!'

I paid him no attention. I knew without turning around that Lukas was right on my heels. Yes, I'd promised him I wouldn't interfere with anything unrelated to the investigation, but I couldn't stand back and watch. I'm not the bystander type.

I strode past Jonas and fixed on William Moss, peering at his face. His eyes looked clear and focused, unaffected by either drugs or alcohol. 'Mr Moss,' I said briskly, 'my name is DC Emma Bellamy. I can get you out of this situation.'

I reached for his manacles. I could probably pull them free from the wall if I yanked hard enough.

Three burly human security guards approached me but Jonas shook his head. 'It's okay,' he said mildly. 'Let the little police lady do her thing. And don't worry about the crossbow – she's only allowed to shoot supes. You'll be safe.'

I flicked him a look. His expression matched his tone of voice: he wasn't in the least perturbed by me or my actions.

As I reached for the chains, Moss shook his head in alarm. 'Have you been coerced into this, Mr Moss?'

He shook his head more forcefully.

'Why are you here? Why are you doing this?'

He didn't answer, though he looked increasingly nervous.

'If he makes a sound, detective, he loses the game,' Jonas interjected. 'He's not going to speak, not if he doesn't want to forfeit his place.'

I snorted. 'How very convenient for you.'

'You need to ask him the right question, one that he can answer.'

I considered. 'Are you doing this of your own free will?'

Moss nodded without a smidgen of hesitation. I gave him a hard look.

'I think you have what you need, detective.' Jonas smiled at me.

His expression was friendly but my hackles rose. Through clenched teeth I said, 'If I find that you are forcing this man in any way to do this, I will shut you down so quickly that your arse won't know what's hit it.'

Jonas continued to smile. 'I'd expect nothing less. Why don't we step into my office? We need to discuss matters that are unrelated to Mr Moss.'

Fine. I folded my arms and nodded tightly.

Lukas stepped up next to me. 'We appreciate your help,' he said clearly.

Jonas hadn't helped us, not yet, but I reminded myself that it was easier to catch flies with honey. 'We do,' I said.

Jonas's smile flickered and his mask slipped for the first time. 'It should be me who's saying thank you,' he said. 'I think I'm the one who needs help. Come with me, and I'll tell you everything I know.'

CHAPTER ELEVEN

LUKAS AND I FOLLOWED JONAS THROUGH AN UNOBTRUSIVE GREY door near where Moss was chained and into another room. I sat down on one of the utilitarian chairs and Jonas did the same. Lukas remained standing, taking up position by the door. Without saying a word, he was indicating that I was in charge. I appreciated that a lot.

'Before we get started, would you like another drink?' Jonas asked. 'Or perhaps a snack?'

I wasn't here to be entertained. Or fed. 'No, thank you,' I said, as politely as I could. I wanted to get down to business and get out of here as quickly as possible.

'Lord Horvath? Another vodka? Or some blood, perhaps?' Jonas flicked his long hair over his shoulder and extended his neck. 'You can have some of mine if you wish.'

Vampires only require human blood once a month or so. Jonas knew that Lukas would decline his offer, which was probably why he'd made it. He knew how to schmooze.

'No, I'm fine,' Lukas said, surprising none of us.

Jonas nodded amiably, allowing his hair to drop back into place. I stiffened as I examined him more carefully. Huh. 'You're not a supe,' I said slowly. 'And you're wearing a wig.' It was a good wig, probably custom made, but nonetheless it was a wig.

Jonas didn't appear dismayed that I'd noticed. 'I heard that your investigative powers are almost legendary, DC Bellamy. I'm not disappointed.'

Was he making fun of me? I rose to the bait. 'That little show you put on? The levitation and leaping across the room? That was wires, right?' I twirled my index finger in the air. 'This whole set up is little more than a gambling scam. Smoke and mirrors. Who are you really?'

Lukas winced but kept his mouth shut.

'I'm MC Jonas.' His smile dipped. 'But you can call me Kevin.'

I blinked. 'Kevin?'

'It's my name, though I don't tend to use it. Someone called Kevin doesn't inspire an audience quite as much as someone called MC Jonas.'

Indeed. It was hard to think of him as Kevin. Jonas fitted him better.

'I assure you Fetish is not a scam,' he continued. 'I put on a show, detective. People come here for entertainment and to let their hair down. So to speak.' He raised his hands, removed his wig of flowing green hair and placed it on his lap. 'Nobody is being cheated out of anything and nobody is being forced into anything. I promise you that.'

It was quite astonishing how much difference the wig's absence made to his appearance. His hair was mousy brown and cut close to his skull, and he looked almost normal. I reckoned that if he wiped off his elaborate stage make-up, he could have passed for an accountant. Or a customer service rep.

There was a sharp knock on the door. Lukas frowned and opened it. To my surprise, a familiar face appeared: Phileas Carmichael Esquire, gremlin solicitor to all manner of supes. Well, well, well.

I watched narrow eyed as he strolled in and took a seat next to Jonas. 'Good evening, DC Bellamy.'

My mouth tightened. 'Mr Carmichael.'

Jonas registered my expression. 'It seemed wise to ask my legal representative to attend. Lord Horvath has given his reassurance that my club will remain free from police interference, but this is a delicate matter and I am always prudent.'

I couldn't argue, but Carmichael's presence didn't ease my tension.

'There's no need to look so anxious, DC Bellamy,' Phileas Carmichael said. 'I'm here merely to ease the path between my client's need for certain protections and your desire for information. He made contact voluntarily. He wants to help.'

I'd withhold judgment about that until his 'help' actually manifested itself. 'Very well,' I said briskly. 'Carry on.'

Carmichael placed his briefcase on the floor and smiled at me benignly. 'Mr Jonas only wants what's best for everyone. What he doesn't want is for his selfless help to be thrown back in his face and adversely affect the day-to-day running of his club. Before he continues, we require one or two assurances.'

That was a big ask given the severity of the crimes we were investigating, but from what Lukas had told me about the club being illegal, I could understand it. 'Go on,' I said.

'Any information gathered during the course of the investigation that pertains to the daily running of Fetish will not be used in any future prosecutions against either Mr Jonas, his customers or his business. Fetish does not deserve to be victimised, and neither does my client.'

I grunted. That was fair – I supposed.

'In return,' Carmichael continued, 'Fetish will hand over all relevant documentation, including its security-footage history, guest lists and details of recent special events.'

I frowned.

'Is there a problem, detective?' the gremlin enquired.

Far from it; I'd been expecting to hear much more stringent demands – and that Jonas would want compensation for his trouble. These requests were surprisingly reasonable.

'I don't want to be difficult,' Jonas said. 'I only want to protect my club while helping your investigation.' His hands twisted in his lap. 'I'm trying to do the right thing, especially now there are two killers on the loose.'

I kept my expression blank. 'Two killers?'

'It was on the news in the last hour. Stupid and Cupid? That's what you're calling them?'

I wasn't surprised that particular detail had leaked. But I was disappointed. 'Mm,' I murmured non-committally. I breathed in. 'You have to realise, Mr Jonas, that I'm not in charge of the investigation. It's not my place to agree to anything on behalf of the Metropolitan Police.'

'Do *you* have a problem with our conditions?' Carmichael asked.

'No,' I said honestly. Similar agreements were often made in the pursuit of the greater good.

'The fact is that I trust Supe Squad,' Jonas told me. 'Your team has proved itself. But the Met Police as a whole has a bad reputation. I want to help, but I must be sure there'll be no official blowback. The only way to achieve that is to communicate only with you.'

Murray wouldn't like that, but we had to respect that Jonas had come forward to talk. 'I'll have to make a phone call to check with my Senior Investigating Officer that this is appropriate,' I said, almost apologetically.

Carmichael and Jonas exchanged glances. 'We would like to be present for the call,' the solicitor said.

Fair enough. They'd obviously realised that I wouldn't have the authority to agree to their demands without checking first. My respect for Jonas went up a notch; I certainly didn't feel any urge to giggle at him any longer.

The phone call didn't take long. 'What is it?' Murray barked. 'Have you found something?' He paused. 'Has there been another murder?'

I hoped that wasn't eagerness in his voice. 'I've been approached by someone who knows of a connection between the two victims, sir. It involves a club that both men have visited.' I outlined what else I knew without divulging any details about Fetish or Jonas, and I described the conditions that Carmichael had laid out.

Murray didn't hesitate. 'Agree to it all. I need all the information I can get if I'm to find these two killers.'

There was no I in team, unless you were DCI Murray. I should have been grateful for small mercies: at least he wasn't obstructive in the face of reasonable requests. 'Yes, sir.'

'Somebody leaked to the press that we're searching for two murderers,' Murray spat. 'It's unconscionable.' He didn't bother to ask if I'd leaked the news. In that instant, I knew it was Murray himself who'd spoken to a journalist.

'Yes,' I said. 'It's shocking that somebody in our police force would risk more lives by divulging information that could help us prevent more murders.'

There was a beat of silence. 'Indeed.' Murray sniffed. 'Don't think,' he added darkly, 'that any information you uncover from that club means you're off phone duty tomorrow. You have a lesson to learn, detective.'

Yeah, yeah. I sighed to myself, ended the call and nodded at the two men. Done.

'Well,' Jonas said, 'he sounds...' he paused, trying to think of the right word '...committed.'

From his position by the door, Lukas snorted.

I suppressed a smile. 'He is.'

Phileas Carmichael nodded, apparently happy that I was meeting all the conditions. Just as well.

'Now,' I said, 'let's get to the matter in hand. You contacted

Lord Horvath today concerning the two murder victims, Gilchrist Boast and Peter Pickover.'

'Yes.' Jonas seemed almost eager to talk about them. 'I was truly shocked to hear of their passing. Both of them have frequented my club in recent weeks.' He shuddered. 'Such violence.'

I said nothing. I wanted Jonas to fill in the blanks for me.

'I've known Pete for a long time – he's been coming here since we opened four years ago. He participates in a lot of the games,' Jonas gave a rueful smile, 'and he often wins.' Then he grimaced. 'He often won.' He looked down.

'How much money do you think he's won?'

'A whisker short of a million.'

I stared at him. Bloody hell.

'I looked it up before you arrived,' he said helpfully. 'I thought you'd want the exact figure: £973,000.64p.'

Even Phileas Carmichael looked surprised.

'That's a lot of money,' I said. More than enough to pay for his swanky flat. No wonder Peter Pickover didn't seem to have any other hobbies.

'He never boasted about it,' Jonas told me. 'He wasn't the type to brag. I took the liberty of printing out all the games he'd participated in together with details of his opponents. Maybe someone was a sore loser.' He passed over a sheet of paper.

I glanced at it and stiffened. 'This is the last game he took part in?' I tapped the top of the list. 'An eating challenge?'

'Yes.' Jonas's voice dropped to a whisper. 'He only played against one opponent. Gilchrist Boast.'

'And Boast won?'

Jonas nodded. 'Pete couldn't win 'em all.'

No wonder Jonas had decided to get in touch. Within forty-eight hours of that 'game', both men were dead. 'Your other customers betted on the outcome?' I asked.

'Yes. We don't keep notes on side bets, but I went through the security footage and identified everyone who was involved.' He gave me another sheet of paper. There had to be at least fifty names on it.

I exhaled. 'Peter Pickover was human. How did he come to learn about your club?'

Jonas shook his head. 'How does anyone? Word of mouth, I imagine. He knew someone who knew someone who … you get the picture.'

'Did he have any dealings with Gilchrist Boast other than this game?'

'I honestly have no idea. I've not witnessed anything between them, and I couldn't find any interaction on the CCTV footage – but I didn't get a lot of time to look.' He held up a memory stick. 'Every single minute from every single camera for the last month is on here. I want you to find whoever did this, detective. If there's a connection between their deaths and this club…' Jonas's voice trailed off.

He didn't need me to tell him that it seemed likely. 'Thank you,' I said. 'This is really helpful.'

Jonas licked his lips and looked nervously at Carmichael.

'What is it?' I asked. 'Is there something else?'

He shifted uncomfortably in his chair. 'I received a letter. It was hand delivered this afternoon after I'd contacted Lord Horvath. Somebody slipped it under the gate.' He motioned to Carmichael who opened his briefcase.

The letter had been placed inside a transparent plastic bag. My skin prickled. That didn't look good.

'Three people have handled the envelope,' the gremlin told me. 'Ally Sim picked it up when she arrived for her shift and gave it to Mr Jonas. Mr Jonas opened the letter, so his prints are on both the envelope and letter. Then me. We will all give our fingerprints.'

Uh-oh. I swallowed and took the bag, then reached into my

pocket and pulled out a pair of gloves. I slipped them on so I could check the contents more closely.

The envelope was innocuous enough; all that was written on the front, in block-capital letters, was: *FOR THE ATTENTION OF MC JONAS*. There was no postmark. I lifted the flap and glanced inside. It contained a single sheet of paper. slid it out. From the doorway, Lukas leaned over to see what it was.

I inhaled sharply. Jonas looked down at his feet and Carmichael watched my face.

'*The Paint Challenge*,' I read aloud.

Lukas grimaced.

I gazed at the two photos beneath the title. They were in black and white and had been printed side by side, but there was no mistaking what they were. The first photo was of Peter Pickover, slumped in his own apartment. It was almost identical to the crime-scene photo of his body that Colquhoun had shown me. The second photo was of Gilchrist Boast lying flat on his floor. Propped against his chest was the bloody picture of the double-decker bus, and his severed finger.

'What's written underneath?' Lukas asked.

A shiver ran through me. '*Who wins?*' Sickened, I dropped the paper back into the envelope. 'They want you to decide. Who killed their victim best?'

Jonas nodded. 'That's what I thought too.' His face was pale; Phileas Carmichael looked green around the gills, too.

'I need to take these,' I said.

'Of course.'

I looked at him. 'This changes things considerably. Can you think of anyone who might have done this? An over-ardent admirer? A stalker? Someone with a grudge against the club?'

Jonas shook his head miserably. 'No. I can't think of anyone.'

'Okay.' I held up the baggie. 'Thank you.' I asked a few more questions and took some notes, but Jonas had little more to tell me. The copy of his client list included addresses and phone numbers, but there were more than 5,000 names. I was certain that at least one of those names belonged to a killer but it was a lot of suspects to deal with.

However, it was more information than I'd had before I'd walked in here tonight. The people who'd placed bets on Pickover and Boast's competition would take priority, but I knew that the letter, with its gruesome photos, was the key to everything. Maybe this was the breakthrough we needed.

Feeling guilty for my initial misgivings about him, I thanked Jonas again and gave him my personal number. 'Call me if anything else comes to mind or you receive any more … communications like this,' I said firmly.

'I will,' he said. 'I promise.'

I shook Carmichael's hand and stood up to leave. Lukas nodded respectfully at both men before stepping out. I paused at the door.

Jonas glanced up at me. 'You've thought of something else?'

Not exactly. 'I have one question that's unrelated to my investigation.'

'Go on.'

'You seem like a good person who's trying to do the right thing. Why do you do *this*? Why Fetish?'

'You think it's a tawdry business.'

'I didn't say that.'

'You didn't disagree either.'

Touché. I waited.

Jonas appeared to consider the question seriously. 'The simple answer, detective, is that I like playing games. I enjoy it when there's a clear winner and a clear loser. Competition encourages us to do our best and to push beyond our self-imposed limits. I enjoy seeing what heights people can rise to when they receive the right encouragement. I know what's out there on the club floor sickens you, but there's something for everyone. Stay long enough and you'll find a game that'll sing to you and your own desires.' He smiled. 'I dare you.'

I laughed. 'I'm a bit busy trying to solve a double murder.'

'We're open all year round. We could always come up with a special game that suits your particular talents. You'd make a lot of money – resurrection is definitely a unique talent and you'd draw a large crowd.'

That was never going to happen. Not ever. 'Thanks,' I said. 'I'll bear it in mind.'

He bowed, the twinkle in his eye indicating that he could read my thoughts. 'You're welcome.' Then his expression sobered. 'Find the bastards who did this and keep my other customers safe.' He paused. 'Please.'

'I'll do my best.' And I meant it wholeheartedly.

Jonas seemed to relax. He stepped over to me and, startling me, leaned in and kissed my cheek. 'Thank you, DC Bellamy. Thank you so much.'

CHAPTER TWELVE

I PHONED MURRAY AGAIN AND TOLD HIM WHAT I'D LEARNED, THEN made copies of most of what Jonas had given me and passed them over to the team that remained on duty at Hackney.

Although I knew there would be more than enough officers poring over the client lists and videos, I stayed up half the night watching as much of the CCTV footage from Fetish as I could. Eventually fatigue forced me to grab a couple of hours' sleep, but as soon as I woke I made some coffee and played the section with Pickover and Boast's eating game several times over.

I stared at the faces in the audience – I even recognised a couple of them. There were a lot of people to question. DCI Murray's investigative team was going to be busy – and so was I.

I messaged Murray and offered to participate in the interviews. I received a one-word reply: *phones*. Damn it.

I knew he'd be pissed off if I didn't immediately scoot to Hackney to do his bidding but, notwithstanding he was the Senior Investigating Officer, he wasn't my boss. Not really. I was a Supe Squad detective so, before I crossed the city to return to my position by the phone, I went to the Supe Squad office. There wasn't any particular need to check in, but I wanted to make a point. Whether Murray would understand it – or even notice it – wasn't my problem. It was something I was doing for myself. And it was possible that one of my colleagues might have insights into the Fetish killings.

Liza was at her desk when I walked in, her head bent over her keyboard. She glanced up and pursed her lips. 'I didn't think I'd see you today. Aren't you still on secondment for that double murder?'

'Yep.' I perched on the edge of Owen Grace's empty desk. 'A double murder where one of the victims is supe. And where both victims are connected to a bizarre club called Fetish where—'

'Fetish?' Liza interrupted. 'Jonas's place?'

I raised my eyebrows. 'You know it?'

Two points of colour appeared high on her cheeks. 'I might have frequented it once or twice. Not recently, I hasten to add. In fact, I've not been there for years.'

'Uh-huh. How did you hear of it? I didn't know it existed until last night.'

Liza's embarrassment increased. 'Tony told me about it,' she said, referring to my late predecessor, 'and I was curious.'

'Curious enough to go more than once?'

'This might shock you,' she said drily, 'but this isn't the highest paid job in the world and I have bills to pay. There was a time when competing in some of the games at Fetish seemed like a good way to make ends meet.'

My eyes widened. 'You took part? What did you do?'

She waved her hands. 'Nothing too crazy.' She clearly didn't want to go into any of the gory details.

'You're aware that it's an illegal club, right?'

Shame-faced, Liza shifted in her chair. 'I was unwise to go there, and I can honestly say that I regret it now. But at the time there was something incredibly satisfying about going head-to-head with someone and beating them. When MC Jonas notices you and praises you for your achievement—' She shivered. 'It was quite a thrill.' She stared at me defiantly. 'I'm not saying I'm proud of what I did, but it made me feel good at the time.'

I couldn't pretend I wasn't surprised by her admission. Liza was not the sort of person who'd usually cross the line. Clearly, Fetish was more alluring than I'd given it credit for – and we all have shameful secrets. I bit back the temptation to judge her actions until I knew more. 'Why did you stop going?' I asked.

Liza pulled a face. 'Tony. He found out what I was up to and threw a hissy fit. I think he wanted to shut down the club, but it never went that far. I don't know why. He reported me for going there. It wasn't my finest moment,' she added quietly.

I'd known Tony for little more than a day before he was murdered, but he hadn't seemed like the kind of person who'd have cared about a club like Fetish on the other side of town. If he'd reported Liza for going, there would be case files and a paper trail. It wouldn't be appropriate to ask her to look them out for me, so I'd have to search for them myself.

'Thank you for your honesty,' I said, meaning it. 'You didn't have to own up to visiting Fetish.'

'Yes, I did.'

We exchanged tiny smiles. When I nodded, indicating that the subject was closed for now, Liza's relief was palpable. 'What's happening with Rosie Thorn?' I asked, changing the subject.

'Owen and Fred are interviewing the neighbours. Nobody has reported anything untoward, but Robert Sullivan is still crying foul. He now wants everything in Rosie's flat tested. Owen is doing his best, but we don't have unlimited resources. We can only do so much.'

'What about Thistle Thorn? What does she think?'

Liza grimaced. 'She's allowing a second post-mortem to go ahead, but Fred thinks it's to stop Robert complaining. He can be quite intimidating.'

Thistle Thorn hadn't struck me as the sort of pixie who would be easily browbeaten, but I could understand why she'd allow

Robert Sullivan to have his way. Unless every avenue was explored, part of her would always be troubled by the suggestion of foul play. It was far better to be absolutely sure that her grandmother had died of natural causes – or at least as sure as she could be.

'It can't be easy for any of them,' I said.

Liza murmured agreement. 'True, although our resources could be put to better use. At least your investigation is definitely murder.'

'Mmm. Except I'm not convinced that I'm being put to best use there, either.' I checked my watch. 'I should probably go. I'm supposed to be manning the phones over at Hackney.'

'Call handling? Have you been vexing the SIO already, DC Bellamy?' Liza smirked.

I placed a hand on my chest. '*Moi*? I'm a little ray of sunshine.'

She snorted. 'Whatever you say.' She shook her head. 'Whatever you say.'

I STARTED my shift by trying to be the happy, sunny, helpful person I'd told Liza I was. Unfortunately, less than twenty minutes in it was proving remarkably difficult to maintain the façade. I didn't even have many biscuits left to support me; I'd eaten most of my stash the day before.

'I live near to where that bloke was killed,' a caller told me in a quavering voice. 'I thought I should call.'

'Did you witness anything unusual that day or night?' I asked, sitting up straighter.

'There was a fox wandering down the street at dusk.' The caller hesitated. 'I don't suppose that's relevant.'

'Probably not,' I said. 'Although information is always useful. Did you see the victim at all?'

'No, I've never seen him before. It wasn't until I saw the news that I knew he existed. I don't know any of my neighbours.' Her voice took on a mournful note. 'He looked like a nice chap. He didn't deserve to die.' She sighed. 'I can give you a DNA sample, if you like.'

'Pardon?'

'I'll give you a DNA sample so you can rule me out of your investigation. I'll do anything I can to help.'

Someone had been watching too many television crime shows; blanket DNA testing was prohibitively expensive and time-consuming. 'That's very much appreciated, ma'am. We don't require any DNA samples right now, but if that changes I'm sure someone will be in touch.' She was trying to be helpful and I couldn't knock her for that.

I sighed and answered the next call. 'Good morning. You've reached the Metropolitan Police tip line concerning the murders of—' I didn't manage to finish my sentence.

'Hello, Musketeer.'

I half-choked. 'Zara.' I sat bolt upright.

'You remembered my name. I'm touched.'

This was an anonymous tip line, so the call wasn't being recorded and no trace had been set up. I had to persuade Zara to give me as much information as possible so we could find her. 'Of course I remember. It's a beautiful name and you made quite an impression. I didn't catch your surname, though.'

She laughed, as if she were genuinely enjoying herself. 'That's because I didn't tell you it.'

'Can you tell me now?'

Zara laughed again. 'No.'

'Why not?'

'Come on, detective, you're not that stupid. You know why I don't want to be tracked down. I'm sure your boyfriend told you what he thinks of my kind. It's not my fault that I can see things others can't. I can't control my prophecies and I can't control the future, but people always want to shoot the messenger. I've been hounded out of my home before because of my gift. I won't let it happen again.'

'I can make sure that you're protected, Zara.'

'Don't insult my intelligence, Musketeer. You're better than that. Besides, I didn't call to talk about me.'

My stomach tightened as a curl of dread wound its way around my body. I'd wanted this call, I'd wanted to get some information that the investigation could use, but that didn't mean I'd enjoy hearing it. 'Why *did* you call, then?'

'You will be a busy girl,' she said, her voice tinged with sadness. 'They'll kill again. Soon.'

I clenched my fists. 'When you say "they",' I asked carefully, 'do you mean there's more than one killer, or are you being non-gender specific?'

Zara hummed lightly, ignoring my question. 'When a thief kisses you,' she said, 'count your teeth.'

What? My brow creased. 'What do you mean by that?'

'Eighteen-fifteen, Musketeer.'

'Zara.' I ground my teeth in frustration. 'You're not making any sense.'

'I can only tell you what I see. White coat. Black chair. And echoes. Echoes. Echoes. Echoes of eighteen-fifteen.' She paused and her tone altered. 'Detective,' she asked with what sounded like nothing more than vague curiosity, 'do you floss?'

Before I could formulate an answer, I was confronted with a familiar dull buzz. Zara had already hung up.

'EIGHTEEN-FIFTEEN.' DCI Murray rubbed his chin. 'Quarter-past six, right?' He looked at his watch. 'That leaves us less than seven hours.'

I chewed the inside of my cheek. 'She said *echoes* of eighteen-fifteen. Zara may not have been referring to the time.'

'What do you think she was referring to?' he asked.

'I don't know, sir.'

He pursed his lips. 'Hmm. Well, she also mentioned a white coat. That's a doctor. It has to be a medical professional who murdered Peter Pickover, so she was obviously talking about Cupid and Stupid.'

I cleared my throat. 'She asked me if I flossed. And she said that when a thief kisses you, you should count your teeth.'

'White coat, black chair,' Colquhoun said. 'Not a doctor – a dentist.'

Murray's mouth flattened. 'How many dentists are there in London?'

'Thousands,' Colquhoun answered. 'Too many to get around between now and six o'clock.' She glanced at me. 'If that *is* our deadline. As DC Bellamy said, eighteen-fifteen might not be a reference to the time. At this point, we can't know for sure.'

'That ridiculous woman has been too vague!' Murray protested. 'We could look into dentists who've called in sick today. That'd give us a start.' He sounded as doubtful as I felt.

'What about the Fetish guest list?' I suggested. 'Are there any dentists on that?'

Colquhoun brightened. 'We can check. There are a lot of names, but it'll give us another way of narrowing down suspects.' She paused. 'Or victims,' she added more darkly.

I pulled back my shoulders. 'There aren't many dentists who deal with supes, and we already know that supes are involved in these murders as much as humans. I can focus on the dentists who have supe clients.' Unsurprisingly, both vampires and were-wolves pay close attention to their teeth.

Murray looked at me, and for a moment I thought he was going to order me back to the phones. Thankfully, for me and for the public at large, he nodded. 'Good idea. We can't know whether this Zara is telling the truth, or what she was referring to. We don't know if she's pointing us towards dentists as either victims or killers, but it's a start. I'll rally the troops.'

There was a glint of excitement in his eyes. 'Maybe this is the lead we've been looking for. Goodness knows, none of the statements we've taken from the other Fetish customers have helped.' He whirled out of the small office, already yelling at the other police officers to gather round.

I swallowed.

'You don't look thrilled,' Colquhoun commented. 'But Murray is right. This might well turn out to be the information we need.'

'Perhaps.' I ran a hand through my hair. 'But when Zara spoke to me before about Gilchrist Boast, it was already too late to save him. Even if she'd been specific, given me his name and address and I'd acted immediately, I couldn't have reached him in time. What if this is the same?'

'All the more reason for us to get out there and find as many dentists as we can,' Colquhoun replied grimly.

I reached for my phone. This time I would call on the entire supe community to help.

CHAPTER THIRTEEN

Tallulah did me proud. In a mere whisker over thirty minutes, we reached the centre of Soho. She seemed to recognise the urgency of the situation and didn't once complain or stall.

I pulled up on a corner and jumped out. Lukas was waiting for me on the pavement with a brooding expression on his face and his hands in his pockets. He looked exactly how I felt.

We didn't waste time on any soft hellos or snuggly kisses. 'There are three dentists who work with my vampires,' he said. 'I've rounded them up and they're waiting inside. Two are vamps and one is human.'

'Do you know them?'

'Naturally, I know the vampires,' Lukas replied. 'And I'd vouch for them in a heartbeat.' He shot me a rueful glance. 'But I will always vouch for my people, you know that.'

'The human?'

'I've never heard any bad reports about her. She's had vamp clients for the better part of twenty years. She wasn't particularly happy about being pulled away from her afternoon appointments.'

'She will be if she's a potential target, rather than a cold-blooded killer.'

'Hmm.' His scepticism was obvious. 'Except she's only here because of vague mutterings from that damned Cassandra.'

'That damned Cassandra was bang on the money last time,' I said quietly.

Lukas was silent for a moment. 'You're the detective,' he said finally. 'I won't argue with you.'

'But?'

'Have you considered that she might be one of the killers? Or that, at the very least, she might know them?'

'Of course. But why would she approach me, if that were the case?'

Lukas grimaced. 'Cassandras enjoy their little games.'

I gazed at him. 'She frightens you,' I said, suddenly understanding. 'That's why you dislike her so much.'

He shook his head. 'No, she doesn't frighten me, D'Artagnan – she terrifies me. If she's a true Cassandra – and I don't yet believe that she is – then the power that she can wield is monstrous.'

I reached for his hand and squeezed it. 'I don't think she means anyone harm.'

'It doesn't matter what her intentions are.' His mouth tightened. 'Seeing the future is wrong.' His lips drew back over his fangs in an involuntary snarl. 'There was an artefact, you know. A ring. It does the same thing that a Cassandra does, albeit only twice a year during each solstice. I sent Scarlett to Italy to retrieve it for the princely sum of five million pounds because nobody should possess that sort of power. *Nobody.*'

I gripped his hand more tightly. I rarely saw him display such fervent conviction. 'Where is it?' I asked. 'Where's the ring now?'

'I destroyed it,' he said simply. 'I paid a fortune to be able to remove it from our world.'

Blimey.

There was a sudden loud honk from the end of the street that forestalled further conversation. I turned in time to see a large SUV careening towards us, tyres screeching. I winced as it swerved around a cyclist, almost taking him out with its wing mirror. Then the brakes were slammed on and it came to sudden halt right beside us. The driver's door flew open, revealing Buffy. Beside her was Robert Sullivan.

'Detective Constable Bellamy!' she trilled. 'How wonderful to see you!' She jumped out and curtsied, first to me and then to Lukas. She added a girlish giggle for effect. 'I'm so lucky to be able to help you out. Being in your presence always makes me feel rather breathless and giddy, you know? It's even worse when you're together. You're such a power couple. I think you should wear matching outfits – you'd look super cute. I can help you shop, if you like. I have a great eye for fashion.' She giggled again.

Lukas and I simply stared at her. Robert walked around the front of the car and joined her. 'Drop the act,' he growled.

'Act?'

He glared at her and Buffy grinned. 'Sorry,' she said. 'Sometimes I simply can't help myself.'

Yeah, yeah. I shook my head and pointed to the back of the car. The windows were tinted so I couldn't see who was inside. 'Do you have them?'

'Four supe dentists,' Robert said. 'As requested.'

'Thank you. I know rounding people up off the street isn't much fun but, believe me, it could make all the difference.'

Robert held my eyes. 'Quid pro quo,' he said. I didn't need to ask what he was referring to.

Buffy stepped closer to me. 'Personally, I don't know what you're talking about,' she said with a flick of her head. 'Rounding people up off the street is great fun. Especially when they're dentists.' She drew her lips back over her teeth, revealing a set of perfectly straight, brilliant-white canines and molars. 'That'll teach them to give me fillings.' She reached for the back door of the SUV and yanked it open, revealing four pale faces.

I stared at the occupants. 'Buffy,' I said heavily, 'it wasn't necessary to tie them up.'

'You said that they might be *in* danger or they might *be* dangerous.' She sniffed. 'I was merely taking precautions.'

'They're bound and gagged.'

Buffy beamed. 'I know. Ain't it great?'

I counted to ten in my head, then apologised profusely to all four trussed-up dentists. I gestured to Robert and Buffy to untie them. 'Is this everyone?' I asked Lukas in an undertone.

'Yes.'

'Can you—?'

He inhaled deeply before pointing at the oldest of the bunch. 'That one. He smells of blood.'

Buffy removed the man's gag, and he immediately began to splutter. 'I performed three tooth extractions this morning! Of course I smell of blood!'

I glanced at Lukas. 'It's only a faint odour so he's probably telling the truth,' he said.

'I'm not lying!' the dentist objected.

I nodded. 'I appreciate that, sir. If you'd like to come inside, hopefully we can clear this up as quickly as possible.'

One of the two female dentists, a dark-haired woman wearing glasses, folded her arms. 'I'm not going anywhere until you explain what's going on.'

I looked at Buffy. 'You didn't tell them?'

'I thought time was of the essence.' Buffy blinked innocently. 'Isn't that what you said on the phone?'

I ground my teeth and turned back to the group. 'Again, my sincere apologies. Follow me and I'll explain everything.'

SEVEN DENTISTS OF VARYING ETHNICITIES, ages and sexes, stared at me.

'You're telling us,' a white-coated werewolf wearing the colours of clan Carr said, 'that you suspect at least one of us is a crazed killer?'

I glanced at his name tag. 'I think, Dr Simpson, that it's more likely one of you is an intended *victim*. It's conjecture right now, but we need to do everything we can to keep both you and the public safe.'

'Are you rounding up all the dentists who work on humans, too?' asked a vamp dentist whose pearly canines were extraordinarily white.

'There are too many of them, but my colleagues in the Met are trying to contact them.'

'And what if it's not us who are in danger? What if it's our patients?'

This time Lukas answered for me. 'We've posted guards at all your clinics. Anyone who comes by will be informed and have the choice of remaining with the guards or returning home.'

We had to consider every scenario, and there was always the chance that drawing the dentists away from their surgeries would create the opening the killers wanted. I knew from looking at their faces that they weren't particularly comforted by our hastily cobbled-together plan. I didn't blame them. My control over the situation felt fragile indeed.

Another of the werewolves stepped forward. 'My name is Alicia Fairweather,' she said softly. 'While I think it's appalling that you're putting this much faith in a Cassandra, you need to give us more information. We know our craft, detective. We can help.' She looked at the others. 'The more we help, the faster we'll get out of here. Right?'

I gave her an appreciative nod. 'The Cassandra asked me if I flossed, and said that when a thief kisses you, you have to check your teeth. She also said something about echoes of eighteen-fifteen.'

'That's it?'

'She made mention of a white coat and a black chair.'

All of the dentists exchanged glances.

'Have any of you noticed anything unusual recently?' I asked. 'Has there been anything out of the ordinary?'

They shook their heads.

Dr Simpson spoke. 'No, there's been nothing. Does that mean one of us is likely to be one of your killers? We've all seen the news. We all know who you're looking for. Do you think I'm Cupid?' he sneered. 'Or Stupid?'

Buffy sidled up to him. 'Maybe I should rip your throat out now, Stupid,' she said sweetly, 'and ask questions later.'

'Enough!' Robert snapped at her. He glared at Simpson. 'DC Bellamy is trying to help you. Stop being obstructive, and maybe we can get to the bottom of this mess!'

I tried not to think of Robert's hands wrapped around my throat. 'I understand that tempers are fraying,' I said. 'Your patience is very much appreciated.' I nodded at Buffy and, with a pout, she moved away. 'What about new customers?' I asked. 'Have any of you had any new dental patients sign up this week?'

'I've had a few kids from the McGuigan clan,' the dark-haired woman said. 'Both under ten.'

'I've had a couple of humans who moved to the area recently,' Dr Fairweather told me. 'I doubt either of them are killers, though. Why would somebody sign up as a new patient and record their name and address before they proceeded to murder one of us?'

Yes, I was clutching at straws. I tried a different tack. 'Do any of you know Fetish? It's a club on the outskirts of the city?'

Simpson averted his gaze. Ah-ha. 'Dr Simpson?' I prodded.

'I've heard of it.'

'Have you been there?'

When he didn't immediately answer, Buffy darted forward and kicked him in the shin.

'For fuck's sake!' I yelled. 'Stop that!' I waved at Robert. 'Get her out of here.'

Robert took her arm and hauled her towards the door.

'Don't tell me that you don't want to kick him too, DC Bellamy,' Buffy said.

'I'll kick *you*,' I muttered under my breath, albeit loudly enough for her to hear me. She beamed with delight.

'We'll wait outside,' Robert growled.

At least three of the dentists looked relieved. Lukas had also clocked their expressions. 'I'll wait outside with them,' he murmured.

I was glad he'd volunteered, otherwise I'd have had to throw him out. The dentists might speak more openly without him in the room. Although I was with the police, I was far less scary than supes like Robert, Buffy or Lukas.

Once the door had closed, I said, 'Let's try again. How many of you have been to Fetish?'

Three of them raised their hands. One vampire, one human and one werewolf. Then Simpson reluctantly did the same.

'Recently?' I asked.

'Last month.' He glanced at the others with a question in his eyes before proceeding. 'We were all there together. It was my birthday.'

Was there anyone who hadn't been to that bloody club? 'And were you there as observers?' I asked, keeping my expression non-judgmental. 'Or as participants?'

'Is that relevant?'

I had no need to lie. 'Yes. There is a strong link between the previous victims and the club.'

One of the two humans raised her hand nervously. 'You really think we might be involved in these killings, don't you? That if we're not murderers, we might become victims?'

I held her eyes. 'At this stage I'm not prepared to discount anything.'

Simpson shoved his hands into his pockets and looked me in the eye. 'We had a few drinks, made a few bets and went home. That was it.' He seemed to be telling the truth; if he weren't, it would be easy to cross-check against the information that Jonas had given me.

'Okay,' I said. 'Thank you.'

Fairweather wrapped her arms around herself. 'Well, detective? Can you give us a straight answer? Is someone going to try and kill us or not?'

'Honestly? have no idea. And until I do, it's better if you all stay here and make yourselves comfortable. We don't want to take any chances.'

Simpson rolled his eyes. 'What if nothing happens? Will you keep us here until somebody dies?'

I hadn't thought that far ahead. 'Let's wait and see what happens between now and this evening to begin with.'

'You mean until quarter past six. Echoes of eighteen-fifteen? What if the Cassandra was referring to the year 1815 and not the time?'

Dr Fairweather frowned. 'The Battle of Waterloo,' she said. 'That was 1815.'

My knowledge of history was sketchy at the best of times. 'Napoleon?' I asked. 'And the Duke of Wellington?'

Simpson's expression had altered from irritated to thoughtful. 'And dentures.'

'Dentures?'

Fairweather's hand went to her mouth. 'Oh,' she said. 'Oh.'

I looked at both of them. 'What?'

Simpson grimaced. 'Waterloo teeth.'

Fairweather nodded. 'Before porcelain teeth were used, rich people had dentures made from real teeth. Living donors weren't always easy to come by. Neither were dead ones for that matter, unless you happened to be wandering through a battlefield littered with corpses.'

I swallowed. 'You mean—?'

'Yes. People extracted teeth from dead soldiers and sold them to dentists to use as dentures. They were called Waterloo teeth because that's where a lot of them came from.' She spoke matter-of-factly, but I wasn't the only person in the room who shuddered.

Blood had been taken from Peter Pickover and used at the murder of Gilchrist Boast. What if the same thing was now happening with two more victims – but instead of blood it was teeth? My own blood ran ice-cold.

I dug out my phone and called Colquhoun. 'I'm with the supe dentists,' I said as soon as she answered. 'We've got a new theory. Eighteen-fifteen could refer to Waterloo teeth which—'

She interrupted me. 'I was about to call you.'

Something in her voice made me pause. 'What is it?'

'We've got another victim,' she said.

I flinched. Oh no.

Colquhoun reeled off the address of a dentist's surgery not far from where Peter Pickover had lived. 'Time of death is recent – very recent. Whoever you're with at the moment can't have been involved. You should get here. And you should bring your boyfriend along too,' she added darkly.

I sucked in a breath. 'Why?'

'Because the victim appears to be a human male who's been given his very own set of recently extracted vampire fangs.'

I closed my eyes. Waterloo teeth indeed. Shit. I felt no surge of triumph that I'd had an inkling of this before Colquhoun told me. Lukas would not handle this news well. 'I'll be there as soon as I can.'

I hung up and looked at the dentists who gazed back at me with a mixture of fear and expectation.

'What is it?' Simpson asked, his earlier bravado gone. 'What's happened?'

'You're all off the hook for now,' I told them. 'You can go

home but stay wary. Don't let any strangers into your houses and keep your phones to hand, just in case. Thank you for your help and your patience.'

'Won't you tell us what's happened?'

I didn't answer. Knowing Murray, it would be on the news before too long. 'Thank you,' I repeated lamely, then I walked outside without looking back.

On the pavement, Buffy was leaning against a lamppost, chewing gum and gazing into the distance. Robert appeared to be lecturing Lukas. 'You see,' he was saying, 'my Rosie couldn't have died of natural causes because—'

Lukas's black eyes landed on me and he moved forward swiftly. 'What's happened?'

I swallowed. 'We have to go. I'll tell you in the car.'

My expression must have betrayed me because even Buffy kept away from wisecracks. 'We're done here?' she asked.

I nodded. 'The dentists are free to leave.'

Robert folded his arms. 'Quid pro quo,' he reminded me. 'Will you speak to DS Grace now? Make sure he sends everything from Rosie's flat to the laboratory for proper testing?'

'Rob.' Buffy's voice was soft. 'Not now.'

'But—'

She put a hand on his arm and he fell silent. Under any other circumstances I'd have been fascinated to see Buffy dominate a superior wolf from her own clan, but right now I couldn't muster up the interest.

I pointed to Tallulah. 'I'll drive,' I said to Lukas.

A muscle jerked in his cheek but he didn't argue. I clipped on my seatbelt, started the engine and drove away from Buffy, Robert and the pale-faced dentists who had joined them on the pavement.

'Go on then.' Lukas's voice was dark enough to make a ghost shiver. 'What's happened?'

CHAPTER FOURTEEN

ON A NORMAL DAY, THE LITTLE DENTIST'S SURGERY WOULD HAVE looked ordinary. Bright Smiles wasn't part of any of the bigger chains so it had retained its own quirky identity. The exterior was welcoming, with a smiley-face logo and healthy, leafy plants in the window, and there was a large, resin statue of a cheery dentist by the door. Unfortunately, the crime-scene tape, and the lack of bright smiles on the faces of the many police officers outside, had dramatically removed the surgery's quiet appeal.

At least the uniformed policewoman manning the cordon recognised me and waved Lukas and I through without a murmur. There were some bonuses to being vaguely famous.

Although it was small, the surgery waiting room felt bright and airy – as long as you ignored the forensic guys dusting for prints, and the grim-faced detective tapping away at a computer behind the reception desk.

I swivelled around, slowly taking in the scene, while Lukas clenched and unclenched his fists. I knew it was taking everything he had not to shove everyone else out of the way and barge towards the murder scene. Under the circumstances, he was displaying incredible restraint.

DS Colquhoun emerged from a side door, looking neither pleased nor dismayed to see us. I recognised her attitude: she was far too focused and business-like to allow something as distracting as emotion to derail her from the matter in hand. Compartmentalising was something we both had to do.

'Hey,' I said softly. 'What have we got?'

'We're awaiting final confirmation of the victim's identity, but it appears that his name is Samuel Brunswick. Caucasian human male, thirty-two years old. He had an appointment for a root canal at three o'clock this afternoon.'

My eyes strayed to the clock on the wall: it wasn't yet 3pm. 'Is there an estimated time of death?' I asked, pretending not to notice Lukas's coiled tension as he stood next to me.

'The pathologist has yet to make an initial determination based on the body,' Colquhoun said, 'but it had to be between 12 and 1pm. The surgery was shut then, and all three members of staff were having lunch at a nearby café.'

'Is that usual?'

'The dentist said they lock up the surgery and go out for lunch together every Friday.'

So the routine was well established. The killer must have known they'd have unhampered access to the surgery during that time. I glanced at the front door.

'The lock's not been tampered with,' Colquhoun told me. 'But there's a back entrance, and a small window next to it has been smashed.' She paused. 'All the shattered glass has been removed. The dentist, the hygienist and the receptionist believe that it was intact before they left for lunch.'

Exactly like the scene at Pickover's home.

She held up an evidence bag. 'We found this in the victim's coat pocket.'

I squinted.

'It's a letter,' Colquhoun murmured. 'Purporting to be from

the surgery and requesting that Brunswick's 3pm appointment be moved to 12.15pm.'

'Leaving enough time for the killer to break in after the staff left but before Brunswick arrived,' I said grimly,

'Exactly.'

The level of planning and the attention to detail was chilling.

Lukas drew in a sharp breath; he couldn't stay quiet any longer. 'Take me to him,' he bit out.

Under any other circumstances, I was certain that DI Colquhoun would have politely but firmly told Lord Lukas Horvath to fuck off. He wasn't in the police, even though she'd told me to bring him along. Vampire lord or not, he held no sway here. But we all knew why she'd told me to include him.

'Maybe you can tell us where the teeth have come from.' Colquhoun hesitated. 'Or rather *who* the teeth have come from.'

I winced but Lukas didn't move a muscle.

'This way.' She motioned towards the inner door. 'He's through here.'

The black dentist's chair was pitched at an angle in the centre of the room. Samuel Brunswick was lying on it as if he were merely waiting for a check-up. His eyes were closed but his mouth was wide open, and speckles of blood marred the collar of his white shirt.

I stared at the fangs that had been crudely inserted in place of his own canines, then my eyes flicked to the white counter along the far wall. Brunswick's original teeth were lying there in a small pool of blood. My stomach turned.

Lukas hissed under his breath before stepping back, pale-faced, to look at DI Colquhoun. 'How did you know that he's human and not vamp?' he asked evenly,

It was a good question. At first glance, most humans would have registered the fangs and assumed bloodsucker, despite the two bloodied human canines on the counter. Of course there were plenty of other physical indications of vampirism other than fangs, but most people focused on the first thing they saw and jumped to conclusions.

Colquhoun opened her mouth to answer but it was DCI Murray who spoke up. He'd been standing in the corner murmuring quietly to a white-coated woman, whom I assumed was the on-scene pathologist. 'The dentist told us. He examined the victim only last week and he knows his teeth. He told us that there was no way those fangs were natural. Dr Sims confirmed the victim was human when she arrived.'

It was a small thing that mattered little, but it bothered me that Murray called Brunswick 'the victim' rather than using his name. It de-personalised him – and it irritated me – but I knew better than to allow my feelings show.

'Where is the dentist now?' Lukas asked.

'He's been taken to the station for tea, biscuits and a hell of a lot of counselling,' Colquhoun said. 'His colleagues are with him. They have confirmed that they all returned to the surgery shortly before one and they didn't see anything or anyone. The first indication that anything was wrong was when the dentist opened the door and saw the body.'

'The killer worked fast.' I glanced at the pathologist, Dr Sims. 'Have you established a cause of death?'

'It looks like a heart attack, but I can't say for sure until I make a proper examination. And I don't know what brought on the heart attack, though I think at this point we can assume it was deliberate.'

'Everything about this was planned out and premeditated, ' Lukas muttered. 'The heart attack was deliberate – count on it.'

Murray straightened his back and gazed around the small room like a politician giving a speech. 'The Cupid Killer thought about this,' he intoned. 'He knew what he was doing and left nothing to chance. However, he shouldn't get too cocky. We will leave no stone unturned in our search for him. He will be apprehended. This poor man deserves justice.'

It sounded like a rehearsal for his next press conference. I was surprised that Murray didn't punch the palm of his hand when he finished speaking.

'This poor man isn't the only victim.' Lukas's tone of voice was casual, almost pleasant. Uh-oh.

'Yes.' Murray didn't seem to recognise the danger. 'Can we confirm yet whether those fangs were taken from a live or dead vampire?'

Dr Sims glanced at Lukas. 'It's time to find out,' she said quietly. 'Step back please.'

We did as she asked. Using tweezers, Sims leaned over Brunswick's body and carefully extracted the first fang. It slid out from his mouth with disturbing ease. We watched as she held it up and examined it. 'It's a healthy tooth. Whoever it originally belonged to, it appears that they were alive until recently.'

'Do you think,' Colquhoun asked carefully, without looking at Lukas, 'that it was extracted post-mortem? Are we looking for another dead body?'

'I can't say for sure,' Dr Sims said. 'Not yet. Obviously, the removal of the fangs wouldn't have caused death. The original owner might still be alive somewhere.'

Murray could barely contain himself. 'It seems unlikely that a vampire would allow someone to simply extract their own fangs, so they must already be dead. Four victims,' he breathed. 'In less than a week, we have four victims and two killers. It's extraordinary!'

In a flash, Lukas was by his side. 'Extraordinary?' he growled.

'Well, it's hardly ordinary, is it? When was the last time somebody was able to attack a vampire like this? Unless I'm mistaken, your kind are incredibly strong.' He rubbed his chin. 'At least one of our killers must be a supe. How else could they achieve this? Unless the tales of vampiric strength are exaggerated?' he asked innocently,

I sidestepped and nudged Lukas with the toe of my shoe. This wasn't the time to let his temper get the better of him.

'Are any of your people missing, Lord Horvath?' Colquhoun asked, her even tone defusing the tension slightly.

Lukas stared hard at Murray, then backed away. He slid out his phone. 'I will let you know.' He left the room while Dr Sims bent over Brunswick to retrieve the second fang.

I watched him go, wondering whether I should follow and make sure he was alright. Lukas took the job of protecting his own people very seriously – but he didn't need me hovering over him. He needed to find out which vampire was missing. Or dead. But it was daytime and it wouldn't be that easy to find who was involved.

Something tugged at the back of my memory, an annoying itch that I couldn't reach. I grimaced and focused on something else, hoping the thought would clarify before too long. 'Somebody killed Peter Pickover,' I said quietly. 'A human.'

Murray nodded self-importantly. 'The Cupid Killer.'

'Somebody else took the blood from that murder and used it after killing Gilchrist Boast. A supe.'

He nodded again. 'The Stupid Killer.'

'Now somebody has attacked or killed a supe, taken their teeth and possibly a different person has used those teeth after killing Samuel Brunswick. The order has been reversed.'

Murray tapped his mouth. 'First Cupid then Stupid. Now Stupid and then Cupid.'

'They're taking turns.' I thought of the letter Jonas had received. 'Maybe it's to keep the competition between them—' I hesitated over the word because it felt nauseating to say aloud '—fair. Have you checked Brunswick's name against the list of Fetish clients?'

Colquhoun grimaced. 'Yes. He's on the list. He's been to the club.'

'Fetish is the link between them all.'

'I'll send a couple of officers there to keep an eye on the place,' Murray said thoughtfully. 'Your Mr Jonas might receive another letter.'

He wasn't my Mr Jonas.

I watched as Dr Sims bagged the second fang. So did Murray. 'Grim,' he said, shaking his head. 'And some poor sod of a vampire is also dead and toothless.'

Not necessarily dead, I thought irritably. Probably dead but not definitely. Then I froze. 'Toothless,' I said. Oh.

Murray gazed at me. 'That's what I said. What about it?'

A shudder ran through me. Without bothering to answer him, I turned and left the room. I looked around until I spotted Lukas; he was standing on the pavement outside the dental surgery with his phone pressed to his ear. His hair was mussed and his expression was grey. It didn't look as if he knew which of his vamps was missing.

When I joined him, he grimaced. 'Hang on, Scarlett,' he said into the phone. 'I'll call you back.' He disconnected then looked at me questioningly. 'What is it?'

I swallowed hard. 'That first night. When Zara came to Heart.'

Lukas's black eyes narrowed. 'What about it?'

'Christopher was on the door. He barred her way.'

'Yes. And?'

I licked my lips. 'Zara called him a toothless idiot.'

Lukas stiffened, paled, and then jabbed at his phone. 'He's not picking up,' he said with an edge of desperation. 'Christopher's not answering.'

'Do you know where he lives?'

He nodded. 'I'll send somewhere there straight away.'

'We should head there too.' I glanced at Bright Smiles. 'I'll let Colquhoun and Murray know.'

'Okay.' Lukas paused. 'Emma?'

'Yes?'

'Hurry.'

CHAPTER FIFTEEN

DI Colquhoun came with us, jammed into the back of Tallulah. She didn't complain about the lack of space; in fact, she didn't say anything. None of us did until Lukas's phone rang, harshly breaking the silence and making us jump.

He answered it tersely. When he hung up, his expression was even darker. 'Christopher isn't at his flat. There's no sign of him there. I've got people speaking to his friends and family.'

I nodded and pressed harder on Tallulah's accelerator.

Even though it was the middle of the day, there were more vampires outside Christopher's home than there had been police and crime-scene experts at Bright Smiles. It was an indication of how seriously the vampire community was taking Lukas's call to arms.

I pretended not to notice the looks of relief on their faces as Tallulah screeched to a halt. They expected me to find Christopher and solve whatever crime had been committed, and they thought that Lukas would be able to make everything else right again. I doubted either of us could live up to their expectations.

Lukas jumped out almost before the car had stopped. I took more time, and helped Colquhoun extricate herself from the tight space behind the driver's seat. 'Emma,' she said in a low voice, 'at the risk of asking a stupid question, should I be concerned here?'

I registered her expression. She wasn't scared of walking into a nest of vampires, she simply wanted to know what to expect. I shook my head. 'You'll be fine. The supe community's opinion of the police has changed in recent months. And you don't have to be worried about being human – they'll respect your position here. Treat it in the same you would any other potential crime scene. There might be the odd vamp who's irritated that we're here, because normally they take care of their own problems, but this is part of a larger crime that involves all sorts of victims – and suspects. We have a right to be involved.' I hesitated. 'And a duty.'

She nodded. 'Thank you.'

I managed a tense smile and we joined Lukas.

'What can we do?' a burly vamp asked. 'How can we help?'

Lukas glanced at me and I nodded. We'd find Christopher faster with their help. 'We'll begin a street-by-street search,' he said. He started to divide up the group. 'You lot, bang on doors between here and the church. You six, take the western side.'

As he continued to give orders, I stepped past him and walked into Christopher's flat with Colquhoun beside me.

I couldn't profess to know Christopher well, but the flat felt like him. It was more cosy than sleek, more comfortable nest than bachelor pad. There were photographs on the carefully painted peach walls, but they weren't posed studio shots; most seemed to be of Christopher with friends and, I was pleased to note, his family who were all human. They'd not disowned him when he'd turned vamp. He had a strong support network of people who would be desperate to find him.

I noted the photos of Christopher at work at Heart, including three with Lukas. There was even one framed picture of the two of us deep in conversation outside the club. I couldn't recall when it had been taken, or what we were talking about, but I was touched that he'd chosen to put it on his wall.

'He seems like a nice guy,' Colquhoun murmured.

'He is,' I replied, painfully aware that we were referring to him in the present tense.

'He might not be the victim we're looking for. Maybe he's gone out for a walk.'

Maybe. I sighed. 'If it's not him, it's somebody else. Somewhere in London, there's a vampire whose fangs have been forcibly removed.' I swallowed. And who was probably dead.

I glanced at the photos again. Christopher looked happy in every single one of them; he was even smiling in the photos where he wasn't looking at the camera. I stepped back and gazed at them. Lots from Heart, some from restaurants, a couple in pubs that I recognised from their décor. None from Fetish. Then I remembered that Lukas said that Christopher had complained about the very existence of the club. Interesting. I filed the thought away for now and poked my head into his bedroom.

I wasn't going to rummage through Christopher's belongings; until we knew more about where he was, he deserved his privacy. As Colquhoun had said, he might be fine. I registered the undisturbed bed with its smoothed sheets and undented pillows and pulled a face.

'He works at Lord Horvath's club?' Colquhoun asked.

'Yeah.' I stared at the neat bed. 'He covers the busiest shift, from 9pm until 5am. If he'd come home, he'd be here asleep. Most vamps are nocturnal, regardless of their jobs.'

'Does he have a partner? A girlfriend or boyfriend who he might be staying with?'

'Lukas would know for sure.' I rubbed the back of my neck. 'But I don't think so.' I sighed again. 'Come on. Let's check the kitchen.'

Colquhoun made a beeline for the fridge and poked her head inside. I smiled faintly; Fred had done the exact same thing at

Rosie Thorn's place. 'Well stocked,' she said. 'And everything looks fresh.' She peered at me. 'No blood though.'

'He probably drinks straight from the vein. Most do.'

Colquhoun arched an eyebrow. 'Does your boyfriend do that, too?'

From the kitchen doorway, Lukas snapped, 'Yes, I do. Do you have a problem with that?'

'Lukas,' I chided. 'DI Colquhoun is one of the good guys. She was only asking. There's nothing wrong with honest curiosity.'

Colquhoun bit her lip. 'No, it was flippant and I apologise. It's none of my business.'

Suddenly Lukas looked very, very tired. 'You don't have to apologise. I'm the one who's sorry.'

I reached for his hand. 'We'll find him.'

His eyes were filled with pain. 'Not alive, we won't. I've sent all those people off to search for him, but we all know the truth. He's not walking back in here. He's already dead.'

'Fuck off.'

Both Lukas and I stared at Colquhoun. 'Come on. We've all dealt with death before.' She pointed to me. 'You certainly have. Peter Pickover and Gilchrist Boast and Samuel Brunswick and Christopher the vampire don't need our sympathy, they need us to find the fuckers who are behind this and stop them. You've had your moment of wallowing. Now it's time for action.'

I snorted. 'You're better at speeches than DCI Murray.'

Colquhoun rolled her eyes. 'Ain't that the truth.' She looked around. 'Christopher's not here. There's no sign of a struggle and other people are already out searching for him. Why don't we—?'

Her words were drowned out by the sound of a heavy lorry reversing down the back lane next to Christopher's kitchen window, its loud beeps indicating that people should get out of its damned way. I glanced out of the window. So did Colquhoun. She frowned, then her expression changed abruptly. 'Check the bin,' she said.

I suddenly realised what she was thinking. I opened the lid of the pedal bin. 'Empty,' I said. 'With a fresh black bag.'

'It sounds like a Hollywood cliché, but it happens. I've lost count of the number of times a victim's rubbish has helped in our investigations. We should stop that bin lorry.'

Lukas was already disappearing out of the back door. Colquhoun and I followed him.

Two binmen wearing hi-vis orange were hauling the first wheelie bin from outside the block of flats towards the rear of the lorry. Lukas marched up to them, and Colquhoun pulled her warrant card.

I hung back, checking the remaining wheelie bins to see if I could establish which one belonged to Christopher. A few of them were numbered with crudely daubed paint, but none of them were Christopher's.

I moved to the first unnumbered bin. I flipped open the lid, peered inside and hauled out the first black bag. Almost instantly the bottom split, sending used kitchen towels, cigarette butts and the remnants of an Indian takeaway spilling across the road. I cursed and bent down to scoop it all back up. Then I stopped.

'Hey!' I called. I stared more closely at the ground and called again, more urgently. 'Hey! Get over here!'

Lukas and Colquhoun were by my side in a second. 'What is it?' Colquhoun asked.

I pointed at the dark splotch. 'Lukas?'

He sucked in a breath. 'It's blood.' He knelt down and sniffed. 'Vampire blood.'

'Is it his?' Colquhoun's question was urgent. 'Is it Christopher's?'

Lukas shook his head. 'I can't tell. Without a sample of his blood to compare it to, I can't know for sure.'

I straightened up. 'Get those binmen out of here,' I said to Colquhoun. 'I'll start knocking on doors.'

Colquhoun pointed at the red door opposite. 'Start with that one,' she said. 'It's got a RingCare video doorbell.'

The three of us exchanged looks, then we sprang into action.

THE MIDDLE-AGED PIXIE who opened the red door was desperate to help. 'It records whenever it detects motion,' she told us. 'My husband thinks it's stupid and an invasion of privacy, but I got it anyway. Now I'm glad that I did.'

She led us through to a small study crammed full of books and papers. She reached for the dusty computer sitting on a narrow desk and turned it on. 'I can show you all the footage.'

'We really appreciate this, ma'am,' Colquhoun told her.

'No problem! No problem at all!'

We gazed at the computer, willing it to spring to life. It made several groaning noises but didn't appear to be in any rush. 'I'm afraid it's an old machine,' the pixie said apologetically.

I resisted the temptation to smack the screen in a bid to speed it up.

'Are you working on Rosie's case as well?' the pixie asked.

'The rest of Supe Squad are,' I told her.

'Poor Rosie. I knew her a little. I never thought she'd go out that way, you know? Was she really murdered?'

'We're looking into it.'

The pixie tutted. 'Terrible business. And now this vampire, so shortly after the goblin. Christopher is a good neighbour. He's always got a smile on his face and a friendly word. Everyone round here likes him. I don't know what the world is coming to.'

Neither did I sometimes. The computer screen finally lit up. 'Here we go,' she trilled. She tapped on the keyboard and opened up the RingCare app. 'Ooh. It was activated at 6.34 this morning.'

A thrill of anticipation zipped through me. That time fitted perfectly with Christopher returning home from his shift at Heart. I leaned forward; so did Lukas and Colquhoun.

The view from the RingCare doorbell didn't include Christopher's back door. All the same, we held our breaths – until a sauntering cat flickered into view. A curse exploded from Lukas.

'It's okay,' the pixie said. 'There's more.' She clicked on the mouse. 'Here – 6.58am.'

We stared at the screen again. Colquhoun sucked in a breath. 'There,' she said. 'There he is.'

She was right. Christopher came past carrying a black bag. He must have entered through his front door, emptied his bin and walked out of the back door to drop the rubbish in his wheelie bin for the pick-up later on.

'He came home,' I said. 'He didn't go to an early-morning pub or to somebody's house after his shift. And this is only five hours before Samuel Brunswick was murdered across the city.'

The pixie blinked. 'Oh my.'

I glanced at her. 'Perhaps it's best if you wait in the other room while we view the rest of your footage.'

The pixie wrung her hands. 'Um…'

Colquhoun flashed her a reassuring smile. 'It's a good idea. There might be things on this video that you don't want to see.' Her tone was soft but her meaning was clear.

The pixie blanched, nodded and skittered out of the study, closing the door after her.

Lukas barely noticed her departure; his attention was focused on the video. A van had pulled up, blocking the RingCare camera's view. There was a flicker on the far side of the screen as the van's driver jumped out. Unfortunately, he walked away from the camera rather than towards it, so all we got was a glimpse of his feet. Less than three minutes later, the van pulled away, leaving the street empty again. There was no longer any sign of Christopher.

'Do you think…?' Colquhoun didn't finish her sentence.

'Rewind the video.'

Lukas did I as I asked. He didn't look at me or say anything – his anguish cut too deep and he didn't want reassurance or platitudes, even from me. He wanted answers. I glanced down and saw his taut, white knuckles, then I looked back at the screen.

We watched the video again. Lukas paused it briefly in the half-second before the van appeared. The road was unmarked but, after the van trundled off, there was something on it. It was faint, but it was there. Blood marked the spot.

'That's him,' I said in little more than a whisper. 'That's our killer.'

'One of our killers,' Colquhoun corrected.

'And all we can see,' Lukas said, his voice vibrating with rage, 'is that he wears generic jeans and cheap black trainers and drives a dirty white van.' He slammed his fist into the wall, and plaster and paint flew in all directions. Then he spun round and stalked out, swerving round the pale-faced pixie.

She gazed at us. 'Is everything alright?'

I lifted my chin and met her eyes. 'It's all fine,' I lied. I flicked a look at the dent in her wall. 'But we do owe you some money.'

CHAPTER SIXTEEN

BY THE TIME COLQUHOUN AND I HAD APOLOGISED TO THE PIXIE and assured her that the damage to her home would be repaired as soon as possible, Lukas had vanished.

'You know he can't be involved now,' Colquhoun said to me. 'He's too close and too emotionally invested.'

I was emotionally invested too, but I hid it better. 'He can still help,' I said.

'How?' She looked up and down the street. 'Where's he gone?'

I turned right. 'This way – the way the van went.' I started jogging. I knew where Lukas would be.

Proud Produce, the small shop at the end of Christopher's street, was renowned in the supe community. From the outside it looked like any other corner shop in London, but inside it was a veritable cornucopia of strange objects and even stranger food.

Technically this area was still Soho, so the shop offered a selection of flavoured blood 'treats', which were adored by hundreds of Lukas's vampires. I couldn't say that an O negative lollipop with a jalapeno twist was to my taste, but I wasn't the target customer.

The shop catered for werewolves as well as vamps and

seemed to do a roaring sale in 'costumes for the shifted form'. I thought that dogs wearing tiny T-shirts, custom-made jackets and bow ties looked odd, but that was nothing compared to the sight of a fully grown werewolf in animal form doing the same. Obviously, my lupine fashion sense wasn't up to par.

The array of products for the supernaturally inclined encouraged goggle-eyed humans to drop by. For the most part, the shop's owner didn't mind because the humans often bought bits and pieces as joke presents for their loved ones. A human's money was just as good as a supe's. When anti-supe sentiment had been on the rise, though, things occasionally turned ugly. I'd been called out to the shop on several occasions when a foul-mouthed human had taken things too far.

We'd advised installing extensive CCTV both inside and outside the shop. It was rarely required in these calmer times, but I didn't think the owner, Bartimaeus Proud, would have dismantled the cameras. After all, there was no telling what the future might hold.

The door jangled as I entered and the strong scent of verbena-laden incense tickled my nostrils. Colquhoun stared round with wide eyes. 'What kind of shop is this?' She picked up a red candle that I knew was laced with blood.

I left her to examine it and strode up to Lukas. He was standing by the counter, his hands shoved in his pockets and a brooding expression on his face. 'Are you—?' I started.

'I'm fine.' He sighed deeply. 'Sorry, D'Artagnan. He's *my* vampire. He's my responsibility. I have to find him.'

I put my hand on his arm. '*We* have to find him. And we will.' I ignored the heavy weight pressing down on my shoulders. Right now, Lukas's well-being – and the search for Christopher – took priority.

'I was furious, you know,' he said distantly. 'When I heard what Robert Sullivan tried to do to you, it took everything I had not to march round to the Sullivan clan residence and call him out. I know you can look after yourself and you don't need me to step in for you, but that wasn't what stopped me.' He sighed. 'It was understanding what it feels like to lose someone that held me back. How do you do this, Emma? How do you deal with this sort of misery on a day-to-day basis?'

I tightened my grip on his arm. 'Remember what Colquhoun said? No wallowing. Let's focus on finding Christopher and the fuckers behind this. That's how I deal with it.'

'Amen,' Colquhoun murmured from behind us. 'Where's the shopkeeper?'

As if he'd heard her, Bartimaeus Proud emerged from a small door behind the counter. Colquhoun was professional enough not to comment on his otherworldly appearance; even MC Jonas, with his flowing green wig and wired acrobatics, couldn't compare to Bartimaeus Proud.

He couldn't have been more than an inch over four feet tall, but his lack of height in no way diminished his presence. I had no idea what manner of supe Bartimaeus was, and when I'd once asked him, he'd neatly sidestepped the question. Whatever he was, there was considerable power beneath his small frame.

I'd never seen him outside the shop, so maybe it was the building itself that imbued him with confidence. His pride in his business was the reason he took it so personally when a human decided to overstep the line and cause trouble. Truth be told, I had the feeling he'd called Supe Squad when there were problems because he wanted to protect the numbskull idiots who were pushing for a fight rather than deal with them himself. I had little doubt that Proud could look after himself.

For once, Colquhoun couldn't maintain a blank-faced façade and she just stared at him.

Bartimaeus nodded a greeting at me and offered her a smile, but his deference was reserved for Lukas. 'Here.' He placed a laptop on the counter and spun it around. 'Here's this morning's footage.'

Colquhoun and I leaned over Lukas's shoulder. The time stamp was 6.57am, a minute before the van arrived outside the pixie's home and Christopher's back door. The picture was crisper than the RingCare footage. I crossed my fingers, hoping this would give us the lead that we needed.

'There,' Colquhoun said suddenly, as the van flashed into view. It passed Proud's shop in the blink of an eye.

'Can you pause it?' Lukas asked.

Proud nodded. With expert fingers, he replayed the same scene, stopping the video at the exact moment the van went past.

Lukas didn't bother to moderate his temper. 'Fuck!'

Fuck indeed. The rear of the van was visible – but the number plate was splattered with enough mud to completely obscure it. There was little doubt that had been done deliberately.

Proud pressed play again, and again we all leaned into the screen. Somewhere beyond the camera's vision, Christopher was being attacked. The van reappeared, travelling in the opposite direction. This time, we didn't need to ask Bartimaeus Proud to pause the video.

The front number plate was obscured in the same fashion as the rear one. We could see the van driver, but his head was down and he was wearing a hat that obscured his face. We might have captured him on camera, but there were no obvious details to help us capture him in person.

Lukas's shoulders dropped. The hopeful anticipation that we'd find something useful followed by swift disappointment was almost too painful to bear.

We watched the footage five times., but at no point was the vehicle or the driver identifiable.

I shook my head. 'This isn't opportunistic. That man – that killer – must have targeted Christopher. He was waiting nearby for Christopher to return home from Heart.'

'I realise DCI Murray doesn't particularly impress either of you, but surely he had a point when he mentioned vampiric strength? How does someone who's not a supe overpower a vampire?' Colquhoun asked.

'Christopher might have had a few drinks after he knocked off work,' I explained. 'He could have been attacked from behind. We know that the kidnapping happened quickly. If he was taken by surprise and the attacker had the right tools, anyone could have done it.'

Colquhoun looked at me.

'But, yeah,' I conceded reluctantly, 'it was probably a supe.'

Lukas seemed not to be listening to our conversation. 'You've told me before, D'Artagnan, that the devil is in the detail. Criminals are caught because they don't cover all the bases and something gets over-looked.'

'Yeah.' I glanced again at the computer screen and frozen image of the van driver. In the split second before he pointed it out, I realised what he was talking about and so did Colquhoun. On the van's dashboard, and in full view of Proud's camera, was the detritus of a half-eaten breakfast.

'Zoom in,' Colquhoun breathed.

Bartimaeus was already on it. He tapped the mouse and enlarged the image. Half a bacon roll with its wrapping hanging off and a large disposable coffee cup sat precariously next to the windshield. I squinted at the lettering on the cup. Not all of it was visible. Something House. There was a logo of a blue coffee bean underneath.

'—ind House,' Lukas read aloud. 'Wind House?'

Colquhoun frowned. 'It's a café. It'd be more like Unwind House. Or Kind House. Somewhere you'd go to relax, something caffeine related.'

'How about Grind House?' I suggested.

Bartimaeus spun the laptop back towards him and typed the words into his search engine. 'Here!' he crowed, jabbing at the third entry down. 'That's the same logo, right?'

I sucked in a breath. There it was.

'It's less than five miles away,' Bartimaeus said helpfully. Lukas, Colquhoun and I were already running for the door. 'Good luck,' he called out.

I acknowledged him with a smile before I left. The truth was that we were making our own luck – and not very successfully.

COLQUHOUN UPDATED DCI MURRAY, Lukas rallied some of his troops away from the search, and I drove like a demon. The traffic was increasing as the day wore on, but the busy roads were no match for Tallulah, not when she was in the right mood. We zipped in and out of the lines of cars, and I ignored the angry beeps and horns from other drivers.

Adrenaline was rushing through my veins, borne out of the desperate desire to find Christopher alive, whether he possessed his fangs or not. Maybe there was a chance we'd find out who his kidnapper – and Gilchrist Boast's killer – was. If he'd gone into the Grind House to buy his breakfast and their CCTV was half as good Bartimaeus Proud's, maybe we'd see his face. He wouldn't have been expecting us to track him to the coffee shop and might not have taken the same precautions to cover his face. Third time lucky, I promised myself.

'We're gonna get you,' I whispered.

Colquhoun spoke up from the back. 'Murray is sending people over and he's coming, too. He wants us to wait outside the coffee shop until he gets there with a warrant.'

Lukas growled, 'I don't work for him. I can do what I want.'

'Except,' I said, begrudging every word, 'if we get a clear identification of the killer, we need to ensure every rule is adhered to so we can build an airtight case. It's not a supe business like Proud's Produce. You can't barge in there and demand to see the cameras.'

'Humans and their damned rules,' he muttered. 'Christopher might still be alive. If we delay…'

'Murray won't be far behind,' Colquhoun said. 'No matter what you think of him, he wants the same as we do. He can't afford to mess this up.'

I spun into the small car park next to the Grind House and pulled Tallulah into the first empty space.

'In that case,' Lukas replied, 'he shouldn't have any objection to us using the time appropriately and going in to speak to the staff.'

I turned off Tallulah's engine. 'We're not going into the coffee shop,' I said quietly.

'Emma—' Lukas started.

'Look,' I said. I raised my finger and pointed.

The Grind House was situated on the side of a busy road, in a great spot to nab customers going to and from work. On the other side of the road, to the right, there was an industrial estate filled with car showrooms and branded businesses. On the edge of it, a smaller building was set apart from the larger ones. It looked empty and rundown, as if it were slated for demolition so the space could be used more profitably.

Directly outside it was a dirty white van. If I craned my neck, I could just make out the mud-covered side and rear. 'If his van is still there,' I said, my veins pulsing with the need to spring into action, 'then he probably is too.'

And the killer's continued presence here meant that Christopher might still be breathing.

CHAPTER SEVENTEEN

'I KNOW YOU'RE NOT GOING TO WANT TO HEAR IT, BUT DCI Murray will want you to wait,' Colquhoun said as she handed me my crossbow.

She was right. The sensible plan was to wait – I'd only just been arguing with Lukas about waiting – but the situation had suddenly become more urgent. 'Both you and Murray said it makes sense that a supe brought Christopher down,' I told her. 'That means going into that building is Supe Squad's responsibility.'

'And mine,' Lukas added darkly. 'We take care of our own.'

Colquhoun put up her hands. 'I'm not arguing with you, but it would be wise to hang on for the cavalry. You don't know what to expect in there and you'll need backup. And this is a joint investigation – humans have died, too.'

'Christopher might still be alive,' I said. 'He's the one who needs back up, not us.'

She sighed. 'You know the chances that he's not dead are slight.' Then she took a step back and I knew what she'd say next. 'Go. I'll wait two minutes before I call it in. Whatever you're going to have to do, do it quickly.'

I flashed her a grateful smile and turned to Lukas. 'I can only see one entry point.'

His features were set and focused. 'It makes our job easier.'

'I'll take the lead.'

He opened his mouth to argue but I shook my head. 'You know it's safer that way.' Translation: if there were booby traps or somebody waiting with a gun, I could die but I'd recover. Lukas wouldn't. I could see following me galled him, not because of his ego but because he believed that looking after Christopher – *saving* Christopher – was his responsibility. But he wasn't stupid and he knew it made sense.

'All for one,' I reminded him.

His eyes held mine. 'Don't die.'

I pushed myself onto my toes and kissed him. 'I'll do my best.'

Then, without another word, we were both running across the road towards the van and the ramshackle building next to it.

We knew what to do without needing to communicate. We approached the van as silently as possible, which was easier for Lukas than for me even though I kept to the balls of my feet and muffled my footsteps as much as I could. Lukas took the driver's side while I headed to the passenger door. I raised the tip of my crossbow and aimed through the glass. Nobody was there.

I looked at the messy interior; it wasn't just his murder scenes that were bloody and careless and in stark contrast to his competitor's efforts. He'd finished his breakfast roll and the Grind House wrapper was balled up on the passenger seat, together with several other wrappers and a lot of crumbs. I counted four empty coffee cups. That was good: if he was a repeat customer at the coffee shop, he was probably spending considerable time in the building next to the van. He might be there now.

I tiptoed to the rear of the van and pressed my ear against the back doors, listening for any signs of life. Nothing. Lukas rattled the handle on his side but the door was locked. I tried the rear doors – also locked. It would have taken us seconds to break in but it wasn't our priority.

I dipped my head around the van and motioned to Lukas. He nodded and headed to the left of the building while I went right. Eventually we met in the middle.

My initial assessment held up: there was only one door leading into the building. The windows were high, and too small and narrow for anyone to escape through them. All the same, I didn't want to take any chances and I held up a finger to Lukas, asking him to wait.

I ducked around the corner and beckoned to Colquhoun over the road. She raised her hand and said something into her phone before tucking it away and jogging over to join us. She knew better than to speak. She motioned to her phone and pulled a face. Yeah, yeah. Murray could be as pissed off as he wanted to be.

I wasn't going to ask Colquhoun to come in with us, not because she'd be disobeying Murray's orders if she followed us but because she'd be putting her life in danger if this killer was indeed a supe. She was entirely human, and that made her far too vulnerable. But I didn't want to leave anything to chance.

I pointed at the door. Fortunately, Colquhoun understood. There was a slim chance that the killer would manage to get past both Lukas and me, but if he did she'd be waiting for him. I hoped she wouldn't try to apprehend him because she wasn't armed, but at least she could get a look at him.

Colquhoun backed up and crouched some distance away where she was relatively safe but still had a clear view of the door. As soon as she gave me the thumbs-up, I glanced at Lukas. He was ready. We both were.

I stepped in front of the door and stopped for a second, listening hard. Lukas shook his head. Nope, he couldn't hear anything either. I reached for the rusty door knob and inhaled sharply when it turned and the door opened an inch. It wasn't locked. Maybe this guy deserved the moniker Stupid Killer after all.

The hinges were as rusty as the doorknob, so I only nudged the door open until it was wide enough to slip through. Inside it was dark, with only the faintest light seeping in through the grimy windows.

Heart beating faster, I edged inside. The air was thick with the scent of mould. I sniffed. I didn't need to look at Lukas to know that there was also the tang of blood under the earthier smells. We were in the right place.

Lukas edged in beside me and looked at the door with a question in his eyes. I nodded and he closed it.

We could head left or right. I checked the floor to see if there were any footprints on the dirty carpet but saw nothing. I pointed: Lukas would go right. The gloomy shadows made his features look even grimmer but, despite his set jaw and dark expression, there was a spark in his eyes that was probably reflected in my own. We both had the same sliver of hope that Christopher was in here and alive.

I crept towards the end of the hallway and turned right. Another hallway stretched in front of me. An old calendar proclaiming the year to be 1992 clung to one wall, alongside some tattered posters of scantily clad women, the sort you'd have found in any lads' mag two or three decades ago. It didn't look as if this building had been put to any good use since then.

I ignored the lurid images and focused on the doorway halfway down the corridor. There was a chink of bright light coming from it. There. That was where I needed to go. I made my way silently towards it.

I was about a metre away when I heard a long, guttural groan.

I gripped my crossbow tightly, double-checking that it was loaded and ready to go, then I nudged the door open with the toe of my shoe.

The illumination was coming from a large skylight, which

hadn't been noticeable from outside. It was bright enough to light the room – and the body strung up in the centre of it. I couldn't see his face, but I knew it was Christopher.

He was hanging upside down, suspended by his feet. His arms hung loosely and the tips of his fingers were scraping the floor. He wore boxer shorts and nothing else, and his skin appeared to be covered in blood like Peter Pickover's had been.

My instinct was to cut him down but instead I scanned the room for any other signs of life. Was the killer still here? There was an odd prickling sensation across the back of my neck; I felt as if I were being watched.

There was a pile of boxes along one side of the room. A chair stood five metres away from Christopher, positioned so that whoever sat in it would be facing him. The killer must have sat there and watched him, perhaps even chatted to him. I shuddered.

I searched for anywhere someone might be hiding, but the rest of the room was empty. Despite my misgivings, nobody else was here. That meant the groan I'd heard only seconds before had come from Christopher; he was still alive.

I wasted no more time. I sprang towards him and crouched beside his head. His eyes flickered open and he flinched.

'Shh,' I said. 'It's okay. It's me, Christopher. It's Emma. I'm going to get you out of here.' I stared at the dried blood round his lips. His mouth was open wide enough for me to see the dark gaping holes where his fangs had once been.

'Uhhhh…' he managed.

'Don't try to speak.' I pulled back and gazed upwards. He was being held by some kind of steel wire that was wrapped around his ankles. I followed it with my eyes; it led across the ceiling towards the far corner of the room where it trailed down the wall. Now I understood: it was a pulley system.

'Fuck!' Lukas's voice exploded from the open doorway. He

sprinted forward. 'Christopher!' He cupped the younger vampire's face. 'Christopher!'

'Uhhh…'

Lukas let out a shuddering breath. 'He's alive. Praise be – he's alive. Don't worry. We'll get you down. You're safe. You'll be alright.'

Christopher's eyes bulged and he groaned again. He was shaking from head to toe. He must have been strung up for hours. Given the blood loss he'd suffered, not to mention the exposure, it was a wonder he was even conscious.

I reached for the pulse in his neck. It was faint and ragged. 'He's barely clinging on,' I murmured to Lukas. 'We have to get him down. You stay here with him and I'll release the pulley.'

'I'm ready. I won't let him fall.'

I knew he wouldn't. I darted over to the wall. The catch to release the pulley seemed simple enough; all I had to do was flip it up to release the wire and try to ensure a controlled drop so that I didn't do Christopher's battered body any more damage.

I placed my hand on the metal catch. 'On a count of three,' I called. 'One, two—' I hesitated.

Lukas's voice drifted over. 'Is there a problem?'

My hand hovered over the taut wire. 'It's too easy,' I muttered to myself.

'Emma?'

It didn't feel right, and I still had the sensation that we were being watched. It was hours since Christopher had been taken. Why had the killer risked leaving him alive? Unless…

I shivered. 'Give me a moment,' I replied.

My gaze fell on the pile of boxes in the corner. I moved over to them and stared at them more closely.

'Emma.' Lukas sounded strained. 'He doesn't have long.'

'Bear with me. This is important.' I pulled down the box at the top of the pile. It was empty. I grabbed the second, then the third.

Also empty. I tossed them aside. Maybe I was imagining ghosts where there were none.

I reached for the fourth box then I halted. A hole was cut into its side where there shouldn't have been one. It was small but it was definitely there. I crouched down and poked my finger at it. Shit.

'What is it?'

'I think it's a camera,' I hissed. I flipped open the lid. I was right: a small digital camera was taped inside the box, its lens pressed to the peephole and a thin cable linking it to a power bank. Chillingly, a red light indicated that it was recording. We were indeed being watched.

I chewed my lip, then returned to the pulley. Pulling out my phone and turning on the torch function, I held it upwards to shed more light. Even so, I almost missed it.

'Uhhh...' Christopher's grunt sounded weaker. He was definitely fading.

'There's a second wire,' I said. I stared at the thin silvery line that led horizontally from the pulley. It was taut and barely noticeable, but it was there for a reason.

I tracked its length from the pulley. It led all the way around the cobweb-covered walls until I was opposite Christopher. The concealed, spring-loaded system and the sharp blade were designed to be released as soon as the pulley was loosened.

I clenched my teeth. It was a fucking booby trap. This entire setup was designed for Christopher to be killed in front of our eyes at the very moment we thought we were saving him. And somewhere, the killer was watching us. I wondered if he was enjoying the show.

I turned back to the box with the hidden camera and knelt down to face the lens. I held up my middle finger. *Screw you. You're not going to win.* 'I will find you,' I told the camera.

'Emma—'

I didn't look at Lukas. 'As soon as I'm gone, get Christopher down. I'll see you in twelve hours.'

I didn't wait for a reply. Instead, I positioned myself in front of the blade and reached for the wire.

I'd be back.

CHAPTER EIGHTEEN

I WAS VAGUELY PLEASED WHEN I OPENED MY EYES AND REALISED I was lying on a fire-retardant blanket. Removing scorch marks from a floor was a pain in the arse, so it was good that Lukas had the foresight to put me somewhere sensible, even if our lounge floor wasn't particularly comfortable.

The reek of sulphur was as strong as ever, however, and I grimaced as I wondered how long it would take to get rid of the stench. Then I remembered what had happened and why I was here. Goddamnit.

I sat up, grabbed the dressing gown that had been left beside me and joined Lukas at the window. 'You promised me that you wouldn't die,' he said.

Nope. 'I promised you that I would do my best not to die. If time hadn't been of the essence, I'd have found another way.' I paused, afraid to ask the question but desperate to know the answer. 'Christopher?' My voice wobbled slightly.

'Alive. The moment that blade hit your heart, I got him down. It was in the nick of time,' he added darkly.

I shuddered with relief. 'Has he said anything? Did he recognise who did this to him?'

Lukas was holding himself stiffly and I already knew what his answer would be. 'He's in a bad way, so he couldn't say much about anything. He's being looked after by our best people but it's too early to question him.' He glared out of the window. 'That's not stopped DCI Murray from calling in every hour to check.'

'I don't like him,' I said quietly, 'but he's only doing his job.'

'I want to hear what Christopher has to say as much as he does. I want to catch the bastard who did this. But Christopher can't talk yet. As soon as he does, we'll all know about it.' Lukas's voice simmered with barely held fury, though I knew it wasn't directed at me, or Murray. His rage was reserved for Christopher's would-be killer.

I wrapped my arms around myself. 'It was a trap from the start. He knew we'd track down the van and find that damned building. He wanted us to find it so he could film us cutting Christopher down and killing him in the process. He wanted to make a show of it. He wanted to see our faces when Christopher died.'

'He very nearly did,' Lukas muttered through gritted teeth.

I buried my head in his shoulder. His arms went around me. 'He didn't succeed,' I said. 'He didn't win.'

'Neither did we.' Lukas held me tighter. 'And neither did Christopher. Three people are dead and one is maimed for life. If this is a competition, those two killers are winning.'

The thought of winning competitions led me to ask another question. 'Lukas, has Christopher been to Fetish? You said he'd complained about the club, but had he actually been there? Did he participate in any games?'

'His name is on the list that Jonas handed over.'

I cursed. 'It always leads back to that damned club.'

'And,' Lukas replied in a low voice, 'it always starts with that damned Cassandra.'

'I don't believe she's one of the killers,' I said. 'And neither do you.'

'Perhaps not. But either her visions are true, in which case we need her close to hand for the next ones or, more likely, she's being drip fed information by the killers. *She's* the key, not the club.'

'You're prejudiced against her because of what she is.'

He didn't argue. 'Yeah, I am. I'm sorry if that makes you uncomfortable but my prejudice doesn't change the fact that she's involved in some way. You can't deny that we need to find her. *I* need to find her.'

'Lukas—'

He pulled back and met my eyes. 'Do you believe I'll harm her?'

No. His antipathy towards Zara disturbed me but I knew he wouldn't deliberately hurt her, either physically or emotionally. I shook my head and sighed. 'She's a person like you and me. She can't help what she is, Lukas.'

'Unless she's lying about what she sees.' At my look, he grimaced. 'Fine. Do you want to find her and talk to her?'

'Of course.'

'Then once I locate her, I won't approach her. I'll tell you where she is and you can speak to her. Does that make it better?'

'Thank you. She's not the enemy here.'

'Is she the enemy if she knew more about Christopher than she told you?'

I didn't look away. 'We both know better than to deal in what ifs.'

Lukas gave me a crooked smile that didn't quite meet his eyes. 'What if you don't find the killers?' I opened my mouth to answer but he continued, 'What if you *do* find them?'

'Justice,' I told him.

'Whose justice?'

This time I didn't reply.

COLQUHOUN ANSWERED on the first ring. 'Emma?'

'Hey,' I said, sounding altogether too cheerful given the circumstances. It was a side effect of dying and being re-born that I was unable to control.

'Oh. My. God. It really does work. You can't actually die.'

Colquhoun didn't sound like herself and I didn't like her awe-struck tone. I preferred her sombre, taciturn side. 'Yeah,' I said briskly, 'it's a thing.'

'Unbelievable. I saw your body. You were bloody dead.'

'And now I'm not,' I said. 'I'm mortal. I still age and I will die for real at some point. Everyone does.' And then, because there were far more important things to talk about, I asked, 'Where are we up to?'

Fortunately, Colquhoun got the message. 'Fucking nowhere,' she muttered. 'The computer techs are checking the camera. They know the feed went somewhere but they can't tell where. About twenty seconds after you died, it was completely cut off.'

Damn it. That wasn't helpful at all. 'Fingerprints? DNA? That was a big old building. Something must have been left somewhere.'

'Oh, we've found fingerprints galore. They're all over the building and the van, and they match a couple of partials we found at Gilchrist Boast's house. But there's nothing on any of our systems that matches them. The guy's a ghost. He's certainly never been picked up for anything in the past, and he's not in the military.'

That wasn't good news. 'And the coffee shop?' I asked. 'The Grind House? What about their cameras?'

'They don't have any. The owner doesn't believe in invading his customers' privacy. We think that's where the hand-off between Cupid and Stupid happened. The baristas can't remember seeing anyone suspicious, though. The shop was busy and they served a lot of customers. Even so, Murray ordered a thorough search of the place.'

'And?'

'And we found a paper napkin in one of the outside bins that was stained with blood. It's a match for Christopher. The fingerprints match those found inside the building, but there's only one set. Our working theory is that Christopher's attacker took his fangs and left them somewhere outside the coffee shop. Maybe he wiped the blood off them with the napkin, or maybe there was blood on his fingers. Either way, that was when Samuel Brunswick's killer picked them up to use at Bright Smiles.'

My hand tightened around the phone. We knew so much about the how, and so little about the who or the why. 'So we have nothing that will lead us to either killer. All that, and we still have nothing.'

'We have Fetish. Murray has put more people onto looking through the stuff you got from there, and he wants to visit the club with you and talk to the owner. What's his name? Kevin Jonas?'

'Yeah.' I checked my watch. It was barely 7am. Fetish had closed less than two hours earlier and wouldn't open again until the evening. I had no qualms about getting Jonas out of bed, however. 'Okay. I can head over there now.'

'Murray's in a meeting that might take a while. And,' she added drily, 'he has some press calls to make.'

Of course he did. Still, I supposed it would give me time to check in with Phileas Carmichael so he could green light the visit. I didn't need the gremlin solicitor's agreement but it would help to keep him – and Jonas – on side. They had both explicitly requested to limit the involvement of the Met after all. 'Midday, then. I'll check in with the club's solicitor, then confirm the address with Murray and meet him there.'

'I'll let him know. Anything from Christopher yet?' Colquhoun asked hopefully.

'He's still out. As soon as I hear anything you'll be the first to know,' I promised, crossing my fingers tightly that he'd be able to talk soon – and that he'd have some information for us. I didn't think that the killers were planning to stop unless we got to them and ended their sick games. My stomach turned at the thought of more murders.

I ended the call and plastered a fake smile on my face as if I could pretend that everything was fine and walked into the Supe Squad building. Home sweet home.

I paused inside the door and inhaled the scent of verbena and wolfsbane. I'd missed it more than I'd realised. I'd missed my desk and my coffee mug, Liza's cakes and her sharp tongue. I'd missed Fred's easy smile and Grace's constant attempts to maintain order. Hell, at this point, I even missed the paperwork.

I shook my head. Next time another police station required Supe Squad representation, they could have DS Owen Grace. I wanted to stay here.

As soon as that thought entered my head, I heard the shouting. 'For fuck's sake! Why won't any of you idiots listen to me?'

I passed a hand over my eyes. Robert Sullivan. I should have guessed. I squared my shoulders and strode into the visitors' room. Robert was on his feet, his face red. Patches of fur were erupting on his cheeks, and I knew with a sinking feeling that he was inches away from shifting into a wolf. Again.

Owen Grace was next to him with his hands up, palms facing outwards in a placatory gesture. Fred was shielding Thistle with his body, but it looked to me as if the pixie was as involved as Robert was.

'You great oaf!' she yelled at him. 'We *have* listened to you! I've done nothing *but* listen to you! She died. Neither post-mortem found anything untoward. I'm sorry she's dead, but there's no evidence she was murdered. You need to let it go!'

'I can't!' he roared back. 'I loved her!'

She clenched her fists. 'You don't have a monopoly on love! She was my gran. I loved her too!'

'We all need to calm down,' Grace said, twitching at the chaos occurring right in front of his eyes. 'We've investigated every-thing, Mr Sullivan. There's nothing that suggests foul play.'

'Oh yeah?' Robert sneered. 'What about the lipstick? I told you about the lipstick, right?'

Fred cleared his throat. 'I looked into that. She bought it as part of her costume for her birthday party. The only fingerprints on the lipstick are hers. Mr Sullivan, I'm sorry for your loss but Rosie died naturally.'

'It's not possible!'

I gazed at Robert. He wasn't in control of himself, and nothing about this situation boded well. I strode forward and placed my hands on his shoulders. 'Robert,' I said softly.

His head snapped towards me, misery and rage and grief etched on every line of his face. 'You have to help me,' he pleaded. 'You have to help Rosie.'

I nodded, then gestured to the others to leave the room. Grace looked like he wanted to refuse but then he glanced again at Robert's face and nodded. 'Get him to see sense,' he muttered. 'We've looked at everything. She wasn't murdered.'

I directed Robert to a chair. He sat down heavily as the door closed and we were left alone. 'They won't listen to me.' His eyes welled up with tears. 'They won't fucking listen to me and they're going to close the investigation. You can make them, can't you?'

I sighed. I knew why he was doing this; he didn't want to believe she was dead. If we closed the case, it was all over and there was nothing of Rosie left for him to fight for. 'There's no evidence she was killed.'

'She was healthy. She didn't die of a natural heart attack, whatever those post-mortems are saying. My Rosie was strong. She had regular check-ups.' He glared at me, stubborn denial shining from his eyes.

'Her GP confirmed that she hadn't seen him for two years,' I told him. 'Her next-door neighbour checked her blood pressure, but that was about it. She died of natural causes.'

He shook his head. 'No. Someone could have slipped her something, poisoned her. There are chemicals and compounds that are undetectable. Something caused her heart attack – someone killed her!' He wasn't going to listen to anything I said, no matter how true it was.

He went on, 'Her next-door neighbour. Alan Harris? What did he say? Didn't he tell you that her blood pressure was perfect?'

Apparently Robert expected me to conjure up the answer out of thin air. I sighed. 'I'm not in charge of the investigation. I'm not even supposed to be involved.'

He folded his arms. His fur was receding but his determination was not. 'If Harris said that Rosie was perfectly healthy, that's proof enough. You need to keep looking for the person who did this to her.'

Goddammit. He couldn't seem to let this go. 'Wait here.'

I left him in the visitors' room and went into the office. Fred was on the sofa next to a weeping Thistle. Between hiccupped sobs she said, 'He's making out that I didn't care about her. I know I didn't see her much, but I still loved her. It doesn't mean she was murdered. And it doesn't mean I didn't love her.'

Liza and Grace looked at me. 'Well?' Grace asked. 'Is he going to back down?'

'Um … there is one thing.'

Grace's shoulders sank and Liza sighed loudly.

'What did the neighbour say?' I asked. 'Alan Harris? He'd been taking her blood pressure regularly and giving her vitamins. If he can confirm that Rosie wasn't quite the picture of health that Robert thinks she was, maybe Robert will back off.' Or double his efforts. At that point, anything felt possible.

Grace ground his teeth. 'Robert Sullivan is not in charge here. We don't jump to his tune. That's not how we work, Emma, and you know it. We've spoken to the neighbour – he came in the day after Rosie died and gave us a statement. Robert knows all that.'

Thistle blew her nose and gazed at Grace. 'Did Alan Harris

keep any records we could show Robert? I need to get him off my back because I can't cope with any more of this. He won't leave it alone.' She shook her head in defeat. 'He won't leave *me* alone.'

My eyes narrowed. Despite Robert's strength of feeling, he shouldn't have been harassing Thistle.

'Harris didn't have anything with him the first time he came in, but he said he'd kept notes and that he'd look them out and drop them off.' Grace looked at Liza and she pursed her lips.

'He's not been in yet,' she said. 'He phoned to say he'd found the notes, but he's not dropped by with them. I can call back and remind him.'

I thought about the look in Robert's eyes. 'That would be best. Robert won't go away quietly. Not yet.'

'Aren't you too busy dealing with a couple of serial killers to be worrying about errant werewolves?' Liza asked archly. She picked up a piece of paper from her desk. 'And didn't I just get a report of your recent untimely death?'

Owen Grace blinked, then gave me a look that could only be described as disappointed. 'Again? Really?'

I chose not to react.

He tutted. 'Never mind. I'll deal with the neighbour and get the notes from him, but that's the last thing we do. There have been two post-mortems, rigorous searches and interviews. Even by my standards, there's been an exhaustive investigation. I'm sorry about Rosie Thorn, I truly am, but she died of natural causes. This will have to be the end of it.'

Thistle wiped away a tear. 'You're right. You can't keep pandering to Robert. I had my doubts before when he kept going on about it. Her funeral is early next week. As soon as it's over, I'm booked on a flight out of here.' She glanced at us. 'Unless any of you are suspicious about how she died.'

None of us said a word. Thistle sniffed. 'That settles that then.'

Fred looked at Grace, and so did I. He nodded. 'We'll speak to the neighbour again. Unless we discover anything earth-shattering in his notes – and I can't imagine that we will – this investigation will be closed.'

'I'll make sure Robert understands.' I looked at Thistle. 'And I'll make sure he stops bothering you.'

'Any more trouble on that front from him, and I'm going to Lady Sullivan,' Grace told me.

I doubted that would help the situation in the slightest. 'I'll let him know.'

CHAPTER NINETEEN

My visit to Supe Squad wasn't what I'd expected, but it reminded me that I'd meant to follow up on what Liza had revealed about her own trips to Fetish.

I pulled Tallulah up outside the club and saw a parked car containing two plain-clothed officers watching the place. There was no sign of DCI Murray, so I decided to use my waiting time effectively.

'Are you calling to tell me that you died again?' Detective Superintendent Lucinda Barnes enquired coolly when she picked up. 'Because I've already read the report. I know what happened.' She didn't sound impressed.

'I wish people would stop harping on about my death, ma'am. It wasn't a big deal.'

'Sure.' Her sarcasm was obvious. 'Dying repeatedly and coming back to life isn't a big deal at all.'

'It was a necessary evil to save someone else's life.'

I could almost hear her frowning. 'Emma, I'm beginning to think that Lord Horvath is rubbing off on you, and not in a good way. Necessary evil?' She snorted.

I bristled. 'My decisions are my own,' I said curtly. 'Anyway, that's not why I'm calling.'

'So let me guess again. You want to know why a glory hound like Donald Murray ended up in charge of the highest profile murder investigation we've dealt with in years.'

Well, yes, but that wasn't why I was calling. Murray courted the press, and a great deal of police business these days dealt with perceptions rather than reality. I suspected that had a lot to do with it. Unless he was going to be replaced by someone less interested in how things played out on the evening news, there was little point in passing comment. 'No,' I said. 'I'm calling because I want to know what happened with Tony and Fetish.'

'Tony?' Barnes sounded surprised.

'Supe Squad's sole detective before I arrived,' I said unnecessarily.

'I know who you mean. I knew him better than you.'

Everyone had known Tony better than me; he'd died on my first day with the squad. 'I was told,' I said carefully, unwilling to mention Liza, 'that he tried to get Fetish shut down but his attempts were blocked. I want to know why.'

There was a pause before Barnes answered. 'You really have changed. Once upon a time, you'd have approached me with a question like that while adding a pretty please with rainbow sprinkles on top.'

I pursed my lips. 'Oh wonderful boss lady, can you tell me why an illegal club wasn't shut down when a serving Met police detective made efforts to close it? Pretty please with chocolate shaving and whipped cream and glacé cherries and fairy dust on top?'

There was another pause. 'It's getting to you – the crime, the darkness. You're sounding bitter, and you're still only a baby detective. What will things be like in five years?' she asked. 'In ten? I think you ought to see one of the police counsellors.'

I was big enough to admit that she might be right, but she still hadn't answered my question. 'Ma'am—'

She sighed. 'Tony couldn't get Fetish shut down because the club isn't illegal. All its paperwork is in order and every legal loophole and pesky licensing law is covered.'

That was not what I'd been expecting. 'Really? Because the owner suggested otherwise. Liza believes it's illegal too, and she is usually spot on. In fact, even Lukas thinks it's an illegal club.'

'I can't speak for what other people think,' Barnes told me. 'I can only tell you what I know. And what I know is that Fetish is completely above board. I've seen the paperwork.'

Now I was more puzzled than ever. 'Thanks for your help, ma'am.'

'You're welcome. Anything else?'

I scratched my head. 'No, I guess not.'

'Good. I'll book you an appointment with a counsellor. Our guys know what they're doing.'

I murmured vague agreement and said goodbye just as DCI Murray appeared. He pulled up behind Tallulah in a sleek black car that must have cost more than my annual salary. I unclipped my seatbelt and got out of Tallulah.

Murray didn't bother with hello. He was clasping a brown envelope in one hand and gestured to my little purple Mini with the other. 'Is that your car? We're obviously not paying you enough.'

'I wouldn't criticise Tallulah if I were you, sir,' I said.

'Tallulah?' he snorted. 'Now I've heard it all. If you want to get ahead in the Met, Emma, you need to think carefully about your image. How you present yourself is as important as what you do.'

I bit my tongue hard.

He continued blithely. 'It's bad enough that your boyfriend is a vampire – you should re-think that, for a start. But you need to dress better, and you definitely need to arrive at important interviews in a something better than that purple monstrosity. You could have a great future in the Metropolitan Police if you tried harder.'

He looked at me earnestly. 'And you should stop dying all the time. At best, it looks like you're showing off. At worst, it appears that you're incredibly careless.'

I considered and discarded several replies. I couldn't discount the possibility that Murray was baiting me. 'Uh-huh.'

'Now,' he said, 'where's this damned club?'

'Before we go in, I have to tell you that I was just speaking to Detective Superintendent Barnes and—'

'We're late,' he interrupted. 'Tell me later. Let's speak to Jonas. I told you already that appearances are important. Being punctual falls in that category.' He snapped his fingers. 'Take me to the club.'

Fine. I gritted my teeth. 'It's right here, sir.'

Murray turned towards the gated driveway. 'This is Fetish?' he asked doubtfully. 'Well, ring the damned bell then. I want to hear what this Jonas chap has to say for himself.'

The gates opened smoothly before I touched the doorbell; of course they did. I glanced at Carmichael, who was standing at the front door to greet us. Murray swept forward with his hand outstretched. 'Mr Jonas. It's a pleasure to meet you.'

'This is Jonas's solicitor,' I said quickly. 'Phileas Carmichael.'

The gremlin glowered. 'Phileas Carmichael *Esquire*.'

I suppressed a grin. I'd known that.

'Oh.' Murray seemed surprised. 'Why has Mr Jonas brought you along? I hope my colleague told you that this is only a friendly visit to find out more about why his customers are being targeted.'

'She did.' Carmichael didn't miss a beat. 'That's why my client agreed to the meeting. But there are certain caveats that we would like you to observe. For one thing, those two police officers in the car out there need to move further down the street.'

'They are there for a reason. If another letter is delivered—'

'I know why they're there,' Carmichael interrupted. 'But I want them to move back. They're too obvious parked where they are. No more letters will be delivered if the killers see them.'

'And I guess that few customers will want to come inside if they see them out there either,' I said drily,

The gremlin gave me an irritated look. 'There's nothing wrong with wanting to maintain a profitable business. Mr Jonas has done everything to help you.'

'It's not a problem,' Murray said. 'I'll move them twenty metres down the road.'

'Fifty.' Carmichael folded his arms. 'They'll still have a clear view of anyone who approaches the gates.'

A muscle jerked in Murray's cheek. 'Very well.'

'Furthermore,' the gremlin said, 'any information that is gathered during the course of the investigation and pertains to the daily running of Fetish will not be used in any future prosecutions against either Mr Jonas or his business.'

'Yes, yes,' Murray said dismissively. 'That has already been agreed to.'

'It bears repeating.'

'No information will be used unless it's pertinent to the current investigation.'

'Excellent.' Carmichael inclined his head graciously. 'Follow me.'

I half-expected to be accosted again by a teenage truth seeker, but this time the club was empty. It felt gloomy without people or the thump of music, but I liked it better that way. With nobody there, I could be sure that nobody was being scammed.

When Jonas met us, I barely recognised him. He wasn't wearing his wig, his face was bare of make-up and his clothes were casual; he looked nothing like the bold, confident club owner I'd met before. I wondered if we would meet the real man this time.

I glanced round. The detritus from the night before was still there – scattered chairs, overfilled bins and empty glasses. I was grateful that there wasn't any fresh blood in evidence.

Murray slowly spun in a full circle, taking in the scene. 'Busy night?' he asked.

'No more than usual.' Jonas offered a wide smile. 'It's nice to meet you. I saw you on television the other day talking about the investigation. If you hadn't called, I was planning to get in touch. DC Bellamy is very capable, but I think perhaps I should have requested more police involvement. I wanted to protect my business and avoid any future harassment.'

'That was a sensible move,' Carmichael growled.

'The last thing I want is for anyone else to wind up dead,' Jonas said quietly. He shuddered. 'Do you have any leads?'

'We're chasing down several clues,' Murray replied. 'But it's clear that your club is involved in some way. Every victim has been here – and, of course, there is matter of the letter you received.' He pointed to one of the cleaner tables. 'Shall we sit down? I've got some questions for you.'

Jonas nodded and we all sat down. He placed his phone on the table next to him. 'I'll do whatever I can to help. I've got nothing to hide.'

I leaned back in my chair. 'That's not true.'

Phileas Carmichael's eyes snapped to mine, Jonas stiffened slightly and his smile wavered, but it was Murray who spoke first. 'Emma?'

I gazed at Jonas. 'Everyone thinks this is an illegal club, and you and Mr Carmichael did nothing to dispel that belief when I came here.'

'Ah.' Jonas suddenly looked guilty.

I continued. 'I've been reliably informed that everything you do here is above board.' I glanced at the wall where the shackles hung. 'Hard as that is to believe.'

Carmichael sniffed. 'I did not say that Fetish was illegal, and neither did Mr Jonas.'

'You didn't deny it,' I returned. 'And you definitely implied it with your conditions.'

'Why would I do such a thing to a serving police officer? Why would I pretend my client is breaking the law when he isn't?'

Jonas placed a hand on Carmichael's arm. 'It's fine. I'll deal with this.' He raised his chin. 'Yes, there is a rumour that Fetish is illegal. I didn't start it, but I do nothing to dispel it. To be honest, it's a good marketing ploy. When the whispers that we were outside the boundaries of the law started, I thought that the club would be dead in the water within six months. Instead our guest list increased threefold. I guess that sometimes people want to be naughty.'

Smoke and mirrors – again. Jonas certainly enjoyed his play-acting.

'Why didn't you tell me the truth?' I asked. 'Under the circumstances, it would have been prudent.'

Jonas's looked even guiltier. 'If it had become an issue, I'd have told you. But you came here with Lord Horvath and you're in a relationship with him. You'd have told him that Fetish is completely legal. Once he knew, all the vampires would know, and once the vampires know, everyone knows. My guests would think I'd lied to them. They'd think I'd cheated them.'

I crossed my arms. 'You have.'

'Only by omission.' Jonas ran a hand through his hair. 'I apologise, detective. I should have been honest with you from the start. It was an error. I didn't think it would matter.'

'This is a multiple murder investigation. You don't know what matters. What else haven't you told us?'

'I have nothing else to hide. Nothing, I promise.'

I didn't look away.

Murray straightened his shoulders, keen to take back control. 'Where were you yesterday morning between the hours of 6am and 8am?'

Jonas's mouth dropped. 'I'm a suspect now? Do you think I murdered someone? That I'm one of those sick killers?'

'This is not what we agreed to,' Carmichael snapped. 'I think you should both remember that Mr Jonas contacted Lord Horvath in the first place. He volunteered the information that two of Fetish's clients were involved in the first killings. He's not tried to hide that fact, and he's passed over every piece of evidence that he could. This line of questioning is ridiculous!'

To his credit, Murray didn't react. 'We can continue the conversation down at the station, if you prefer.'

Jonas grimaced. 'I'll answer your questions. I was here, alright? Check the CCTV footage if you don't believe me. The last guests left before 6am. I stayed behind for a brief chat with some of my staff, then I waited for an early beer delivery. That arrived about 7.30, then I went upstairs to bed. I've got a flat above here. I slept until about four in the afternoon, then I got up to prepare for the club re-opening.'

'So from 7.30 onwards you were alone?' I asked. That meant there was nobody to vouch for his whereabouts when Samuel Brunswick was being killed at Bright Smiles.

'I didn't say that,' Jonas replied. He sighed. 'I've been seeing someone. It's a casual thing, but we've spent a lot of time together recently. She was with me for most of yesterday. Her name is Adele Jones. Speak to her – she'll confirm what I've told you.' He hunched over in his chair, as if resigned to the fact that he was now being questioned as a potential murderer.

'Very well. We will do that.' Murray leaned forward. 'Do you have enemies, Mr Jonas? Is there anyone who would wish to harm your club?'

'Not that I can think of,' Jonas mumbled. 'There are plenty of people who've lost money, but I can't imagine any of them would be angry enough to start killing other guests. If they were that pissed off, why wouldn't they target me instead?'

'Perhaps by targeting your guests they *are* targeting you,' DCI Murray said.

I glanced at him in surprise. He wasn't as daft as he appeared. Not all the time.

Jonas swallowed. 'So it's my fault? I'm not the killer, but it's still my fault they're dead?'

'I'm not saying it's your fault but we are looking for two killers who, on the face of it, appear to be playing some kind of game between themselves. Some kind of game that's not so different from the games you play here, legally or otherwise.'

Jonas was silent for a long moment. When he finally spoke, he sounded resigned. 'I should close Fetish down, at least until this is over.'

Murray nodded. 'It's not a bad idea, but it's up to you. It would send a warning to your customers that they need to take care of themselves and be wary of anyone who approaches them. And it means those two friendly officers out there can remain twenty metres away.' He smiled, but there was iron behind it. He wasn't the pushover I'd imagined. 'Not fifty.'

Jonas looked at Carmichael. 'We'll do it now. We can't afford not to.'

Murray looked pleased. He opened the envelope he was holding and slid out several photographs. 'From the CCTV footage and your guest lists, we have identified some people we'd like to talk to.' He slid a photo across the table.

I looked at it with as much interest as Carmichael and Jonas. I'd not had anything to do with the official searches into the Fetish customers, so I knew as little as them about who'd been identified as a potential suspect.

The photo was of a dark-haired man, and it appeared to have been taken from the CCTV footage. 'He's one of our regulars,' Jonas said. 'Human. I forget his name, but I know he's lost a lot of money recently.'

'He also has a criminal record for aggravated assault,' Murray said. 'When was the last time he was at Fetish?'

Jonas pursed his lips. 'Last week – Monday, I think. He said something about going on holiday and that he wouldn't be back for a while.' He evidently had a good memory. He didn't even hesitate.

Murray's brow creased. 'Hmm. That'll explain why we've not been able to locate him.' He placed down another photo. 'What about this woman?'

Jonas squinted. 'She's a werewolf. I think she's only been in once or twice. I don't know any more than that.'

Murray indicated another picture, this time an e-fit rather than a photo. 'And this one?'

I barely avoided drawing in a sharp breath. It was a mocked-up image of Zara.

Jonas looked puzzled. 'I don't know her. I've not seen her in the club.'

'You're sure?'

He frowned. 'Positive. Who is she?'

Murray shrugged. 'Someone we're looking into,' he said vaguely. 'Her name is Zara.'

'I can double-check, but I don't think there is anyone on our client list called Zara. Do you have a last name?'

Murray didn't answer. 'Tell me,' he said instead, 'have you ever consulted or spoken to anyone who claims to be a Cassandra?'

Jonas jerked. 'A Cassandra?' His eyes flew to mine. 'You mean—?'

I didn't react.

'No,' he said faintly. 'I don't know any Cassandras. I didn't think they were real.' His phone buzzed and he picked it up absently. He gazed at the screen, then his face paled. 'Oh,' he said. 'Oh.'

'Is there a problem?' I asked.

Jonas showed his phone to Phileas Carmichael, who turned as white as a sheet.

'There's been a text message.' The gremlin swallowed. 'I told you they wouldn't send a letter with those officers so close to the gates.'

Murray and I sat bolt upright and Jonas turned the phone in our direction. 'It's a video.' His voice was barely audible. He pressed play and handed it to Murray. I felt my stomach drop to the soles of my feet.

The video started with the familiar sickening image of Christopher hanging upside down. His body was still and he looked to be unconscious. A gloved hand gripping a pair of pliers reached inside his mouth. I flinched but forced myself to keep watching. Then the video cut and Lukas and I flickered into view, standing in front of Christopher's hanging body. I watched as my image walked over to the pulley and hesitated. If I'd not noticed the second wire in the nick of time, this video would be showing a very different outcome.

Jonas's phone pinged again and Murray thumbed open the message. This time it was an image of Samuel Brunswick, dead in the dentist's chair at Bright Smiles with his mouth wide open. Christopher's fangs looked even more out of place than they had in person.

There was one final text: *Who wins?*

Jonas's hand was clamped over his mouth, and Phileas Carmichael looked as if he were on the verge of throwing up. I wondered if the killers had sent their horrific messages now because they knew Murray and I were there.

'Do you recognise the number?' Murray asked urgently.

Jonas shook his head.

I jumped in. 'How many people have your phone number?'

'Everyone,' he said helplessly. 'I like to be available to all my customers.'

Fuck.

'The text and video were probably sent from a burner,' Murray muttered. 'But we still need to trace it.' He took out his own phone, contacted the team at Hackney and read out the phone number.

I stared at Jonas's phone as if I could reach in and pluck the killers from inside it. 'We should answer,' I said suddenly.

Murray glanced at me. 'What?'

'They want an answer to their question. They want to know who wins. If there's a winner, maybe they'll stop. Maybe nobody else will die.'

'Who then?' Murray asked. 'Who wins?'

Christopher was still alive. 'The second one. The picture of the dentist's chair.'

Indecision flickered on Murray's face but he did as I suggested. Carmichael and Jonas watched silently as he keyed in: *Number 2.* He pressed send.

All four of us held our breath. It didn't take long before the phone dinged again.

Murray read the text message out loud. *'Best of three.'*

CHAPTER TWENTY

'BEST OF THREE.' MURRAY MUTTERED IT OVER AND OVER AGAIN. 'Best of fucking three.' He glared although I knew his rage wasn't directed at me. 'They're playing games.'

Unfortunately, that seemed to be the whole point.

He clenched his fists. 'They will kill again. They're making a fool out of me and I won't have that. Do you hear me?'

'Yes, sir.'

He checked his watch. 'I need to get this phone to the IT guys, then I'll call everyone together and update them. Somebody must have a bloody lead on these two!'

I prayed that was true. 'What shall I do?'

'Speak to the girlfriend and confirm Jonas's alibi. I'm sure he's telling the truth, but we need to check. Then meet me back at the Hackney station. We'll figure out next steps from there.' He paused. 'I know what you think of me – what you all think of me – but I get results. And I'm going to get these two murderers. Watch this space.'

I didn't say anything; DCI Murray wasn't expecting an answer.

The Fetish gates re-opened. As I walked onto the street, I

noted that the two officers watching the building had moved further away. I heard a loud expletive from Murray and glanced back. Oh.

'You didn't put your handbrake on!'

I had put the handbrake on, but there was no point telling him that. Tallulah had rolled back, hitting the front of his car and creating a considerable dent in the front bonnet. Of course, I couldn't see any damage on Tallulah herself.

'I can only apologise, sir,' I said, inwardly cursing my daft car. She was far too touchy. Not that I could blame her.

He glowered. 'I'll see you back at the station,' he spat.

I sighed. Just when I'd been starting to think we'd found some common ground and were working together effectively... Oh well. I nodded and climbed into Tallulah's front seat. It was probably better to leave as quickly as possible.

FROM THE WAY Jonas had spoken about her, I wasn't sure if I could classify Adele Jones as his girlfriend. Whatever label I attached to her, she wasn't what I expected. I suppose I thought she'd be more like Jonas, someone brash and outgoing who was larger than life and who enjoyed dressing up.

When I walked into the café where she worked and saw her name tag, I was genuinely surprised. She looked completely normal. She had smooth brown hair tied into a neat ponytail, and wore a simple white shirt and black trousers with a modest gold necklace round her neck. Her smile was friendly and genuine and went beyond a mere welcome. I had the sense that, unlike with Jonas, what you saw with Adele was what you got.

'Welcome! Would you like a table for one?' she asked in a faint London accent.

I flashed her my warrant card and her smile dipped. 'Actually,'

I said, 'I'd like to ask you a couple of questions. My name is Detective Constable Emma Bellamy.'

'You're here about Kevin and those terrible murders.'

Hmm. Interesting that she'd been expecting me. 'I am. Did Mr Jonas tell you I'd be coming?'

'I was with him yesterday and he said the police might want to speak to me.' She knotted her fingers together and looked at me anxiously.

'Did he say anything else?' I asked. Jonas struck me as someone who liked to control every aspect of his life and I wondered if he'd coached her on what to say.

She shook her head. 'No. Just that I should be honest with you.'

I smiled warmly at her. 'That would be very much appreciated. I won't take up much of your time. Do you mind if we sit down?'

We moved to an empty table. I took out my notepad and waited while she made herself comfortable. 'You mentioned that you were with Kevin yesterday,' I said. 'When was that exactly?'

'Uh … I was off yesterday so I met him at his club once he'd finished work. I think about seven in the morning? I'm an early riser. He cooked me breakfast and we ate together, then he went for a sleep.'

I sat up. 'He slept? But you didn't?'

She smiled slightly. 'I keep more regular hours than he does. I stayed with him, though. He says he likes having me around while he sleeps, and I had plenty to do. I'm studying to be a nurse, so I did some revision until he woke up. Then I returned the favour and cooked him breakfast and left maybe around 6pm, before Fetish opened again.'

'He didn't leave at all during that time?'

She blinked. 'No. I was right next to him and he was out for the count.' She leaned in as if about to tell me a secret. 'He snores really loudly. I keep telling him he should see a doctor about it.'

I tapped my mouth with the end of my pen. 'Adele, have you been to Fetish? I mean, obviously you've been inside the building, but have you been to the club when it's open?'

She laughed. 'It's not my kind of place. I went once but...' She wrinkled her nose. 'I didn't enjoy it very much.'

I looked at her curiously. 'Forgive me for asking, but you and Jonas aren't very alike. You keep different hours, have different interests...'

'You want to know why we're together? I guess opposites attract. It's nothing serious, though. We've only been seeing each other for a couple of weeks and I can't see myself taking him home to meet my mum and dad.'

I tried – and failed – to imagine Jonas in his green wig sitting on a flowery sofa, sipping tea from a china cup and making small talk with the parents of someone like Adele. 'I need you to come along to the police station at some point in the next few days and sign a statement.'

'No problem. Anything to help. I can't believe those poor people who went to Jonas's club were murdered.' She shuddered. 'It's too horrible for words.'

Yeah. And there were two more murders coming our way soon. I repressed my own shudder.

My phone rang as I was leaving the café. Lukas. I felt a warm ripple at seeing his name on my caller ID, followed by a flash of foreboding that he was calling because something was wrong. 'Hey,' I said softly, crossing my fingers that I wasn't about to hear more bad news.

'Hi, D'Artagnan.'

I breathed out. It was a good sign that he was using my nick-name. 'You've got news?'

'Christopher is awake and alert.'

I immediately straightened. 'He's talking?'

'He is indeed. You should get over here. I'll wait till you arrive before I start asking questions. We both need to hear what he has to say, and I won't make him repeat his story. He's been through enough trauma as it is.'

'I'm on my way now.' I picked up the pace and jogged over to Tallulah. What Christopher could tell us might change everything. I could only hope.

THE HOSPITAL where Christopher was being treated wasn't open to the general public; it was only for supes and, as such, was considerably smaller than most human establishments. That helped my cause considerably. As soon as the automatic doors swished open, the receptionist smiled and directed me to Christopher's room. I didn't even need to introduce myself – she knew who I was and why I was there.

As a rule, vamps heal quickly. If their wounds are superficial, their saliva will clear up any infection and close the skin. Occasionally a vampire might drink from a sick human being and become infected, then require treatment. And, as in Christopher's case, there were rare times when a vampire came close to knocking on death's door, but that happened so rarely that there were plenty of medical professionals in his private room to see to his every need. I was glad of that, especially when I saw his face and the faint colour on his cheeks. He was alright. He was going to recover.

Lukas was sitting by his bedside, together with an older couple whom I recognised as Christopher's parents from the photos in his flat. Everyone was smiling, although whether that was to keep his spirits up or the emotions were genuine, I couldn't have said for sure.

I stepped past a nurse who was scribbling on a clipboard and approached the bed. 'Hey,' I grinned. 'You're looking great.'

Christopher opened his mouth, revealing the ragged gaps where his fangs had once been. 'Am I?'

His mother swallowed and patted his arm. 'Your teeth can be fixed, Chris. The doctor told you that.'

'Whoever heard of a vampire with dentures?' he asked in a weak, thready voice. My stomach tightened. He might have some colour in his cheeks but the road to recovery would not be a fast one, whether he was a vampire or not.

'I'm sorry,' I said, meaning it with every part of my being. 'I'm sorry this happened to you, and I'm sorry we couldn't get there faster.'

Christopher's father looked at me. 'You got there. That's what counts.'

His gratitude made me uncomfortable. With both killers still on the loose, it felt undeserved. I shifted my weight and cleared my throat. The best thing I could do was to ask my questions quickly then allow Christopher the space, time and comfort from his family that he needed to heal. 'Thank you.'

I glanced around the room. 'If it's possible, I'd like to speak to you in private, Christopher. I won't take long, but there are questions I have to ask.'

A white-coated doctor nodded. 'We've been expecting you, but he's already quite tired and needs to rest. I'll have to limit you to fifteen minutes.'

I murmured my thanks and waited for everyone to depart. Christopher looked at his mum and dad. 'You should go too.'

His dad started to protest but his mum understood. There were going to be details of Christopher's ordeal that he wouldn't want them to know. He didn't want to see his own pain reflected back at him every time he met their eyes. 'It's okay, Frank,' she said. She gave me a shaky smile. 'Be gentle with my boy.'

'I will,' I promised.

Lukas stood up. 'I'll leave too, if you prefer, but I'd like to stay. It's my responsibility to find the man who did this to you as much as it is Emma's.'

Christopher looked away but he nodded. His parents left, carefully closing the door behind them.

I sat on the chair closest to Christopher's bed. 'Why don't you start from the beginning?' I said softly.

Christopher swallowed. 'I'm not sure what time I got home from work. After six, I guess, but I didn't look at the clock. I had a few drinks after I finished my shift. Once I got home, I was planning to hit the sack straight away but I knew it was bin day so I emptied the rubbish bin first and went out back to put the bag in the wheelie bin. Nothing seemed different. I had no sense of anything wrong.'

He sighed heavily. 'I'd dropped the rubbish in the bin when I heard a van pull up. To be honest, I didn't pay it any attention. I just wanted to get to bed.' His voice trailed off and his eyes took on a distant sheen. 'I didn't think I'd be in any danger. It didn't occur to me that I could be a victim. I'm a vampire,' he said bitterly. 'I'm supposed to be strong.'

'This isn't your fault.'

He nodded but I wasn't convinced he believed me. 'As I turned to go back into the house, I heard footsteps behind me and then something hit me from behind.' His hand went involuntarily to the back of his skull and he flinched.

'The doctor said his skull was fractured,' Lukas told me.

I grimaced. That was some blow; whoever had attacked him had possessed considerable strength.

'When I woke up, I was upside down.' His voice cracked. 'My fangs were already gone. I tried to get free.' He choked. 'I tried so hard. But there was a man...' His jaw worked as he struggled to find the words to explain. 'He was cutting me. All over my body,' he whispered. 'He cut me everywhere.'

'Did you see his face?'

'Yeah.' He raised his eyes to mine. 'That's how I knew he would kill me. He made no attempt to hide who he was. He laughed the entire time and kept telling me he would win. That he had a trick up his sleeve and he was going to win.'

The video. That's what he'd been talking about. The cold-hearted bastard.

'He showed me my fangs,' Christopher said dismally. 'He had them in the palm of his hands. He told me he would leave me alone because he had to give them to someone else. That's when he left. And I knew … I knew I was going to die there.'

His whole body was shaking. I held up my hands. 'Can I?'

He nodded. I reached out, took both his hands and squeezed tight until the shaking stopped. It took far longer than any of us wanted. Once he could speak again, Christopher lifted his head. He looked at Lukas, not at me. 'He's a vampire,' he whispered. 'He's one of us.'

CHAPTER TWENTY-ONE

THE PHOTOGRAPH OF MARCUS LYONS LAY ON THE DESK BETWEEN Murray and me. Colquhoun stood in the corner, her arms folded and her expression grim. Lyons grinned out of the image, a cheeky, boyish smile that suggested madcap nights, fun escapades and a big heart. He didn't look like a cold-blooded killer – but we all knew that you couldn't judge someone on their appearance. Anyone could kill, whether they looked sweet and angelic or swarthy and dangerous.

Murray smacked his lips in satisfaction. 'The Stupid Killer,' he pronounced. 'Finally.'

'Do you know him?' Colquhoun asked.

'His face is vaguely familiar,' I said. 'I've seen him around.' That didn't mean much. There were only about a thousand vampires in London and, apart from the odd law-breaking exception, most of them lived in and around Soho. Sooner or later, I'd seen all of their faces. 'I've probably passed the time of day with him but I don't know much about him.' I held up a manila folder. 'However, Lukas has plenty of information.'

'How is he taking the news that a vampire is responsible?' Colquhoun asked.

My mouth flattened. 'He's been betrayed by one of his own. It's the worst possible scenario for him.'

Lukas was more than shaken, he was devastated. He had ranted and raved; more than anything, he'd wanted to know *why*. What could have driven Marcus Lyons to murder and torture?

'Mmm.' There was a flicker of sympathy on Colquhoun's face. I wondered if the massive inroads we'd made as a community into integrating with the humans were now disappearing in front of our eyes. Whoever the other killer was, there was no doubt that Marcus Lyons, fully-fledged vampire, was a cold-hearted, ruthless murderer.

Murray folded his arms. 'Does your boyfriend know where Lyons is?'

I met his gaze. As soon as Christopher had identified Lyons, Lukas had sent people round to find him instead of waiting for the Met police to grind into action. He was within his legal rights to do so and it made sense. Who better to catch a vampire than another vampire?

'There's no sign of him at his house, and his neighbours haven't seen him for the last day or so,' I said. 'The whole vamp community knows that Christopher survived, which means Marcus Lyons knows, too. He'll be aware that the gig is up and every vampire in the city is looking for him. I'd be very surprised if he shows his face anywhere in Soho or Lisson Grove.' If he did, I doubted he'd last an hour.

Murray frowned. 'It's not only every bloodsucker who is looking for him. I have his identity – he won't escape me for long.' One could only hope.

Colquhoun flipped through the papers in front of her. 'He's been to Fetish many times,' she said grimly.

We exchanged glances.

'The video footage will tell us more,' Murray said. 'I'll get a team onto it so they can find the dates. Maybe there will be something on the club's CCTV that can help.'

'Maybe we'll be able to identify the second killer from the people Lyons interacted with,' I said quietly, '

Murray nodded. 'I'll make it a priority.'

'What else do you know about him?' Colquhoun asked. 'What's in that folder? Why is he doing this?'

I pushed back my hair. 'I can't speak for the why. There's nothing in his history to suggest a reason. He turned vamp about forty years ago, when he was twenty-nine.' I pointed at the photo. 'Nowadays he looks only a few years older than that. His parents passed away several years ago and he's got no siblings. Any close contacts he had before he became vamp are no longer valid. I've spoken to a few people who knew him well. They said he has a reckless streak, but they're shocked that he's killed.'

'We know who Stupid is. Is there any indication that the Cupid Killer is a vampire, too?'

I looked down. God, I hoped not for Lukas's sake. 'At this point, anything is possible. Given the amount of blood at Pickover's flat, it seems unlikely. A vamp would find it hard to remain in control while painting a whole floor with human blood. But I can't say for certain that the second killer *isn't* a vamp.'

Murray pursed his lips. 'Very well. We'll release Lyons' photo asap, and maybe that will shake out something about the Cupid Killer. At least the Stupid Killer's face will be emblazoned across the city. I'll catch him before the day is out.'

Perhaps Marcus Lyons would indeed be in handcuffs in hours, but it wouldn't be Murray pounding the streets to find him. If another supe didn't find him first – if it happened to be a human police officer or, heaven forbid, a member of the public – things could get very messy.

'Marcus Lyons is a vampire,' I said. 'He's stronger and faster than any human. And we know that he's not afraid to maim, torture and kill. He is a dangerous supe.'

'Noted,' Murray said tersely.

He would make sure the public were warned about Lyons. He

couldn't afford the PR if anyone died whilst pursuing or trying to capture; the rest of us couldn't afford any further loss of life.

As long as Lyons was brought into custody as soon as possible and nobody else got hurt, nothing else mattered.

You'd think it would be difficult for a vampire to hide in a city when his face was plastered across every television screen and social media news feed, but you'd be wrong. Several hours after my meeting with Murray and Colquhoun, there was still no sign of Marcus fucking Lyons. Lukas's vampires had scoured every supe haunt, and Murray's police teams had spoken to hundreds of people, but there was no whisper of the damned man anywhere. It was as if he'd vanished into thin air.

Neither had anything useful emerged from the Fetish CCTV cameras. Murray's people had identified all the recordings that included Lyons, but there was no obvious second suspect. Interviews were still going on, but I wasn't holding out much hope.

Footsore and incredibly weary, I met Lukas on the edge of Lisson Grove. For someone who usually took pride in his appearance, he looked terrible. His hair was rumpled, his clothes were wrinkled, and the stubble around his jawline was less designer and more a reflection of his state of mind. I didn't need to ask him if there was any clue as to Lyons' whereabouts. It was obvious from his pursed lips and his tired eyes.

'You should go home and rest for an hour or two,' I suggested. 'I know you want to be out here searching, but you won't do any good if you're too exhausted to think straight.'

'Are you going home to rest, D'Artagnan?'

I looked at him.

'Well then,' he murmured softly. 'That answers that question.'

I heard a polite cough and turned to see all four werewolf alphas. A couple of years ago, Lady Sullivan, Lady Carr, Lady

Fairfax and Lord McGuigan might have displayed a certain glee that the vampires were having problems, but these days we were more of a community. We knew that what harmed one of us harmed us all. They were here to help, not to gloat – at least for now.

'We've covered every street and public place in a three-mile radius using the scents you gave us from the wanker's flat, ' Lady Carr said. 'It's not rained, so we can say with a fair degree of certainty that he's not anywhere near here.'

McGuigan nodded. 'My people included a wide area around the warehouse where your Christopher was found. Lyons must have left in another vehicle because the scent trail leads only to the coffee shop and the building itself. We found a bicycle next to the coffee shop that stank of him but,' he gestured helplessly, 'he's nowhere nearby.'

The bike that he used when he went to pick up Pickover's blood, I thought grimly.

'In short, we can't find him anywhere,' Lady Fairfax said. 'He's gone to ground. He's an experienced vamp, and he knows we'll get involved. He understands our methods. He's covered his tracks well.'

The only sign that Lukas registered their words was a faint muscle throbbing in his cheek.

Carr sniffed. 'We will keep looking – we'll find him sooner or later. He can't stay hidden forever.'

No, he couldn't, but I dreaded to think of the people he could hurt before we got to him. 'Thank you for your help,' I said. 'It's much appreciated.'

The werewolf alphas started to withdraw until only Lady Sullivan remained. She looked at Lukas. 'It's not your fault, you know,' she said. 'You can't control everything that your people do, no matter how much you might like to.'

I tried not to look too surprised at her sympathetic words. That was the trouble with Lady Sullivan; you never quite knew where you were with her.

She turned to me. 'I realise you have other worries, Emma, but I am concerned about Robert. Has there been any progress with the investigation into Rosie Thorn's death? I need a line drawn under it. He needs to move on.'

Ah. I wondered if her kind words to Lukas were because she wanted my help with her beta. I shook off my suspicions and answered her as honestly as I could. 'I'm only peripherally involved in that investigation. There's only so much I know and am at liberty to tell you.'

'I'm his alpha,' she snapped. 'You can tell me everything.'

No, I couldn't. I smiled gently. 'I will tell you that as far as I'm aware, there is no indication that Rosie died of anything other than natural causes. Supe Squad are pursuing one or two final leads and then the case will probably be closed.' My gaze didn't waver. 'Robert will need your care and support.'

Her mouth tightened. 'He always has both.' She muttered a curse under her breath. 'Look,' she said, 'he trusts you and respects you.' That was news to me.

Lady Sullivan continued. 'When the investigation formally ends, he will take it better from you than from that other silly detective. It would help me if you could break the news to him. It would probably help your team, too.'

'Because if Robert decides he doesn't like the news and attacks as a result, I won't be permanently damaged?' I enquired.

'He's doing better now. He won't attack anyone.' She leaned forward. 'But perhaps it's better to be safe than sorry, hmm?'

I sighed. She wasn't asking for much and I knew she'd do whatever she could to keep Robert on an even keel. Whatever else Lady Sullivan did or didn't do, she protected her own. She and Lukas were more similar than they realised. 'I'll do what I can, but I'm not in charge. Ultimately it's up to DS Grace, so I'll have to discuss it with him first.'

Sullivan pursed her lips. 'Fair enough.' She glanced again at

Lukas. 'Obviously,' she murmured, 'there is a lot going on right now. Do you know when Rosie's investigation will be closed?'

'When I get the chance, I'll find out and let you know.'

'Thank you. I will not wish either of you luck in finding these two killers. I do not believe in luck – but I do know you will find them. However, I will ask that you take care of yourselves in the process.' Before I could reply, she drew away.

Lukas sat down on a low wall and rubbed his eyes. 'You know things are bad when Ma Sullivan is being kind,' he said.

I pulled a face and sat next to him, leaning into his shoulder.

'I'm glad you're with me, D'Artagnan,' he said. 'And I know you understand how I feel.'

'Scared,' I said. 'And angry and desperate. Yeah.' I sighed. 'I know how you feel. I feel it too.' I reached for his hand and squeezed it. 'Marcus Lyons is doing this in spite of you, not because of you. This isn't your fault, and it's certainly not your failure. He's one of your people, Lukas, but he's not *you*. Even with all the hindsight in the world, I'm not sure you could have done anything to stop these murders.'

A trace of a smile crossed his mouth. 'You know me too well. Sometimes I wonder if mind reading is one of your skills.'

Ugh. 'I'm glad it's not. I have more than enough on my plate as it is. I don't want – or need – any more supe skills.'

'Amen to that.' His thumb caressed the back of my hand. 'Is there anything on the other killer?' He wasn't asking to deflect from Marcus Lyons. We all had the same thought – find one of these bastards and we'd find the other.

Unfortunately, the news on that score wasn't any better. 'I spoke to Colquhoun on the way here. She reckons they've tracked down more than eighty percent of the people on the Fetish client list. They're looking into several of them, including the ones who interacted directly with Lyons, but,' I grimaced, 'nothing has come up so far.'

'We're chasing our damned tails and waiting for those two

bastards to make another move. At this point, we're relying on them fucking up in some way.'

I wished I could disagree with him but I couldn't. 'We still have leads to follow.' Tenuous leads, admittedly.

Lukas drew in a breath. 'Yes. We do.' His black eyes glinted with determination as he stood up and withdrew his hand. 'Marcus Lyons isn't our only target.'

I knew from his expression who he was referring to. 'Zara isn't one of the killers, Lukas.'

'You don't know that for sure. She's been keeping herself hidden for a reason. That bloody Cassandra knows far more than she's let on. If we can't find Marcus, maybe we can find her.' He nodded towards the conclave of werewolves. 'And maybe they can help.'

I stayed where I was and watched with a sinking sensation as Lukas marched towards the wolves and started to wave his hands around. Finding Zara might help but I doubted she would provide the answers we were looking for. But Lukas couldn't bear running around London in an aimless search for Lyons. He needed something – or in this case some*one* – to cling onto and focus on.

I bit my lip as Lady Carr and Lord McGuigan nodded. They'd help him locate Zara. I'd have to remind them both that she wasn't a suspect. She didn't deserve to be hurt, even if speaking to her in person could help us all.

CHAPTER TWENTY-TWO

IT WAS A LONG NIGHT. LUKAS AND I DRAGGED OURSELVES HOME when it became apparent that there wasn't scent, sight or sound of Zara or Marcus Lyons. Despite only a few hours' sleep, however, I was itching to get back to the search. That was one of the reasons why the phone call from Grace irritated me – though it wasn't the only reason.

'Robert Sullivan,' he grunted, 'won't stop calling. He got my personal number from somewhere and decided that 3am was the perfect time to demand how the investigation was progressing. If Thistle Thorn doesn't kill him soon, I expect that Liza will. I contacted Lady Sullivan to get him to back off. She told me in no uncertain terms that you were handling it, and that I was to leave it all up to you.'

I closed my eyes briefly. Bloody hell. 'That's not exactly how our conversation went.'

'I figured.' His tone was dry. 'I know you have your hands full with the Cupid and Stupid killers. We will officially close Rosie's case today. I don't wish to pass the buck, this is my case and I can deal with Robert…'

'No.' I pinched off a headache. Lady Sullivan had been right: I

178

was the best person to break the news. 'It's fine, I'll do it. Call him again. I'll come into Supe Squad and deal with him first thing before I go back to Hackney. I'll tell him what's happening with the case.'

It had taken Robert a while to calm down last time, but once I'd laid out that the investigation was on its last legs he'd been fairly reasonable. Sort of. He wasn't in a good place but he was maintaining a slightly better hold on his emotions. He'd be okay – eventually.

'I take it that the next-door neighbour was a bust. His notes didn't reveal anything unexpected?' I said.

'Alan Harris? No, he didn't give us a single thing that was helpful, other than proof that Rosie Thorn had high blood pressure and should have seen her damned GP. He dropped by earlier and gave us his notes. And because I knew that Robert bloody Sullivan would bring it up, I even checked that Harris didn't kill her. He was up north on holiday in the Lake District. I confirmed it myself.'

'Nobody can say you've not been thorough.'

Grace snorted. 'Tell that to Sullivan.'

'I'll do my best,' I promised.

'You can look through the case notes. I've checked everything, but you're free to read through them yourself and make your own assumptions so you can look Robert in the eye and tell him the truth.'

Owen Grace was a good guy. 'Thank you,' I said.

'You're welcome. I'll see you shortly.'

I hung up and went in search of Lukas. He was pacing up and down the living room with a phone glued to his ear. I didn't comment on his simmering rage because I felt the same. Instead I waited until he was done speaking before telling him I had to nip over to Supe Squad. I'd be back as quickly as I could to help with the search for Marcus Lyons.

He nodded. 'Nobody's seen or heard from him. He'll be

working even harder to stay hidden this time, so you do whatever you need to at Supe Squad. It won't make any difference if you're here or not.' He waved the phone. 'I did receive some good news. Someone's reported a sighting of the Cassandra. I need to confirm it's her, but it sounds positive.' He smiled grimly.

I tensed. 'Lukas...'

'I know, I know.' He held up his hands. 'I won't do anything you wouldn't like, and my promise from the other day holds true. If this sighting proves accurate, I won't approach her. I'll contact you first. To be honest, it's probably better if I don't talk to her. Even the thought of what she can do or say creeps me out.'

'You didn't believe that she's a true Cassandra,' I pointed out.

He grimaced. 'I'm trying to set my prejudices aside, but it's easier said than done, Emma. Maybe I don't have it in me to be as good a person as you are.'

'You *are* a good person, you just need some time to work through your unease. And I'm not as good as you think I am, Lukas.'

He grinned wryly, although the black expression in his eyes didn't alter. 'You're right. You're better.'

I tutted. Yeah, yeah. 'We'll make you an open-minded vampire Lord yet.'

Lukas kissed me briefly. 'I can't wait.'

I JUMPED OUT OF TALLULAH, sent a quick wave to Max outside the hotel next door, and dashed into the Supe Squad building. Finding Marcus Lyons didn't depend on my participation but that didn't mean I wanted to be away from the search for too long. Hiding or not, he and his partner could still be planning the next murder. There had been more than enough blood and darkness already. I wanted to deal with Robert Sullivan quickly and move on.

I'd expected to find Grace in the main office with Liza but neither of them were there. Instead, I walked in to see Fred on his own, spinning round and round in his office chair looking morose. When he saw me, he stood up so abruptly that the chair careened across the floor, collided with Liza's desk and sent a pot of pens flying.

'Fred, are you alright?' I asked.

'Yes.' He shook his head. 'No. I mean, yes.'

'Fred—'

'I'm really concerned.' The words burst out of him. 'Everything proves that Rosie Thorn died of natural causes but I don't think Robert Sullivan will accept that. He's a loose cannon, boss. He could have killed you. He has no respect for DS Grace, and he's ignoring everything that Thistle Thorn says. If you tell him the investigation is being closed, he'll flip.'

'He's grieving,' I said. 'His emotions are raw and because of that he's made some mistakes. But he's doing better now.' As soon as I said the last words out loud, I knew I wasn't convinced they were true. I ploughed ahead. 'He's on the mend. He'll understand when we present all the facts.'

'No.' Fred shook his head vehemently. 'I don't think he will understand. We've all dealt with grieving relatives, but Robert Sullivan is going through something different. It's not just the phone calls at all hours and his demands to be kept updated. There's more going on than we realise.'

I gazed at Fred. He was genuinely anxious – and that worried me. 'You know there's no set way to react when someone you love dies,' I said. 'There's no right way or wrong way to behave.'

'I know that.' His eyes remained fixed on mine. 'But we have to be careful with him. He's dangerous. I'm sure of it.'

'He's not the next of kin, Thistle Thorn is.'

'I think that's making it worse,' Fred whispered. 'He held a candle for Rosie for years but she rejected him when she was alive. Now her granddaughter – and we – are rejecting him now

Rosie is dead. Once we close the investigation, he'll be left with nothing. By fighting for her, he's keeping her alive. I don't think he'll back down without another fight.'

He was making sense. I nodded; I'd heard what he was saying and I'd act accordingly. 'Is he on his way in?' I asked.

'He's already here. Liza is sitting with him in the visitors' room.'

'Where's Grace?'

'Upstairs with Thistle Thorn. It seemed wise to keep them apart, and she should be the first to hear that her grandmother's case is being closed. She's expecting it,' he repeated my own words back to me, 'but she is the next of kin.'

A ghost of a smile crossed my mouth. 'Yeah.' I glanced around. 'Grace said I could look through the case files so I can answer Robert's questions.'

'When you tell him the case is closed, he'll interrogate you as if he's leading the Spanish Inquisition and then he'll try and throttle you again,' Fred said darkly,

'Your optimism is encouraging.'

'Boss—'

I put up my hand. 'It's okay. I appreciate the warning, Fred, and I'm not dismissing it. I'm worried about Robert, too, but as long as we handle this properly it'll be okay.'

He looked doubtful as he reached into a drawer and lifted out a heavy folder. 'Here,' he said. 'This is everything Grace found.'

'I only need the highlights but thank you. Call Lady Sullivan. Tell her what's going on and that she should drop by. She'll be able to handle Robert if everything goes tits up.'

'Okay.' Fred blinked rapidly. 'That's a good idea. She's his alpha, she'll stop him from killing us all.'

'He won't kill anyone,' I said. I wouldn't let him. 'Though he might throw a few chairs and damage Grace's new paintwork.'

I flipped open the file and scanned the summary on the first page. The sooner I got this over and done with, the better.

ROBERT AND LIZA were sitting in silence. As soon as I entered, Liza jumped up and darted for the door. 'Great!' she said cheerfully, almost knocking me over in her haste to get out. 'He's all yours!'

Robert sent her retreating figure a doleful stare. 'I didn't need a babysitter,' he growled. 'I wouldn't hurt her.' He wouldn't have dared. Liza might be human through and through, but she was tough. And scary.

'I have to be honest with you,' I said. 'Everyone here at Supe Squad is worried about you and what you might do.'

His shoulders slumped. The blue shadows under his eyes weren't as heavy as they had been a couple of days earlier, and there was a resigned expression on his face. It suggested he knew exactly what I was going to say and would finally accept the outcome.

'I'm sorry,' he muttered. 'I know you've got other things going on with those weird serial killers. I've not been hiding under a rock, despite my appearance.' He waved a hand at his unshaven face and rumpled clothes. 'But nobody else was fighting for Rosie. I had to do something, to make sure...' He choked slightly.

I sat down next to him. 'You fought for her every inch of the way. You did everything you could, you held us to account and made sure we left no stone unturned. You can rest easy knowing we looked into everything. Rosie wasn't murdered.'

'Her next-door neighbour—'

I spoke gently. 'Detective Sergeant Grace interviewed him at length. Mr Harris listened to her heart and checked her blood pressure every month. He recommended that she take more exercise, recommended some herbal teas and told her to visit her GP.'

The old werewolf raised his head. 'I want to talk to him. I want to hear what he has to say.'

No chance. 'You know that wouldn't be appropriate – and you know that pestering Thistle isn't appropriate, either.'

Robert didn't disagree but his shoulders dropped another inch. 'It doesn't seem real. Rosie was so strong, so full of life.' Unchecked tears rolled down his cheeks.

I reached for a box of tissues and handed it to him. He pulled several out in a clump and wiped his face, sniffed loudly, then took out more and blew his nose.

'I should talk to Thistle and tell her I'm sorry for everything I've put her through,' he said. 'And I want to pay for the funeral. I want to give my Rosie the best. She deserves the biggest, brightest funeral that London has ever seen.'

'Thistle is upstairs,' I told him. 'She might not want to talk to you again, but I'll see what she says.'

He sniffed some more. 'I understand. I won't cause any more problems. Tell her it's okay – I'm okay.'

I smiled sympathetically and went to the door. Grace was in the corridor with Thistle. Both of them looked anxious when they saw me, but I gave them a reassuring nod.

'Robert would like to talk to you,' I said. 'He's calm and I don't believe he'll cause any problems, but it's up to you. You don't have to speak to him again. You've lost a loved one too, Thistle.'

The little pixie gazed at me with baleful eyes. I had the sense that she was relieved it was almost over and she could put her grandmother to rest. 'It's okay. I'll talk to him.'

Grace was less sure. 'DC Bellamy,' he started, 'are you sure this is a good idea?'

'I'm sure.' I stepped back into the visitors' room. 'Thistle will talk to you,' I said to Robert. 'You need to be gentle. She's griev-ing, too.'

'I will.' He was still holding the crumpled tissues in his hand. 'Do you have a bin?'

I cast around and saw a small wastepaper basket in the corner. I was picking it up as Thistle walked in with Grace by her side.

'I'm sorry, Thistle.' Robert's voice cracked. 'I'm sorry I've made this more difficult than it had to be.'

Thistle managed a smile. I held up the wastepaper basket to Robert – and then I froze, the blood draining from my face.

'Emma?' Owen Grace asked. 'Are you okay?'

My jaw worked but I couldn't find the words. All I could see was the discarded coffee cup, with its blue coffee-bean logo and the words The Grind House emblazoned across it.

CHAPTER TWENTY-THREE

OWEN GRACE WRUNG HIS HANDS. 'IT DOESN'T MEAN ANYTHING. IT *can't* mean anything.'

Liza, Fred and I stared at the wastepaper basket. 'Sure,' I said. 'It probably doesn't mean anything at all.'

Except that the Grind House was a small business miles away from here. There had to be a thousand coffee shops that were nearer.

'I emptied the bins yesterday morning,' Liza said. 'Other than the four of us, the only people who've been inside the visitors' room since then are Alan Harris, Thistle Thorn and Robert Sullivan.'

Fred's eyes were wide. 'Robert Sullivan is the second serial killer you've been looking for? Bloody hell. He's outside with Lady Sullivan now. Should I arrest him?'

I snapped out my hand to prevent him running to the door. Easy does it. 'Alan Harris was in here?' I asked slowly. Alan Harris was a nurse. He had medical training.

'Not for long. He waited for a couple of minutes while I got the interview room ready next door,' Grace said.

A preternatural calmness descended on me. 'Did he come in with that coffee cup?'

'I…' Grace shook his head in frustration. 'I don't know.'

'The file said his interview started just after two o'clock yesterday afternoon.' That was more than enough time to kill Samuel Brunswick and get here from Bright Smiles.

Liza cleared her throat. 'I called him earlier and asked him to come in. He seemed perfectly happy to do so. He sounded like he wanted to help.'

'When?' I asked. 'When did you call him?'

'About eleven.' She swallowed. 'He agreed to come as quickly as possible but he said it'd be a couple of hours because … because … because…'

Even Grace was growing impatient. 'Because what?'

Liza's voice dropped to a whisper. 'Because he had a dentist's appointment first.'

I CALLED both Murray and Colquhoun as I made my way to Alan Harris's flat.

'Do you have any hard evidence?' Colquhoun asked.

'Absolutely not.'

'Is he our man?'

I drew in a breath. I knew the answer – I knew it deep in my bones. 'Absolutely.'

Alan Harris had medical experience and he fit the profile of the Cupid Killer. I remembered his tidy flat; Alan Harris also liked a tidy crime scene. The evidence against him was circumstantial but I wholeheartedly believed he was our second murderer.

Colquhoun didn't ask me for anything else. 'I'm on my way there now.' She disconnected and I knew she'd be running for her car. That thought was extraordinarily reassuring.

Murray's approach was different, but not a surprise. 'You're not to enter his flat. In fact, DC Bellamy, you're not even to go close to it. We don't want to scare him off. This Alan Harris sounds like our man, but I want to speak to him first.' He paused. 'I will be the one to knock on his door and perform the arrest. I will enter the flat. It's best that I deal with him,' he said self-importantly.

'We've confirmed he's not at work, but he might not be at home,' I started. 'And he could be dangerous.'

Murray didn't hear me; he'd already hung up.

I sighed. I couldn't gainsay his orders. Although Alan Harris might well be responsible for the death of one supe and the torture of another, he was human. I cursed and put away my phone. Lukas was right about the vagaries of the damned law.

I parked Tallulah a few streets away where she could be tucked out of sight. The little purple Mini was well known in this part of town. If Alan Harris saw her, he might realise we were onto him and make a run for it.

I debated calling Lukas then discarded the idea. Harris was human. Bringing Lukas in would only muddy the waters and maybe cause more problems than it solved.

I walked with as much nonchalance as I could towards Harris's street. Murray had told me not to get too close and I'd respect his order – to a point. But I knew how to remain unobtrusive, and I'd get as near to Harris's building as I dared.

I calculated how long it would take either Colquhoun or Murray to arrive, then I crossed my fingers that Alan Harris would come quietly. Maybe, just maybe, nobody else would have to die.

My phone beeped with a message from Fred. He and Grace were heading into Rosie's flat directly opposite from Harris's. Thanks to Robert Sullivan's persistence, both of them had spent enough time there over the past week that their presence wouldn't be a red flag if Harris saw them.

I sent a quick thumbs up and skirted round to one of the side streets. Less than five minutes later, Colquhoun appeared. I shifted my weight from foot to foot as she got out of her car. She noted my agitation and smiled. 'It'll be okay. He won't get away from us.'

'Marcus Lyons has,' I answered, wincing at the growl in my voice.

'So far. Plus, he's a vamp. You're sure Harris is human?'

As sure as I could be. I nodded.

Colquhoun met my eyes. 'If he's in there, we'll get him.'

My phone beeped again. I glanced down and grimaced. '*If* he's in there.' I showed her the screen. 'My colleagues are in the flat opposite and they can't hear anything from his place. He might not be inside.'

Colquhoun was far more experienced at this sort of thing. 'I'll let Murray know. I doubt he'll hold back on entering. If Harris isn't at home, he may be out preparing to kill again. We can't afford to wait too long.' She pulled out her phone and eyed me. 'Anticipation of a potential arrest is the worst part. Once we go in, it'll get better.'

'Promise?'

She flashed me a grin. 'I never make promises.'

In terms of philosophies to live by, that was one of the smarter ones. I dropped my shoulders and tried to relax. It didn't work, but for a while I could pretend.

Although every minute felt like an hour, we didn't have to wait long. When Murray appeared, the broad smile on his face said it all. 'This is good,' he beamed. 'This is very good. All that hard work has finally paid off and I've tracked down the Cupid Killer.'

He wagged his finger at us. 'No press yet, mind? Until we are one hundred percent sure that this is our man, nobody says a dickie bird. Until he's charged, Alan Harris will be helping us with our enquiries. In the unfortunate event that he's not home, I'm having a search warrant prepared.'

He offered a self-congratulatory smile. 'I've arranged for a loose cordon to be placed around this area in case he sees us and tries to make a run for it. His stupid mate might have escaped us, but the Cupid Killer will not. He'll be in handcuffs and confessing his crimes before the day is out.' He nodded sagely. 'Soon the streets of London will be safe again.'

I wondered if it was habit that made DCI Murray speak in soundbites, or if he didn't realise he was doing it.

Colquhoun cleared her throat. 'Should we wait for Armed Response, sir?'

Murray scowled. 'I don't need them. I have considered the matter carefully and I'm confident I can manage Harris myself.' He flexed his fingers, cracked his knuckles, then looked at me. 'Show me where the flat is. It's time to show the Cupid Killer that I mean business.'

We walked towards the building where Rosie used to live and where Alan Harris still did. A cold breeze whistled down the street, adding to the chill in my bones. I could hear birds twittering from the nearby trees and the distant rumble of traffic. A few dried leaves tumbled along the edge of the pavement and caught in a drain nearby.

I noted a couple of faces gazing at us from windows opposite Rosie and Harris's building – in fact, the same windows that Fred had pointed out when we'd first entered Rosie's flat. I looked up, hoping to glimpse Alan Harris inside his flat, but the curtains were closed. If he was home, we couldn't see him.

More police officers arrived. Several positioned themselves at either end of the street, and more headed to different points around the building. There was a mechanical whirr from overhead and I saw a drone hovering above us. At least Murray was making sure that Harris couldn't make a run for it. All avenues of escape were covered.

A uniformed officer marched towards us with his body armour in his hand. His face was familiar, and I realised he was the same guy who'd greeted me when I went to Hackney to meet Colquhoun that very first time. I smiled a greeting, and the tips of his ears went pink.

Murray strapped on the armour. 'Thank you, Norris,' he said. He glanced at his reflection in a window, frowned slightly and sucked in his stomach.

The officer passed an identical body armour vest to Colquhoun. 'I'm sorry,' he apologised to me. 'I only have two. I can get another one for you, if you'd like to wait. We have plenty of spares.'

'We're not waiting. Everyone is in place. If you don't have adequate protection, Emma, you can wait at the end of the road.' Murray pointed down the street.

My eyes followed his finger and I jerked when I saw Robert Sullivan standing there, with Lady Sullivan next to him. Robert had clocked my reaction when I'd seen the contents of the rubbish bin, and he and Lady Sullivan must have seen us tearing out of Supe Squad at high speed. I hoped he didn't believe we were here because of Rosie.

I turned back to Norris. 'I don't need a vest.' I'd have liked one but I wanted to see Alan Harris's reaction when we knocked on his door. I couldn't waste time and risk missing his arrest.

Norris's eyes widened with delight. 'Because if he's armed and he shoots you, you won't die, right?' He shivered happily. 'That's so cool.' He nodded at the building. 'I heard it was you who found Harris. You connected the dots and worked out who he is and what he's been up to. That's amazing. *You're* amazing. In fact—'

'There is a time and a place, Norris,' Murray hissed. 'And this is not it.' He turned on his heel and entered the building without another word.

Colquhoun glanced at me apologetically and followed him. A

time and a place indeed. The young officer looked even more embarrassed and quickly headed in after them.

The door to Rosie Thorn's flat was ajar. As we reached the hallway, I spotted Grace in the gap between the door and the frame. He motioned at us, making it clear that there had been no sign of movement from Harris's place. Murray acknowledged him with a raised hand and turned to Alan Harris's front door. He pulled his shoulders back and straightened his tie. Then he knocked.

It was something of an anti-climax when nobody answered. Murray knocked again. Still nothing. He knelt down to the letterbox and flipped it open. 'Mr Harris!' he bellowed. 'It's the police! We need to talk to you.'

I winced. So much for the element of surprise. If Alan Harris had been in a back room and been taking his time to get to the door, he might well have changed his mind and gone for a window instead. There were no sounds of running feet, however; there were no sounds at all. Alan bloody Harris wasn't home.

Murray sucked air through his teeth; from his expression, he was taking Harris's absence as a personal insult. 'So be it,' he said. 'Let's break the door down and see what's inside.'

CHAPTER TWENTY-FOUR

THE INTERIOR OF ALAN HARRIS'S FLAT WAS AS NEAT AND TIDY AS I remembered it. He obviously didn't appreciate clutter. Or dust. Every surface had been scoured to within an inch of its life. The layout was essentially a mirror image of Rosie's place, although the view from the windows was one of the gardens at the rear rather than the street.

'No computer,' Colquhoun grunted, her vexation beginning to show.

From his position in the centre of the living room, Murray frowned. 'No blood. No death paraphernalia. No crime-scene souvenirs.' He glared at me. 'Maybe Alan Harris isn't our man after all.'

I glanced at the bookshelf with its array of alphabetically ordered titles. *How To Beat The Odds: Volume One. A Winner's Mindset. Dice Man.* No; I was still convinced that Harris was the bastard we were looking for. 'He's on the Fetish client list,' I said. I'd already checked.

There was a small desk next to the bookshelf. Using gloved hands, I opened a drawer and squinted at the notepad inside. Alan Harris might enjoy a tidy home but his handwriting was a messy scrawl. *'The pink house,'* I read aloud. What did that mean? *'P park before 2.'* I grimaced. Whatever the notes referred to, they were a reminder for Alan Harris alone and incomprehensible to me.

From deeper inside the flat there was a loud crash. Colquhoun and I jumped but Murray only rolled his eyes. 'Go and see what that was,' he ordered. Before I'd even left the room, he was complaining about me to Colquhoun. 'She's brought us here on a wild goose chase. This isn't the Cupid Killer. This guy is squeaky clean.'

I drew a deep breath into my lungs and walked into the bedroom. A young tech wearing white forensic overalls gave me a guilty look from the corner of the room. 'I knocked over a lamp,' he said, biting his lip.

I noted the ceramic shards littering the immaculate carpet. 'Don't worry,' I told him. 'I'll help you tidy up.'

I knelt down beside him and started gingerly picking up the pieces of broken lamp. The bigger shards were easy enough, but some small white splinters near the open door of the built-in wardrobe were harder to scoop up. I picked up as many as I could, then leaned back on my haunches to get a better look. I tilted my head, scanned the floor and glanced up at the wardrobe.

'Have you already looked in there?' I asked the tech, pointing at the perfectly straight array of well-ironed shirts.

'We've done a quick check,' he said. 'It seems to be only clothes.'

I gazed at it. 'There's something there,' I said. I wouldn't have noticed if I hadn't been scrabbling around the floor, but there were some unusual scuff marks at the back of the wardrobe. I got to my feet and took a step back, turning my head from the wall to the wardrobe and back again. 'It's a fitted wardrobe,' I said. 'It's designed to maximise space.'

The tech joined me and his eyes widened. 'And if it's designed to maximise space,' he agreed, 'why doesn't it align with the back wall?'

We glanced at each other, then the tech shouted for his colleagues. It took them only seconds to locate the mechanism to slide the back panel aside. When the space was revealed and we saw the contents, I swallowed. 'Go get DCI Murray,' I told the tech. 'He needs to see this.'

The secret space wasn't huge – less than a foot wide – and you'd struggle to a hide a body inside it, but what Alan Harris had managed to hide was damning enough. On a shelf were two wide paintbrushes, a decorator's mask and a set of overalls. It would take Lukas or a proper lab to confirm it, but I was fairly certain that the stains on the overalls were dried blood.

Beneath the shelf was a medicine cabinet with the doors removed. It contained syringes and needles and several bottles of clear liquid. I peered at the largest bottle: atropine. Of course it was. Next to it was a set of small pliers. I couldn't repress a shudder; I'd lay bets they had recently been used to remove Samuel Brunswick's canines.

Murray marched in, stared and gave a low whistle. 'It's a serial killer's starter kit,' he said.

I couldn't disagree. I gazed at the framed photo displayed on the wall next to a set of sharp knives. It was a candid shot of Jonas sitting at the bar at Fetish. It didn't look posed; in fact, he didn't appear to be aware of the camera. I shook my head.

'Look at that,' Murray breathed, pointing at the hand-drawn chart next to the photo. It was a carefully drawn table with two sets of boxes.

'What is it?' the tech asked, baffled.

'It's a score sheet,' I answered. One mark to Marcus Lyons. One mark to Alan Harris. And still everything to play for.

THE DISCOVERY of Alan Harris's murder stash changed everything. The atmosphere in the small flat moved from doubtful to energised. Murray was on the phone, setting up alerts across the city to find Harris and bring him in, and the mood of the entire team was focused and alert. In an ideal situation, Alan Harris would wander in through the door at any moment.

Owen Grace and Fred, who were still hovering outside, had caught the same energy. 'Well done, Emma,' Grace told me. 'Bloody well done.'

Fred bounced from foot to foot. 'The coffee cup and the rest of the contents from the bin are already at the lab.' He blinked at me eagerly. 'Did he do it?' he asked. 'Did he kill Rosie?'

Under the circumstances it was a reasonable question but, in truth, nothing had changed with her investigation. There was no evidence to suggest that Alan Harris had murdered his neighbour; in fact, it seemed highly unlikely. Rosie Thorn's name wasn't anywhere on Fetish's guest list, and the other murders had taken place nowhere near here. It would have been incredibly risky to kill someone so close by, and, from the expression on Harris's face when I'd informed him of her death, he'd been genuinely shocked.

'There's still nothing to suggest she died of anything other than natural causes. And,' I reminded him, 'Alan Harris was away on holiday when she died.'

Grace agreed. 'I checked his alibi myself. It's watertight.'

Murray thumbed off his phone and strode over. 'Who are you?' he asked, looking at my two companions.

Grace extended his hand. 'DS Grace, sir. I'm with Supe Squad.' He gestured to Fred. 'And this is PC—'

Murray interrupted him. 'We don't need more Supe Squad intervention. Alan Harris is human and your presence is not required.'

That was bluntly put, even for DCI Murray. 'Sir,' I started.

Murray shook his head. 'We don't need you here, either,' he

informed me. 'We've got enough on Harris and he'll be in custody soon. But that vampire is still on the loose. I need you to continue the search for Marcus Lyons. You're a supe, you're better placed to find him than the rest of us.'

'We've got no leads on him at the moment,' I protested. 'He's gone to ground. He could be anywhere, sir. There are vampires and police looking for him, but until he pops his head above the parapet we won't know where he is. Our best bet is to wait and see what Harris says about Lyons. He must be in contact with him. We can use what Harris knows to arrest Marcus Lyons, too.'

'Are you saying you don't care that there's a dangerous vampire loose on the streets of London?'

What? 'No! But I think we should use all our resources in the best way that—'

'Find Marcus Lyons, Emma.' Murray turned away. 'That is all.'

Shit. I gazed after him while Fred and Grace looked on, open-mouthed. I knew exactly why Murray wanted me out of the picture, but he should have worked out by now that all I cared about were results. I didn't need any credit.

Colquhoun sidled over. 'I'm sorry, Emma.' She pulled a face. 'You know he's banking on Alan Harris leading us to Marcus Lyons and making both arrests himself.'

'We're supposed to be a team,' I said through gritted teeth.

'We are,' she told me, and I knew she wasn't referring to Murray. 'I'll keep you updated, I promise.'

'You just told me you didn't believe in promises.'

Something twinkled briefly in her eyes. 'In this case, I'll make an exception.'

I WASN'T GOING to sulk. I was better than that. Besides, we needed to locate Marcus Lyons.

There was no point aimlessly walking the streets and

searching for his face, and I'd be wasting my time speaking to vampires because Lukas had that side of the search well covered. I'd only be going over old ground if I went looking for Marcus Lyons' friends and acquaintances.

I tried to think laterally about where Lyons might have gone. He wouldn't be anywhere public. He wouldn't have checked into a hotel or be anywhere his face could be caught on CCTV. I also doubted that he'd be staying with anyone he knew. By now, the entire city was aware that Marcus Lyons was a killer. He was somewhere out of sight.

At some point he would need access to human blood; he'd starve without it. With that thought in mind, I looked up the hospitals in the area and searched for somewhere quiet with a well-stocked blood bank. The blood donor centre at a hospital in Edgeware seemed as good a place to start as any.

I hopped into Tallulah and turned the ignition key. Her engine spluttered but she resolutely refused anything more. I briefly closed my eyes.

'Yes,' I said aloud. 'This is a better place to stay. Wandering around London looking for a vampire who doesn't want to be found isn't a great plan. But there are some empty properties near this hospital and I have to try something.' I paused. 'Please, Tallulah?' I waited a beat and turned the key again.

She choked and spluttered; her exhaust belched out a cloud of black smoke – but her engine still didn't start.

'I'll take you to the car wash later,' I said. I wasn't beyond offering a bribe. 'I'll even upgrade to a wax.'

Nothing. I hissed and prepared to switch from carrot to stick, but before I could tell her that I'd have her stripped for parts and left to rust on a derelict wasteland my phone rang. I sighed and answered it without pausing to check the caller ID. 'This is Detective Constable Emma Bellamy.'

I heard nothing. I frowned. 'Hello?'

'Hi, Musketeer.'

I sat bolt upright. Zara sounded strange – strained. 'Zara? What's going on?'

'There will be two more,' she whispered.

I turned ice cold. 'Two more what? Two more murders?'

'Yes. Two more murders.' She hummed quietly. 'But that's not why I'm calling you.'

'Zara—'

Her tone altered. She didn't sound happy or content, but oddly wistful. 'I think we could have been friends, in another life. You seem like a nice person.'

Now I was alarmed. 'What's going on?'

There was another brief silence, then she sighed. 'I'm calling to tell you I'm sorry. I'm so very sorry. It's not what I wanted, but I can't control it,' she added sadly.

My stomach dropped to the bottom of my shoes.

'I also have to tell you,' she said, 'that the postman doesn't always ring twice. And you should beware of glib tongues and elaborate lies.'

'You need to give me more information. There's never enough time, Zara. I need more details so I can prevent the next murders.'

'Time will be on your side, Musketeer. You take care of yourself.' There was a click.

'Zara? Hello?' I shook the phone as if somehow that would reconnect us. 'Goddamnit!'

It rang again. I scrabbled to answer it. 'Zara?'

'How did you know that's why I was calling?'

I blinked. 'Lukas?'

'None other.' His voice was dry.

My dread didn't decrease. 'You've found her. You've found Zara.'

'Yes. In the absence of Marcus fucking Lyons, the Cassandra is the next best thing. Her last name is Thomas. Zara Thomas. I'm on the way to her place now.'

Oh. 'Lukas,' I said. 'You can't approach her. She's just phoned me, and from what she said—'

He sounded irritated. 'I won't approach her. I already told you I wouldn't.' He paused, before adding, 'Twice.'

'None of your people can go near her.'

'My people,' Lukas snapped, 'will do as they're told.'

Marcus Lyons hadn't. I managed to bite back my retort. Tensions were running high and a petulant remark wouldn't help either of us. 'Where are you? Where is she?' I turned Tallulah's key again and this time her engine started with a smooth purr.

'South of the city,' he said. 'Croydon.' He gave me an address.

'I'll be there as soon as I can.' I drew in a breath. Even though I knew it would annoy him further, I said it again, 'Keep your distance till I get there, Lukas. Please.'

'Yeah, yeah.'

I glanced down the street at Harris's building and the growing kerfuffle of police officers and onlookers. I should tell Murray, but I knew he wouldn't listen to me. Screw him.

I put Tallulah into gear and took off.

CHAPTER TWENTY-FIVE

'THE POSTMAN DOESN'T ALWAYS RING TWICE?' COLQUHOUN sounded as confused as I was. 'I don't know what that means. What else did she say?'

'That she was sorry. And to beware of glib tongues and elaborate lies.'

'For fuck's sake,' Colquhoun muttered. 'I could have told you that last part. She doesn't make things easy, does she?'

'I can't make head or tail of it,' I agreed. 'But if I can talk to her face to face, maybe she'll give me more. We *need* more.'

'Indeed we do. Murray is apoplectic. Harris hasn't put in an appearance, and we don't know where he is.'

I gritted my teeth. We still weren't winning. Not yet. 'Keep in touch,' I said.

'You too.'

I ended the call and focused on the road. I didn't know Croydon well; it is part of outer London and not a place you'd usually find supes. I knew that the area was undergoing considerable regeneration, and that it had a long history dating back to the Domesday book, but that was about it.

Thank heavens for the satnav on my phone that led me to

Zara's street without too much trouble. I slowed down, checking the house numbers and keeping an eye out for Lukas and his crowd of vamps.

As soon as I rounded the next bend, I saw them. In this neck of the woods, they stuck out like beacons. A leafy suburb wasn't the place for a band of bloodsuckers and, from the taut faces at some of the windows of the surrounding bungalows, the residents knew it.

In theory, Lukas wasn't doing anything untoward – he was merely leaning against the door of his car with his arms crossed – but he didn't need to do anything. With his inscrutable expression and rigid stance, he looked dangerous. Hell, in his current mood, he *was* dangerous. Then again, I reflected, so was I.

I looked around. Four other vampires were milling about close by and I knew there would be plenty more out of sight. It had taken this long to track Zara down that Lukas wouldn't risk her slipping away like Marcus Lyons had.

I jumped out of Tallulah and walked towards him. 'You're lowering the tone of the neighbourhood,' I said, trying to lighten the mood between us. It was a poor joke and Lukas barely reacted.

I reached out and placed my hand on his. The other vamps turned away in a bid to give us at least the illusion of privacy. 'Are we okay?' I asked quietly.

'Yes.' He didn't look at me.

I persisted. 'Are you okay?'

'Yes.' Lukas turned to me. His face was shuttered but I registered the pain flickering in the depths of his black eyes. 'Alright,' he conceded. 'I may not be okay. I'm outside the house of a Cassandra because I can't be trusted to go inside on my own. One of my vampires is a serial killer who's on the run, and I can't find him despite my best efforts.'

He clenched his fists. 'I like to be in control – I *need* to be in control. It's the only way I know how to survive.' He shook his head. 'But right now I'm not in control of anything. I can't deal with chaos, Emma. It's not how I work.'

For a second, he looked like a little lost boy. I loosened my grip on his hand and went for a hug instead, wrapping my arms tightly around his body. 'It's okay to not always be in control,' I whispered. 'You're Lord Lukas Horvath. You can deal with everything that life throws at you. You've got people to help you. *I* will help you.'

His arms went round me and his head dropped. 'It's hard when the façade drops and you see the real me,' he murmured in my ear.

'I love the real you. I don't want the façade.'

'God,' he said, 'I love you so much.'

'The real me?'

Finally the smile returned to his voice. 'Always.'

We drew apart and gazed into each other's eyes for a moment, as if we needed the extra reassurance that we were there for each other.

I pushed aside my worry about Zara's last message and took a deep breath. 'Come and see Zara with me. It'll help you feel more in control.' I smiled at him. 'I trust you with her. Truly I do.'

Lukas looked momentarily surprised, then shook his head. 'You shouldn't,' he said. 'You shouldn't trust me in this. I'm trying to think more kindly about her, Emma, I really am. There's enough proof that she's a bona fide Cassandra, and I know it's not her fault that she is what she is. She doesn't deserve how I feel about her, and I've been trying to set those feelings aside.' He sighed. 'But I'm not there yet. I may never be there. It's better for her if I stay outside. The thought of what she is capable of terrifies me. I'm sorry.'

I didn't know many people who would admit that something or someone scared them. 'Don't be sorry.' I touched his cheek. 'You're being honest, not just with me but with yourself, too. I'll talk to her and we'll take things from there. Which house is she in?'

'It's the one at the end,' he said. 'The pink one.'

I froze. *The pink house.* The scribbled note in Alan Harris's house. 'What?' I asked, my voice strained. 'What did you say?'

'The pink house,' he repeated. 'At the end of the terrace.'

I started to run before he finished speaking. I sprinted down the street with all the speed that my phoenix body could muster. By the time I reached Zara's pink house, my heart was hammering hard against my ribcage, not from physical exertion but fear.

I knocked on the door and shouted but didn't wait for an answer. I rattled the door knob, prepared to break the door down if I had to, but it opened easily and I burst in.

It didn't take long to find her.

Zara's body was lying on the kitchen table. She was spread-eagled, with her arms and legs dangling off the sides. Her eyes were closed and, for one desperate moment, I thought she was alright. Then I saw the gaping wound in the centre of her chest and knew that she wasn't.

I gasped, feeling a stabbing sensation in my own heart. It was little more than an hour since I'd spoken to her on the phone.

I heard a shout from the doorway. Feeling sick, I looked back. 'I can smell the blood,' Lukas said, his face pale. 'Is she...'

'She's dead,' I said. Or at least that's what I tried to say; my mouth formed the words but no sound came out. I tried again. 'She's dead.' I swallowed hard. Thank God he was here. Thank God I wasn't alone. 'I was on the phone to her right before you called me. An hour ago, she was fine. When exactly did you get here?'

'I called you on the way,' he said. 'It was maybe another thirty minutes after we spoke that I arrived.'

'Obviously you didn't see anyone go in or come out of the front door after you arrived. What about the back?'

'I'll check. Hang on.'

I didn't want him to go but the killer might still be in the vicinity. It had been minutes, not hours, since Zara had been killed. The bastard worked quickly: Alan fucking Harris worked quickly.

My stomach twisted. I could have stopped this. I *should* have stopped this. I moved back to Zara's body. She'd told me she was sorry, and she'd said we could have been friends. Did she know this was going to happen?

I knew I shouldn't do it – touching Zara's body went against every crime-scene protocol in the book. I couldn't explain why, even to myself, but I reached out and brushed her hand with my fingertips. 'I'm sorry. God, Zara. I'm so, so sorry.'

That was when I felt something. I stiffened. Had her fingers just twitched? Was she still alive? My eyes travelled to the bloody mess in the centre of her chest. It seemed impossible. There was no way she could have survived that. Could she?

I moved round the table, my own blood roaring in my ears, and pressed my fingers to the base of her throat, feeling for a pulse. Nothing. Her skin already felt cool. She was definitely dead.

I swallowed and backed away again. I had to call this in; I had to speak to Murray and Colquhoun.

'A motorbike.' Lukas spoke from the doorway, his eyes flicking to Zara and then back to me.

I stared at him.

'A couple of minutes after my guys took up position at the rear of the house, a motorbike revved up and departed. There was a single rider. They couldn't see his face because of his helmet but he was definitely male. And,' he added grimly, 'he skidded away so fast he almost crashed at the end of the street.'

'That was him.' I exhaled.

Lukas's gaze returned to Zara, lingering on the hole in her

chest. 'He had what looked like a cool box strapped to the back of the bike.'

A cool box? *No.* I'd thought things couldn't get any worse, but they could. They always could. I edged over and peered again at Zara's wound. 'I can't see. There's too much blood.' I looked up at Lukas, my voice a mere whisper. 'Has he taken her heart?'

Lukas drew in a breath. 'It appears so.'

My head spun. 'He'll leave it somewhere for Marcus. And then Marcus will use it when he kills someone else.' Best of three, I thought. Best of fucking three.

I pressed the base of my palms to my temples. I couldn't let my horror get the better of me, there wasn't time. 'The P Park.'

'What's that?'

'Alan Harris, the man who murdered Zara and Peter Pickover and Samuel Brunswick. We found his flat, but he wasn't there because he was here. There was a note. The pink house. And the P Park, before two o'clock. I bet he's planning to leave Zara's heart in the P Park before two o'clock so that Marcus Lyons can pick it up.'

Lukas checked his watch. 'It's already after one o'clock. No wonder he was in a rush.' He shook his head. 'But I don't know any P Park. I can ask the others—'

'No,' I interrupted. 'Wait. Zara said something too.' I tried to get the wording right. 'I should beware of glib tongues and elaborate lies. And the postman doesn't always ring twice.'

'That doesn't make any...' Lukas stopped. His eyes met mine. 'Postman's Park,' he breathed.

I stared at him. 'Of course. We need to get everyone there as quickly as possible.'

'Everyone who's available is out searching for Marcus Lyons. I don't think anyone is close to Postman's Park.'

'Then you need to get them there.' My jaw tightened. 'Now.'

CHAPTER TWENTY-SIX

UNDER NORMAL CIRCUMSTANCES, POSTMAN'S PARK IS ONE OF THE loveliest corners of central London. A mere stone's throw from St Paul's Cathedral, it is a tiny green oasis, a genuinely heart-warming spot. It contains a public memorial and dozens of engraved plaques dedicated to people who died while saving others and whose names might otherwise have been forgotten. The people commemorated in Postman's Park were true heroes – and that made it all the more nauseating that Harris and Lyons' were using it as part of sick game.

'If Murray floods the park with police, they'll both be scared off,' I cautioned Colquhoun as I pressed Tallulah's accelerator to the floor and sped back towards central London. 'This is our chance to get the pair of them. We can't mess it up.'

'For once DCI Murray is way ahead of you. He's taking precautions.' She paused. 'But Harris has a good lead on us. On a motorbike he can navigate much faster through traffic. He might have already been and gone.'

That was a very real possibility.

'Fortunately,' Colquhoun continued, 'the park's location means that the area is always teeming with police. Murray is sending a couple of uniforms through to stroll around. They won't approach Harris if they see him, but they'll tail him if he makes an appearance. Everyone else is keeping an eye open for a bike.'

I breathed out. Okay. Zara had told me that time would be on my side. It hadn't been on hers, but I had to hope that she'd been telling the truth. If she had, maybe we could put a stop to all this horror. 'I'm less than fifteen minutes away now,' I told her. 'Keep me updated.'

'Will do.'

I raced through the next set of traffic lights. Lukas was somewhere behind me in his own car with the vamps who'd gone with him to Zara's place. His car was considerably more luxurious and expensive than Tallulah, and on the open road he'd have left us for dust, but Tallulah had the edge on busy streets. She could nip into narrow lanes and overtake larger vehicles in a way that Lukas's large car couldn't.

'Come on, girl,' I urged. 'As fast as you can.'

Tallulah did her absolute best. By the time the dome of St Paul's Cathedral appeared over the nearby rooftops, there had been a lot of angry horns from other drivers and more than one near miss.

Postman's Park was in touching distance when a bus pulled out in front and I was forced to slam on the brakes. The other side of the road was too busy to overtake, but the bus was going too slow. I cursed and looked for somewhere I could pull up and jump out. It would be faster to run the rest of the way.

My phone rang again. I spun Tallulah's wheel to the left so that she mounted the pavement. An old woman shook her fist at me but I ignored her and answered the call. 'Colquhoun,' I said.

I knew from her voice that it wasn't good news. 'He's been and gone,' she said flatly. 'There's a cool box tucked underneath a tree. The uniforms haven't touched it. They're keeping their distance but they have it in sight.'

I gritted my teeth. 'There's no sign of Harris? No sign of a motorbike?'

'I'm afraid not.'

Shit. I jumped out of Tallulah, crossbow in hand, and jogged past the bus towards the end of the street. 'Alright,' I bit out. 'I'm not far now. I'm on foot and I'll be at the park in less than five minutes.'

'Keep your head down,' she advised. 'We can still get Lyons.'

I nodded as I reached the crossroads and swerved out of the way of a laughing group of teenagers.

'Idiot thinks that because he's on a big motorbike he's flexing,' one of the boys said.

'He almost ran us over,' the girl next to him replied. 'He's a tosser.'

I skidded to a stop and whipped around. There were lots of motorbikes in London, and the chances that they were talking about Alan Harris were slim to none. All the same, I couldn't let this go by. 'What bike?' I demanded. 'Where?'

The entire group stared at me as if I were a madwoman. One of the girls looked down at my crossbow and back up at my face. 'Wait,' she said slowly. 'You're that supe woman. The detective who can't die.'

The first boy's eyes widened. 'Does that mean if we kill you we won't get sent to prison for murder?'

I reached for my warrant card. There was a time and a place for banter with teenagers, and this most definitely was not it. 'The motorbike,' I hissed. 'Where did you see it?'

'Back there.' The boy jerked his thumb. 'At that last turn off.'

'Did you see which way it went?'

One girl pointed right. Another pointed left. Fuck. 'Alright,' I muttered. 'Thanks anyway.' It had been a long shot. I started to move past them.

'Would a video help?' one of them called after me.

I turned. A girl with long brown hair and a freckled face held up a mobile phone. 'He was an arse,' she said baldly. 'I filmed him and thought I might put it on TikTok later. I've got over five thousand followers.'

God bless teenagers and social media. 'May I?' I asked.

She handed over the phone and I fumbled with the buttons before I finally managed to get the video to play.

It was him – his visor was up and it was definitely him. He swore loudly at the kids and spat in their direction before dropping the visor and accelerating away. It didn't take much to reveal Alan Harris's true character. I watched as the shaky video followed the roaring motorbike. The number plate was clear.

'He started it,' she said. 'Not us. He almost ran Drew over.'

I nodded, barely hearing her. My phone was already at my ear. 'I need real-time ANPR on a motorbike,' I said to the police operator. 'Now.' I read out the number plate.

'One moment,' the operator responded.

'Hey,' the kid said, 'if you're famous, can I get your autograph? Can I put you on my TikTok channel?'

I found a business card and handed it over. It was the least I could do. Her eyes widened. 'Cool.'

The operator cleared her throat. 'I've got it. It just turned right onto Goswell Road heading north towards Northampton Square.'

I turned and started to run once again.

He hadn't gone far. I heard the motorbike before I saw it – it had stopped at a set of traffic lights on red and Harris was gunning the engine. He was clearly in a hurry to get away. I wondered if he'd seen something at Postman's Park that had made him realise the game was up. It didn't matter; I had him in my sights now. Then the lights flicked to green.

I pelted after him. I jumped over a Yorkshire terrier sniffing at a lamp post and veered around its owner. When a group of tourists blocked my path, I leapt into the road and hurtled at full speed towards the motorbike. As long as he didn't check his mirrors, I'd catch up to him.

There were more traffic lights ahead. I glanced up. They were changing to red. He'd be forced to stop again – and then I'd have him. I put my head down and pounded the tarmac until I reached the line of queueing cars. Now he was only metres away.

Harris's head turned an inch. For one long second he didn't move, then his body went rigid. He'd clocked me. He *knew*.

He sped forward, ignoring even the most basic traffic laws and jumping the red light. A taxi coming from the opposite direction slammed on its brakes to avoid him, but Harris barely slowed down.

I swore and sprinted after him, past the lights, past the shaken taxi driver. Harris swerved to avoid a pothole and I gained a metre. I could do this. I was the phoenix, I reminded myself. I had speed and power.

I drew closer. Harris was panicking now and his grip on the bike's handles faltered. He obviously wasn't an experienced motorcyclist. As he wobbled and was forced to lose speed to stay upright, I gained on him then threw myself up, leaping into the air and colliding with his back. Harris fell to the right and the motorbike and I fell to the left.

I landed badly. My ankle was caught under the heavy frame of the bike and pain shot through my leg and my shoulder. I hissed and scrambled up as fast as I could, but I'd extended too much energy in catching him up.

He was on his feet much faster than I was and already running away. I started after him but was stymied by the screaming agony that flashed through my body. I faltered for a second too long.

Harris darted round the first corner while I fought a wave of dizziness. I couldn't afford to faint. I clenched my teeth and headed after him, moving as quickly as I could.

It wasn't quick enough. By the time I turned the corner, Alan Harris had gone. Shit.

I wiped away the involuntary tears of pain on my cheeks and made a phone call. This wasn't over yet. I wasn't in the mood for giving up.

'ARE YOU IN PAIN, DETECTIVE?' Buffy enquired sweetly. 'Would you like me to kiss the boo-boo and make it go away?' I glared at her and she laughed. 'Sorry but you really don't look very well.'

'I'm fine.' Sort of. I nodded down the street where Alan Harris had disappeared. 'He ran down that way about twenty minutes ago, so he could be anywhere. He might have jumped on a bus or hailed a taxi, but he's likely still on foot because he'll want to avoid anyone seeing his face. He knows we're onto him and that works in our favour. I don't have anything of his for you to sniff but—'

'Don't worry, I can smell his fear. As long as he's in the vicinity, I can track him.'

I waved at her. 'Then go, as fast as you can. I'll do my best to keep up.'

'Gotcha.' She grinned at me. 'I'll get him for you.'

Buffy took off at high speed and I limped after her. Although it had taken her some time to arrive, I knew she was the best chance I had of catching up to Harris. Tracking a trail was a better idea than dragging aimlessly around the neighbouring streets.

I'd hesitated over calling in others because their scents could confuse matters and make it easier for Harris to escape. Keep it simple, stupid, I told myself. As soon as Buffy located him, I'd tell Murray. I could only hope that he was absorbed in arresting Marcus Lyons.

I forced my way through the pain. The harder I pushed

myself, the easier it became to pretend it didn't hurt. At first I hobbled after Buffy, but after a few moments I started to jog. I'd pay for it later in spades, but for now the adrenaline would keep me going.

I followed her down the first street. At the end of it, Buffy turned left then she turned left again at the next crossroads. Hope flared inside me. Harris was panicking and pretty much running in circles.

My mouth was dry and my legs felt shaky, but I managed to keep Buffy in sight. When she came to a halt and slowly turned, her nose in the air, I knew she had him.

I caught up to her. 'He's in there,' she gestured towards the dark, gaping maw of an underground car park. 'I'm sure of it. Shall I go in and get him for you?'

'No.' This was police business. In pain or not, I would find Harris and arrest him. I nodded my thanks, aware that this was not the favour I owed Buffy. Then I thought of something else. 'Actually,' I said, 'can you do me one other quick favour?'

'What's in it for me?'

'A serial killer off the streets,' I growled.

She pursed her lips. 'Fair enough.'

I tossed her my phone. 'I need you to call DCI Murray. His number is in my phone. Introduce yourself and explain where I am and what's happening.' I wasn't hiding from Murray, just using my time more wisely. I thought some more. 'If Murray won't listen then try DI Colquhoun. Her number—'

'Is also in your phone. Got it.' She grinned. 'Have fun.'

Yeah, yeah. I double-checked my crossbow. Although Alan Harris was human and I had no right to use it against him, I might well need it to defend myself.

I headed inside.

The car park was larger than I'd expected. I wasn't sure what this building was but, judging by the location and the expensive cars it belonged to some sort of high-flying company. That was good. Unless Harris happened to be an experienced car thief and had the right equipment with him, he wouldn't be able to break into any of these vehicles. And even if he did, he wouldn't be able to start the engine. The days of hotwiring cars were all but over.

The place was well lit. I couldn't see any shadows that indicated Harris was moving around, and I couldn't hear anything. Perhaps he'd attempted to steal a car and failed. Perhaps he'd already made his way upwards into the building and found an alternative exit.

Hoping that wasn't the case, I walked forward. When I reached the first row of cars, I ducked down and checked underneath. There were a few pools of oil but nothing that suggested a man was hunkering down beneath the belly of a vehicle. I stood up and continued, checking each corner and shadowy crevice.

I was about halfway down and preparing to peer around a large cement column when I heard the unmistakable beep of a car being unlocked. It could have been an office worker heading out for lunch or a meeting, or someone might have foolishly left their car keys under their wheel arch and Alan Harris had found them. Until I knew otherwise, I would assume the latter.

I pulled back out of sight behind the column as I heard an engine start and a car moving towards me from the rear of the car park. To reach the exit, it would have to pass me. That was perfect. I wasn't in any shape to run after a moving vehicle but, with any luck, I wouldn't have to.

I waited until almost the last moment, steeling my body for what was to come and preparing for the onslaught of further pain. As the car drew level, I jumped out from behind the column, planted myself in its path and raised my crossbow.

It was probably the pain that prevented me from being run over. I grimaced horribly as agony slashed through me. From the expression on Harris's face behind the wheel, he genuinely believed I was about to fire a crossbow bolt through the windscreen and into his skull. He slammed on the brakes and stopped the car inches from me then he stared, his eyes fearful. He was the killer around here; I didn't know why he was the one who was afraid.

We gazed at each for several long moments. Eventually, he wound down the window and called out, 'You're the police. You can't shoot me. You'll get into trouble!' his voice quavered. 'You'll be found out!'

A bead of sweat rolled down my forehead. The pain in my shoulder meant it was difficult to keep my crossbow aimed at him without it wobbling.

I forced my voice to remain strong. 'If you get out of the car and give yourself up, there will be no reason to shoot.' For someone who'd murdered three people, he was remarkably concerned about his own well-being. 'I won't hurt you, Alan. But I do need to arrest you. Without any trouble.'

His face slackened. 'There won't be any trouble.'

I looked at him. Was he actually crying now?

'I'll come quietly.' He hiccupped a sob. 'I promise. I don't want to hurt anyone else.'

'Why on earth should I believe a single thing that you say?' I asked, genuinely curious. 'You've murdered – and not just once.'

He waved his hands around, flapping them in a frantic bid to show that he was telling the truth. 'I didn't kill Rosie! She wasn't mine!'

Was that supposed to mean he was a good guy?

'And the others,' he stammered, 'they didn't feel anything. I made sure they didn't suffer.'

Gee, he was all heart. 'You're a fucking nurse,' I said. 'You're supposed to help people. You're supposed to heal them.'

Harris's hands dropped. 'I'll tell you everything. I'll explain it all. I only wanted to make him happy. He said it would be okay – he said the competition would be fun.'

'Where is he? Where's Marcus Lyons?'

'I'll tell you that, too. Just please, please don't shoot me.' His voice was strained.

'Get out of the car with your hands up.' I was still prepared for him to suddenly accelerate again and barrel the car into me.

A range of emotions flickered across his face. As if he could read my mind, he settled on one last attempt at bravery. 'I could run you over! I could keep going and hit you!'

'You could,' I said calmly. 'And I'd die – but only momentarily. You must have heard about me. I'll die and then I'll come back, and if that happens I'll be pissed off. Very, very pissed off, Alan. I will find you again and I won't be so patient next time. Of course,' I added, 'I won't need a next time if my itchy finger presses down and sends a silver bolt through the windscreen and into your soft, human brains.'

His shoulders sagged. 'Alright,' he muttered.

'Alright what?'

'Alright. I'll get out.'

The car door opened and Harris placed one foot onto the concrete floor and then another. With very slow, very deliberate movements, he got out and faced me.

'Why?' I asked.

He didn't do either of us the disservice of asking what I meant. His eyes dropped and he mumbled, 'I wanted to win.'

I reminded myself that I hadn't been planning to shoot him before and I wasn't planning to shoot him now. Instead I walked forward, managing not to stumble, and pulled a pair of plastic ties from my back pocket.

Harris's eyes widened. I heard the thumping paws far too late. I turned, swinging the crossbow round as a huge wolf belted past me and slammed into him.

CHAPTER TWENTY-SEVEN

I SHOT THREE BOLTS INTO ROBERT SULLIVAN IN QUICK SUCCESSION, but it wasn't enough to stop his sharp teeth ripping into Alan Harris's flesh. I dropped the crossbow and darted forward, reaching for the scruff of his furry neck. Pain screamed through me but I bit down and hauled him off, bloody jaws and all.

'On your belly!' I roared, using every ounce of compulsion I could muster. I prayed Robert would hear me through his red mist of rage.

His lupine body shuddered and I thought at first he'd managed to deny my command. Then, however, he shook and shivered and lowered himself down to the cement floor.

I ran to Harris, pulling my T-shirt over my head so I had something to stem the blood flow. 'Don't you fucking die!' I hissed at him.

Harris's eyes turned to mine. There was no pain in his gaze; he'd gone beyond that point. His mouth curved up in the tiniest of smiles as if to tell me that everything was going to be alright. Then his eyelids fluttered down.

I yelled in frustration. No. I wasn't having this. I glanced at Robert, who remained down, his yellow eyes slitted and watching me. 'Stay where you are,' I snarled. Alan Harris might still make it. He might pull through.

'I don't know why you're attempting to save his life,' said a chillingly dry voice behind me. 'He's a supe killer, after all.'

I pressed hard on the worst of Harris's wounds – there was so much goddamned blood – then I turned my head and glanced at Lady Sullivan. Buffy was behind her, hands in her pockets and her expression nonchalant. It didn't take a genius detective to work out what had happened.

'Call a fucking ambulance,' I spat.

I returned my attention to Harris. He was still breathing but he wouldn't be for much longer if the paramedics didn't arrive soon.

Lady Sullivan nodded at Buffy and she drew out a phone and dialled as I focused on Harris. There were several wounds on his body but the deep bite on his neck appeared to be bleeding the most.

'Robert needs help too,' Lady Sullivan said. 'He's got three bolts sticking out of him. The one in his stomach looks particularly serious.'

'Maybe,' I said through gritted teeth, 'you should have thought of that before you sent him here.'

'It was his decision, not mine. I told you he has both my care and support. He needed closure for Rosie's death and now he has it.'

'Alan Harris didn't kill Rosie.' The T-shirt was saturated with blood. I still couldn't hear any sirens.

'It's a moot point. He killed supes, so what does it really matter?'

'It matters because there another killer is still out there,' I spat. 'We still have to find Marcus Lyons! Alan Harris can tell us where he is!'

'Ah,' Lady Sullivan murmured, unconcerned. 'But Marcus Lyons is killing humans. Plus, he's a vampire. He's not my priority.' At that moment, she was very lucky that I had my hands full. 'We'll tell everyone that you brought Robert down with your crossbow. Nobody needs to know that you compelled him,' she continued.

I didn't answer.

'Emma?'

'Whatever.' I checked Harris's pulse. He was barely clinging on. I'd deal with her later.

The first faint wail finally reached my ears. The ambulance was almost here. Thank fuck.

'I'M NOT surprised you're in pain. You dislocated your shoulder and you've fractured your ankle. You need X-rays, pain meds and several days' rest.'

Not a chance. 'Fix the shoulder, wrap the ankle,' I told the doctor. 'I'll deal with everything else later.' If the worst happened, I could kill myself and use the resurrection process to heal. It wouldn't be the first time, although my repeated deaths were beginning to look like carelessness on my part. I really ought to take steps to avoid dying all the time. And I couldn't afford to lose twelve hours right now.

'It will hurt,' he said. 'A lot.'

What else was new? I gritted my teeth and waved at him to continue. I had things to do and people to talk to. Next time, I'd go to a supe doctor; the human ones were far too cautious and they argued too much.

By the time I limped out of casualty, Lukas and Colquhoun were waiting for me. One look at their faces told me everything I needed to know. 'Lyons hasn't appeared at Postman's Park,' I said.

Colquhoun pulled a face. 'No, there's been no sign of him. Maybe he caught wind of our people and was spooked. To be fair to Murray, he was careful to stop that from happening, but no plan is foolproof.'

I snorted. Yeah. Just look at Alan Harris.

Lukas put an arm around me. 'I think you're allowed a break,' he said gently. 'Let's go home and I'll look after you while you look after me.'

'Lady Sullivan—' I started.

His eyes darkened. 'I'll deal with Lady Sullivan. Right now she's been taken to Supe Squad and Grace is interviewing her. Once he's done, it'll be my turn.'

'She's not your responsibility.'

'She is when she interferes with your work. And mine.' He brushed away a curl from my cheek. 'Don't worry about her. My car is nearby. I'll drive us home.'

I didn't spend the better part of an hour arguing with a doctor so I could go home and put my feet up. 'There's too much to do. Marcus Lyons might still show.'

Colquhoun shook her head while Lukas's arm tightened around me. 'The coolbox hasn't been touched. The other two handovers with the blood and the teeth happened quickly. If Lyons was going to make an appearance, he'd have done it by now.'

I shook my head, not because I disagreed but because I wasn't prepared to give up. 'How is Alan Harris doing?' I asked.

'He's certainly not in any position to talk, if that's what you're asking,' Colquhoun said. 'The last time I checked it was touch and go whether he'd make it. He's in surgery but it's not looking good.'

'Did he have anything on him? A phone?'

She nodded. 'The techs have got it. It's not password protected, but it's a burner and there's only one number programmed into it.'

Lyons. It had to be.

'We've called it,' she said. 'The number's already dead.'

I cursed. They were still ahead of us, even now. I opened my mouth to ask another question but Colquhoun frowned at me. 'This isn't a one-person investigation and you're not DCI Murray,' she said sternly. 'There are hundreds of people looking for Marcus Lyons.' She glanced at Lukas. 'Not to mention a good number of vampires. This isn't all on you.'

I knew she was making a sensible point, but that didn't mean I was prepared to go home and twiddle my thumbs because, as Buffy had said, I had a boo-boo. I scowled.

'What is it?' Lukas asked.

'Buffy,' I grunted. It galled me that she'd gone to Lady Sullivan once she'd located Harris instead of calling Murray as I'd asked, even though that was what she'd been trained to do as a Sullivan werewolf. 'She's got my phone.'

'You can get it later,' Lukas said.

'I'll get it now.' I wanted to look Buffy in the eye and make her realise the consequences of what she'd done. 'Is she at Supe Squad with Lady Sullivan?'

'I think so,' Lukas said.

'Then let's go there.' I glanced at Colquhoun. 'You should probably get back to Murray.'

'Yeah.' She sighed. 'And you should probably go home or back inside that hospital.'

'If everyone did what they should do instead of what they wanted to, the likes of us would be out of a job.'

KNOWING I'd struggle with the clutch in my present condition, I made Lukas drive Tallulah. Neither he nor the car were very happy about it. Tallulah stalled three times for no apparent reason, and Lukas grunted and groaned and shifted around in the narrow driver's seat. At least he knew better than to complain. If he'd attempted any derisory comment, we'd never have made it to Supe Squad.

I was beginning to regret my decision not to go home. Although I'd finally been persuaded to take some medication, it only dulled the worst of my pain and certainly didn't remove it. There was a lingering nausea in the pit of my stomach, which could have been the result of any number of things, and the throbbing pressure behind my eyes was making my thoughts foggy and indistinct. But I did everything I could to act normally. I didn't want Lukas to worry any more than he already was – and I definitely didn't want him to turn Tallulah around.

'If you'd tracked Marcus Lyons to that car park,' I asked, 'would you have attacked him?'

Lukas considered. 'If he was giving himself up without a fight then I doubt it. But I'm not sure you can ever really know what you'd do until something happens. If you'd asked Robert Sullivan a month ago if he'd do everything he could to kill a human being, he'd probably have said no. We're all capable of terrible things when we're provoked.'

He was silent for a moment. 'I'm told that Robert will recover without too much difficulty, although he might be using a stick for quite some time. I expect Lady Sullivan is already petitioning for leniency on his behalf.'

'Sometimes it's easy,' I murmured. 'Sometimes there are guys like Lyons and Harris who are fully evil and deserve what they get. But that's not always the case.'

Lukas nodded. 'For what it's worth, I'm not happy about what happened to the Cassandra. I don't believe she got what she deserved.' He hesitated. 'Zara,' he added softly. 'Zara didn't deserve that.'

Unbidden tears pricked the back of my eyes. 'None of them did. Zara's name wasn't on the Fetish guest list. All the other victims were on there, but not her. I'd have noticed if she were.' I shook my head and thought of Jonas alone in his empty club. 'Who wins now?'

Lukas raised an eyebrow. 'What do you mean?'

'Alan Harris killed his next victim and then was apprehended. He might die himself. Marcus Lyons remains free, but he's not killed and he didn't retrieve Zara's heart from the park. So who wins the game?'

'Nobody. Maybe without the heart, Lyons won't kill anyone else.'

I gazed out of the window. 'Zara said there would be two more murders. Unless Alan Harris actually dies, there's only been one so far.'

Lukas's hands tightened around Tallulah's steering wheel. After that, neither of us said anything else.

CHAPTER TWENTY-EIGHT

There was a surprisingly large number of werewolves outside Supe Squad. Max had sidled inside the glass door of the adjoining hotel, but I saw him peering out and looking rather anxious. He was rarely fazed by supernatural occurrences, although I supposed that dozens of wolves clamouring to be heard was enough to make anyone think twice about lingering next to them. I made a mental note to apologise to both him and the hotel management. It wouldn't be the first time; it probably wouldn't be the last time, either.

As soon as Lukas and I stepped out of Tallulah, the questions and demands turned in our direction. I did my best not to look a physical wreck and pretend that I was perfectly capable of walking, talking and listening to their demands.

'You have no reason to keep our Lady in that damned building,' one Sullivan wolf complained. 'You need to release her immediately!'

'As far as I'm aware, she's not under arrest,' I said. 'She's only answering a few questions.'

Another Sullivan wolf snapped at me, 'What Robert did

wasn't his fault! He should be lauded as a hero for what he did to that murdering bastard! He's no criminal!'

Uh-huh. 'I'm sure we all agree that vigilante justice helps none of us,' I replied calmly.

'She's right!' a highly-placed McGuigan wolf started in. 'We can't afford to go back to the way things were before the supe conference. We need to be seen to administer the highest form of legal justice to Robert Sullivan. He should be in chains!'

'Right now,' I said, 'he's receiving urgent medical treatment. What happens afterwards will depend on many factors.'

'Well,' a Carr clan member hissed, 'this is probably the time for Lady Sullivan to resign. She has to take responsibility for this mess.'

I drew in a breath. By my side, Lukas dipped his head and murmured, 'Do you want me to take care of this lot? It will only take a word.'

It wasn't his place, and the vamps didn't need to get involved. Not in this. 'Thank you, but they have a right to be here and to voice their complaints. If things turn ugly, Supe Squad will deal with them.'

'How? You're barely able to stand up straight, and I don't see Fred, Owen or Liza managing to quell a baying of bickering werewolves.'

'You underestimate Liza,' I told him.

'Yeah,' he said after a moment. 'I probably do.'

We entered the building. The first interview room door was closed with the sign on it turned to red for occupied; no doubt Owen Grace and Fred were in there with Lady Sullivan. I went to the visitors' room and peered in. Liza and Buffy were sitting together on one of the narrow sofas.

'Have you ever thought about applying to become a were-wolf?' Buffy was enquiring. 'I think the Sullivan clan would be thrilled to have you.'

I doubted that Liza's reply would be very friendly. I cleared my throat and they turned in my direction.

'Detective!' Buffy beamed. She glanced beyond me to Lukas. 'And the little Lord! Have you found that murderous vamp of yours yet?'

I felt Lukas's body tense. 'Buffy,' I warned.

'What? It's a reasonable question.'

It wasn't the question, it was her tone of voice. I folded my arms and glared at her. 'You have my phone,' I said.

'Would you like it back?'

'What do you think?' I growled.

She smiled. 'Say please.'

I stared at her. She rolled her eyes and dug into her pocket. 'Jeez,' she muttered. 'It's not like manners cost anything.' She handed over the phone and lowered her voice. 'Look, I'm sorry. My first loyalty is to my clan. I understand you're pissed off, but it's turned out alright in the end, hasn't it?'

'No, it hasn't. It's not over yet. More people may die as a result of what you did.'

Her eyes met mine. 'Would you have caught Harris without my help?'

Probably not. 'Do you want a gold-plated commendation?'

'The keys to the city would be nice.' She winked.

I sighed deeply and felt a wave of dizziness. I swayed slightly and in an instant Lukas was reaching for me. 'It's time to go.'

Nope. Not yet. 'It's fine.' I half-turned. 'I'm going to splash some cold water on my face.'

Liza stood up. 'I'll put the kettle on.'

'Oooh.' Buffy brightened. 'I'll have tea with two sugars, please.'

Liza hissed at her and I smiled slightly despite the situation. I nodded at Lukas. 'I'm okay. I'll be back in a minute.'

Once I was in the Supe Squad restroom, I gripped the corners of the ceramic sink and gazed into the mirror. I looked like shit. It wasn't any wonder: my shoulder ached, my ankle was more painful than I cared to mention, my period was due, and I was still trying to process the trauma of finding Zara's mutilated body.

I stared at my drawn face as another surge of light-headedness overcame me. I backed up until I was pressed against the tiled wall. My knees buckled.

There was a flash of bright, blinding light and I almost cried out. I closed my eyes. Purple velvet. In my mind's eye, I suddenly saw a swathe of purple velvet. There was another flash. *Bite Me.* The words appeared in blood-red script. Another flash. A glint of shining blue and sparkling white.

I started to shudder, convulsing wildly. My head banged against the tiles, sending a shock of pain through my skull.

There was a loud knocking sound. 'Emma!' Lukas's voice penetrated through the fog. 'Emma! Either open this door now or I'll break it down!'

I blinked rapidly and tried to call out. My mouth was dry and my tongue felt like sandpaper. I swallowed hard, pulled myself up to my feet and unlocked the door.

'I heard you moaning. What happened? You're as white as a fucking sheet!'

I stared at him.

'What is it?'

I shook myself. The nausea and the dizziness seemed to have dissipated. My jaw worked as I tried to find the words to explain. 'Uh...' My phone rang, the sound echoing around the small bathroom.

'Leave that,' Lukas said roughly.

'It might be important.' I licked my lips and glanced at the screen. Jonas. I had to answer. I pressed the button and held the phone to my ear.

Lukas grimaced but moved away so I could speak to the club owner in peace.

'It's been all over the news,' Jonas said, after a brief exchange of pleasantries. 'I tried to call the station in Hackney, but they wouldn't give me any information.' He sounded nervous. 'Is it true? Is Alan Harris one of the killers?'

The information was already in the public domain so there was no point in denying it. 'Yes,' I said. 'I'm afraid so.'

Jonas expelled a long rush of air. 'Oh,' he said. 'Oh.' He fell silent.

I waited for a beat or two. 'Jonas?'

He cleared his throat. 'Yes, yes. I'm still here. I'm just...' he paused. 'I'm not sure if I should be relieved or horrified.'

'Did you know him?'

'A little. He's been to Fetish and participated in some games. I always thought he was competitive and a bit of a sore loser, but he didn't seem like the type of guy to kill people.'

Who did? 'We'll need a statement from you about your knowledge of him,' I told him.

'Of course, of course. Whatever I can do to help. In fact, I'm not far away. I had to get out for a while so I've come into town to do a few errands and speak to Carmichael. I'm at his office. It won't take me long to drop round to Supe Squad.' He hesitated. 'Unless I should come round to the Hackney station instead?'

'Supe Squad is fine,' I reassured him. I was sure Murray would agree; he probably had his hands full with press conferences.

'The news said Harris was in hospital. Is he going to make it?'

'I don't know,' I answered honestly. 'We'll have to wait and see.'

'At least those poor victims' families will have some closure now that he's caught.' Jonas's voice dropped. 'Zara might have been a Cassandra, but she didn't foresee her own death, did she? How tragic. I'm glad that you've caught him. One down and...' He stopped suddenly.

'Jonas?' I asked. I heard a crackle followed by a muffled thud. 'Jonas? Are you there?'

His voice came back on the line. 'He's here.' He was whispering, but his fear was palpable.

'Who?' I demanded.

'Help me.'

'Jonas! What's going on?'

'Marcus Ly—' The phone went dead before he could finish saying the killer's name.

I stared at the screen for a second then raised my head and gave a hoarse shout. 'Carmichael's office!' I yelled. 'We have to get everyone to Carmichael's office now!'

PHILEAS CARMICHAEL ESQUIRE'S office was located smack-bang between Soho, where the vamps lived, and Lisson Grove, the domain of the werewolves. I'd dropped by a couple of times but I'd never felt this sense of foreboding before.

I gripped my crossbow and swallowed. There wasn't time to wait for Murray and his troops. We had to act now.

I wasn't the only one thinking that; before I could bring Tallulah to a halt outside the smart blue door, Lukas leapt out and started to sprint. I swallowed back my shout to tell him to wait. Marcus Lyons was his vampire and he had the right to do this – and he would be the best person to stop Lyons in his tracks.

While Lukas kicked open the door and disappeared, I checked up and down the street. It looked normal; there was no sign of Lyons making an escape and the passers-by, who hadn't noticed Lukas's dash, appeared unperturbed.

I licked my lips and allowed adrenaline to take over and propel my body forward. This wasn't the time to feel ill or fatigued; this would be a bloody, violent fight and I had to be ready. I steeled my stomach then ran in after Lukas, ignoring the screaming flash of pain from my damaged ankle as best as I could.

I came to a stuttering halt as soon as I entered the gremlin solicitor's waiting room and took in the scene. We'd arrived in the nick of time – but that didn't mean we would win. I ignored the tremor in my hands and raised my crossbow, taking careful aim. I couldn't shoot yet, but I wanted to be ready.

Marcus Lyons was backed into a corner. He wasn't alone; he had one arm wrapped around Jonas's chest and was holding him up as a shield. His other hand was holding some sort of miniature scythe at Jonas's throat. The sharp blade gleamed as it caught the light from the far window. Blood was dripping down its length, trickling along Lyons' clenched fist and pooling on the floor.

Jonas's head lolled to one side and his eyes were half-closed. He didn't appear to be conscious. He was topless, his white shirt discarded and tossed to one side, and the centre of his chest was bleeding heavily. Lyons had already made his first cut.

Lukas barrelled his way in. 'Release him.' The compulsion in Lukas's voice vibrated the very air. 'Now.'

Lyons neither laughed like a comic-book villain, nor looked scared like someone who knew his time was up. He regarded Lukas with unflinching, expressionless eyes. It was clear he was too far gone with his maniacal bloodlust for any sort of compulsion to filter through, even from his own Lord. 'You can't order me to do anything,' he murmured. 'Not now. I don't belong to you.'

Lukas snarled and bared his fangs. Marcus Lyons merely blinked languidly.

I stepped closer. 'You won't get away, Marcus,' I said softly, matching my energy to his. 'You won't get past Lord Horvath and you won't get past me. Even if you did, there are police and vampires and all sorts of other people outside.' I hoped that logic rather than inflamed rage would encourage him to release Jonas and give himself up. 'You can't run. There's no point in continuing.'

For the first time, Lyons' gaze flickered to me. His lip curled, the flash in his eyes indicating that he thought I was stupid. 'There's every point,' he said. 'No winner has been declared yet. I can still beat him. I can still win.'

He pressed the tiny scythe into Jonas's throat, drawing a line of bright blood. 'I'll kill this one first,' he said. 'Then you can do whatever you want. It won't matter.'

Lukas started forward but I put a hand on his arm. Jonas's life hung in the balance. We couldn't afford any rash moves, not yet. 'Why do you need to win?' I asked.

'Winning is everything,' Lyons hummed. He suddenly looked feverish – or possessed. 'All that matters is to win.'

Lukas could barely get the words out. 'What's the prize?' he hissed. 'What can you possibly win that's worth another person's life?'

'You don't get it.' Lyons shook his head. 'I knew you wouldn't. You can't see the purity of the game because you're too wrapped in the mundanity of existence. The prize *is* winning. There's no trophy,' he sneered. 'There's no money. The game is too perfect to be sullied by a physical prize. It's what inside your heart that counts.'

He smiled. 'That's why I will take *his* heart.' He looked at Lukas. 'I'm going to eat it. If you film it and promise to send me the film afterwards, you can do whatever you want.' He glanced out of the window towards the street. 'I knew I wouldn't escape from here. It's fine. I'm at peace with my ending.' His voice hardened. 'As long as I fucking win.'

Marcus Lyons' single-minded, utterly focused determination to win this sick competition even in the face of death was incomprehensible.

He caressed Jonas's light brown hair then shifted his grip on the scythe. 'Don't worry. I won't take long.' He glanced down at Jonas's face almost tenderly then his brow creased.

I shook my head. We couldn't talk him down; he couldn't be swayed by logic any more than he could be compelled. There was only one way this was going to end. I nudged Lukas with my elbow. We had to put a stop to it all.

As Lyons moved the scythe, Lukas feinted left. The blade sliced into Jonas's throat and Lukas twisted right to grab the weapon. The second that his fingers touched it, I pressed the crossbow trigger.

The bolt's path was true. It slammed into the only part of Marcus Lyons' body that wasn't shielded by Jonas's unconscious form and embedded itself in his eye. Lukas wrenched away the scythe, cutting his fingers as he did so.

Lyons staggered back against the wall, still holding Jonas. I dropped the crossbow and ran towards them, ignoring my pain in favour of hauling Jonas away so I could lie him flat on the floor and stem the blood pouring from the wound in his throat.

The scythe hadn't gone all the way through. He could still be saved. 'He needs an ambulance now. He's losing a lot of blood. Can you—?' I didn't finish the question.

'The wound is too deep. Nothing I can do will seal it. Not now,' Lukas said. He already had his phone out and was raising it to his ear.

Jonas stirred beneath my blood-drenched fingers. He groaned once. 'Hang on,' I told him. 'Just hang on. Help is on its way.'

CHAPTER TWENTY-NINE

IT WAS SEVERAL HOURS LATER WHEN I LIMPED BACK INTO THE police station at Hackney. Norris, the wide-eyed, over-awed young officer, was back on the front desk. He beamed and buzzed me through. 'Well done,' he breathed. 'Bloody well done.'

I didn't know how to react. I wasn't in the mood for smiling and, given how many people had died, patting myself on the back seemed more than rude. It would have felt insulting. In the end, I acknowledged him with a vague 'Mmm', and went in search of Colquhoun.

I found her at her desk, typing away on her computer. She glanced up as I approached and offered a tired grin. 'Hey. Pull up a pew.'

I grabbed a chair and sat down. Thank goodness. The painkillers were wearing off and the jabbing pain in my ankle was becoming hard to ignore. My limits were greater than those of most other people, supes included, but I was reaching the end of my physical tether. I'd pushed myself too hard for too long, and I was paying the price.

'Cheers.' I leaned back, wincing at the less sharp but still annoying ache in my shoulder. 'Any word from the hospital? I've been stuck with the IOPC going over what happened, so I've not heard any updates.'

'I thought that because he was a vamp and you're Supe Squad, the Independent Office for Police Conduct gave you a free pass.'

'They still do their checks,' I said. 'Especially when humans are involved, too. And it's a highly publicised case.' They'd even taken my crossbow away for analysis.

Colquhoun snorted. 'Yeah. Murray's final press conference is due to start any moment.'

Frankly, I was surprised it had taken him this long. 'The hospital?'

'Jonas will make it. Some blood transfusions, far too many stitches both on the wound on his neck and the back of his head where Lyons hit him and knocked him unconscious, but he'll pull through.'

'Anything on Alan Harris?'

'His condition remains the same.'

Shit. I hoped he would make it, not for his sake but for ours. There were still so many unanswered questions, and Marcus Lyons hadn't articulated his reasons clearly enough for any of us. We needed to know how this bloody game had started and why it became so important. How had they reached the point where they killed people for the sake of a competition? It went beyond all morality, logic and reason. Nothing about a murder competition made sense.

'I interviewed the barrister,' Colquhoun told me. 'He's something of a character.'

'Phileas Carmichael? Yeah, he's one of a kind.'

'He said that he'd been called away on an urgent case. A pixie had phoned and asked for his help after she was arrested in Knightsbridge. He left a message for Jonas delaying their meeting and headed off there.'

'Let me guess,' I said drily. 'The pixie doesn't exist?'

'Got it in one.'

I scratched my head. 'All of which begs the question, why try to kill Jonas? He was supposed to be the judge of their sicko competition.'

'It's the ultimate win, right? Kill the judge of your own killing competition? That's got to be worth extra points.'

I shuddered. 'It's all so...' My voice drifted off.

'Pointless? Bizarre? Twisted?'

'Yeah.'

We exchanged looks. We didn't understand either killer but we did understand our feelings about them.

'I should go and check in with Murray,' I said. 'I'll write my reports and send them through, but I probably won't be back in here unless he specifically requests it.'

Colquhoun smiled faintly. 'I imagine you're looking forward to getting back to your own turf. If you ever fancy a change of scenery, you'd be very welcome here. You'd make a great asset to our team.'

I grinned. 'I'd been planning to say the same to you.'

'Not a chance.'

My grin grew. 'Ditto. I won't say no to a pint or two some time, though.'

'I'll hold you to that,' Colquhoun said.

I hoped she would. I stood up, nodded goodbye and wandered towards Murray's office. The door was ajar, so I knocked once and popped my head in. 'Sir, I'm back from meeting with the IOPC and—'

'Come in, Emma.' He waved a hand but didn't look up from his screen. Somewhat surprised, I did as he asked.

I'd barely stepped inside when there was another knock. An officer, whom I didn't recognise, looked in. 'The press conference is due to start, sir. Shall I tell them you're on your way?'

Murray grunted. 'Delay it.'

I stared at him. That was the last thing I'd ever expected to hear from his mouth.

'Twenty minutes,' he said. 'That's all.'

The officer withdrew. Now I was intrigued.

'Have a look at this.' Murray spun his screen so I could see it, and I immediately recognised the CCTV footage from Fetish. 'The techs have spliced together all the sections with either Alan Harris or Marcus Lyons or both. Here. Watch Lyons' face. This is from the first time he visited the club roughly ten months ago.'

I focused on the video. Marcus Lyons was standing in a small crowd of people watching what appeared to be some sort of slapping competition between two humans. I squinted. 'He looks … disgusted,' I said eventually.

'Now look at this from ten days later.' He clicked the mouse.

I watched. Lyons was seated at the Fetish bar. A gremlin approached him, making some sort of overture. Lyons looked reluctant but finally nodded and handed over some money. 'He's making a bet,' I said.

DCI Murray nodded. 'I've cross-checked it with the other details from that evening. He gambled fifty quid that the gremlin could hold his breath in the plunge pool for three minutes.'

'And?' I queried.

Murray clicked the mouse again and brought up another view. Money was being thrust into Lyons' hands. 'He won.'

The vampire looked pleased at his win but not overly ecstatic. 'Okay.' I licked my lips. 'Sir—'

'Bear with me,' he said. 'There are many other instances. Between his first visit and his last, Marcus Lyons went to Fetish at least once a week, by my reckoning.'

I'd looked at the frequency of visits of many of Fetish's patrons when Jonas had first handed over the information. A lot of people went to the club once a week; hell, a lot of people went to the club several times a week.

Murray ignored my expression. 'I want you to watch this one. It's from a couple of weeks ago.'

I did as I was told. Lyons was taking part in a game of snakes and ladders. As far as I could tell, every time a player hit a snake they had to down a shot of some kind of clear liquid. When they landed on a ladder, the liquid was blue. 'Look at his face,' Murray urged.

I focused. Marcus Lyons no longer looked disgusted. There was a fanatical gleam in his eyes that even the CCTV cameras conveyed.

'And his hands,' Murray said. 'Look at his hands.'

On the screen, Lyons raised a shot glass to his lips. His hands were visibly shaking. I rocked back on my heels and looked at the DCI. 'I'm still not sure what you're getting at, sir,' I said. 'We know that he became so enamoured of the competitions at Fetish that he was driven to create his own version, one that was more twisted than anything the club could have come up with.'

'From his expression, he didn't enjoy anything about the club on his first visit.'

'But he enjoyed it enough to go back,' I pointed out. 'Something – or someone – changed his mind.'

Murray clapped his hands. 'Exactly. His mind was changed! But by whom?' He jabbed a finger at the screen. 'His face on his last visit is that of a fanatic, someone's who's been groomed – radicalised.'

'You think Alan Harris was the instigator? Alan Harris groomed Lyons?' I asked doubtfully.

'Harris and Lyons were never in Fetish on the same night. Not once.'

I frowned. 'Oh.'

'Have a look at this. It's one more clip.' He fiddled with the mouse before finding what he needed. 'Here.'

I leaned in. A group of people was standing by a pool table, laughing. Marcus Lyons was amongst them. Suddenly, Jonas appeared, flicking his long green hair over his shoulder and beaming at his guests. He spoke to a woman, charming her enough to make her blush. He patted a werewolf on the shoulder as if commiserating with him for a loss. He paused next to a human male with white hair and chatted for several moments.

'He doesn't talk to Lyons,' Murray said. 'In fact, at no point on any of these videos, does Jonas ever talk to him. He knows all his customers, he speaks to them all, but he never once speaks to Marcus Lyons.'

He raised his eyes to mine. 'The only other person I've found who visits Fetish and whom Jonas never appears to talk to is Alan Harris. Isn't that a little strange? Harris had a shrine to Jonas hidden in his home, but Jonas never spoke to him. Not on camera, anyway.'

'Marcus Lyons *selected* Jonas as one of his victims,' I said slowly. 'That makes it highly unlikely that Jonas was involved too.'

Maybe Lyons had felt slighted by being ignored and that's why he'd acted against the club. Maybe Alan Harris had felt the same, despite his adulation. And then I thought about the odd look on Lyons's face when he'd glanced at Jonas just before I shot him. He'd seemed confused – but confused by what?

'That's true,' Murray conceded. 'And you met Jonas's girlfriend who conveniently provided perfect alibis for him for more than one of the murders.' He pursed his lips. 'And Jonas *conveniently* helped us out by giving us all this footage. I believe he's the one who made the initial contact with Lord Horvath rather the other way around?'

Conveniently. I nodded. The uneasy feeling inside me was growing. Zara had said to beware of glib tongues and elaborate lies. 'Smoke and mirrors,' I whispered.

Murray didn't hear me. He spun the screen away from me and picked up his suit jacket. 'There's more going on here than meets the eye,' he said. 'I'm sure of it. Something to think about,' he said.

He checked his watch. 'I'd better head upstairs for the conference. I need to brief the press on what's happened and release the name of the final victim. Those headline writers will be busy. At least there won't be any more of these murders. We've done good work here, Emma. Good work indeed.'

I stared at him, white-faced.

'What?' Murray asked. 'I am not beyond giving compliments where they are due. You did do good work – in the end.'

I swallowed, ignoring the grudging compliment. 'You said you had to release the names of the final victim. The press doesn't know about Zara?'

'They know a woman was killed, but it's taken more time than we'd have liked to find her family so we could inform them first. They were estranged. Apparently, her loved ones couldn't reconcile themselves to having their futures constantly pointed out to them.' Murray shrugged. 'I don't know why they were so disturbed by it. They could have found out the lottery numbers in advance.' He grinned but his smile faltered as he registered that I was still staring at him. 'What is it?'

'Jonas knew,' I said. 'Jonas knew that Zara was dead. He told me so on the phone right before Marcus Lyons attacked him.'

Murray looked at me.

'What hospital was Alan Harris taken to?' I asked, sounding casual but feeling anything but.

'Bellfield.' Murray tensed. 'And yes. That's where Jonas is, too.' He pulled back his shoulders then strode past me, opened his door and looked out. 'Cancel that press conference,' he said to the first person he saw. 'And muster the troops.'

CHAPTER THIRTY

THE SENIOR NURSE ON DUTY AT JONAS'S WARD ON THE EIGHTH floor was not impressed. 'He was brutally attacked! He can't deal with a posse of police interrogating him. The man needs to rest. He's not going anywhere. You can come back once he's feeling better.'

Murray didn't blink. 'We need to speak to him now. We have reason to believe he's dangerous.'

She paled slightly. 'I doubt that very much. He's incredibly poorly.' Her voice belied her words; she was beginning to sound less sure of herself. 'Two of you,' she said. 'No more than that.'

Murray glanced at the cluster of grim-faced police officers. 'You three wait here. Colquhoun, you head up to ITU. Keep an eye on Harris.'

She took off. Murray raised his little finger towards me. 'Emma, the two of us will talk to Mr Jonas.'

The nurse led the way, her white shoes squeaking on the shiny ward floor. 'You have to be gentle,' she said. 'I can only allow you ten minutes and no more. We can't risk his health.' She paused at an open doorway. 'He needs rest.'

She stepped inside the room and her face fell. 'Oh.'

Murray pushed in after her and I immediately followed. It was a private room with only one bed. There was a neat bedside cabinet, an IV stand, a heart monitor and crisp white sheets underneath a rumpled pillow – but there wasn't anyone in the bed. My eyes flicked to the adjoining toilet. It was empty.

'Well, I...' the nurse stammered. 'I think he's probably been taken away for more tests. X-rays, maybe.' None of us believed that. Not even she did.

Murray unclipped the radio from his belt. 'Shut the hospital down,' he barked. 'Monitor all exits.' He looked at me. 'Get to Colquhoun and Harris. This game isn't over yet.'

I was already on my way to the door, my heart rate rising. I could see the three officers who'd been waiting at the ward's entrance standing by the lift at the end of the corridor. One of them was jabbing at the call button. When the lift didn't miraculously appear, all three of them darted for the stairs.

I gritted my teeth. Phoenix or not, my ankle was still fractured. It hurt and my movements were limited. I hissed, enraged at my temporary frailty. I could limp up the stairs to where Harris was, but the others were already ahead of me and I wouldn't catch them up.

Murray ran past me, calling out over his shoulder, 'We have a potential sighting on the ground floor. I'm on my way there. Continue to Colquhoun!'

It was galling that he could move faster than me. I could only watch as he twisted towards the lift, glanced at its closed door then headed for the stairs.

I reached the stairs moments later. I could lock the worst of the pain away and push past it, but I could only make my bruised body move so fast. I stepped back to the lift and stared at the LED numbers counting up from the floors below. Come on, you fucker. *Move.*

It was only seconds before it arrived, but it felt much longer. As soon as the doors slid open, I stepped inside and frantically pressed the button for the tenth floor where the ITU was located. The doors started to close and I exhaled as they sealed shut and the lift finally started to rise. Two floors. Only two floors.

The lift jolted to a halt on the ninth floor. Goddamnit.

The doors opened, revealing an empty white space. I jabbed at the button again – and again the doors started to close. This was becoming farcical. When they juddered and started to open once more in a stilted fashion that made me want to scream in frustration, I could have killed someone myself. Except that was when I saw the two people waiting on the other side.

Jonas smiled; Colquhoun didn't, but then she had a scalpel pressed to her throat in a fashion that was eerily similar to the way Marcus Lyons had held the scythe to Jonas a few hours earlier. I doubted she was in the mood for smiling.

'DC Bellamy,' Jonas purred. 'Why don't you join us?'

I stared at him, then I stepped out of the lift. It wasn't as if I had much choice.

I glanced to my left. Several white-coated medical professionals were standing in the corridor staring at Jonas. At least one of them looked ready to run forward and play hero. Unless they had hidden supe blood running through their veins, I doubted that would end well. In fact, even if they were supe, I doubted it would end well.

'Keep back,' I said quietly. 'Keep back, look after your patients and stay out of the way.'

Thankfully, they didn't argue. One by one, they pulled back and disappeared. Only when they were all safely out of the way, did I turn back to Jonas and Colquhoun. Jonas was still smiling.

'Alan Harris?' I asked, directing my question at Colquhoun.

'Still breathing,' she answered. 'We arrived in time.'

Despite his grinning façade, anger momentarily flashed in Jonas's eyes. His mask was slipping and he was losing control. I knew then that he'd lured Marcus Lyons to Carmichael's office so that he'd be taken to the same hospital where Harris was clinging onto life. Jonas needed both Harris and Lyons out of the way if he were to slide away scot-free. Or so he'd thought.

'Always looking out for others, eh, detective?' He sucked in air through his bottom teeth. 'I thought I'd won, you know. I thought the game was mine. It appears that I underestimated my opponent after all.'

I watched him carefully, searching for a way to get Colquhoun to safety. Nothing immediately presented itself, but there was a chance if Jonas shifted his weight to the left. I bided my time. Maybe Colquhoun's colleagues were already preparing their own moves.

'It wasn't my suspicions that were raised,' I said almost conversationally. 'It was DCI Murray who thought something was off.'

Jonas raised his eyebrows. 'Really?'

I nodded. 'Really. So you did win. Well done.'

His false, tinny guffaw bounced off the walls. 'Nice try, but I'm not quite ready to call it just yet. I'm not done.' He staggered slightly and I tensed, prepared to spring forward if the right opportunity presented itself. He hadn't moved enough, however; not yet.

Jonas coughed. 'Forgive me. I'm not quite myself. I did lose rather a lot of blood. You're not looking particularly hale or hearty yourself.'

I ignored the last comment. 'Marcus didn't know who you were, did he? Not until the very last moment. Without the wig and the make-up, he didn't recognise you. But you deliberately set yourself up as his victim.'

Jonas looked pleased with himself, though he didn't say anything. I wanted to keep him talking, to lull him into a false sense of security so that either Murray and the others had time to find us, or Jonas let his guard down enough for me to take him down without harming Colquhoun.

'That was a big risk,' I persisted. 'Marcus could have killed you.'

'There's no point gambling unless the odds make it truly worthwhile. Easy wins are boring. Marcus knew that. So did Alan.'

My lip curled. 'You set up the competition. You were in control. They were only your tools. You were the real killer.'

'I haven't killed anyone.' He smiled almost tenderly down at Colquhoun. 'Yet.'

She glared. She didn't look scared; she was trembling, but I was fairly certain it was from rage, not fear.

'In fact,' Jonas said, 'as you know, I have an alibi for all the killings. Adele is very happy to help, and I can assure you that she's telling the truth. She's an honest person. Dull, but honest. Everyone has their uses.'

I couldn't prevent the growl from escaping my throat. 'Why?'

'Why Adele? I'd have thought that was rather obvious.' He smirked. 'She served a particular purpose and put a stop to questions about my involvement.'

'Not her. Why the competition?' I snapped. 'Why do it?'

'I told you the first time we met. Competition encourages us to do our best. It pushes us beyond our limits. I do like to see the heights people can rise to when they get the right encouragement.'

He gave a look of pure satisfaction. 'Although Alan didn't take much encouragement. He'd have done just about anything I asked, even though he balked at allowing anyone to feel pain. Marcus was a harder case, but I so enjoyed making him my creature. He had such potential for violence locked away inside him. I'm surprised nobody else noticed it.'

His expression was akin to that of a proud father. I could barely repress a disgusted shudder. 'Of course,' he continued, 'both Marcus and Alan lost their competitions in the end. But the real race was never between them, it was between you and me.'

I'd met some cold-hearted bastards but Jonas was easily the worst. I looked again at Colquhoun. Her hands were by her sides but her fingers were twitching.

'Bringing you into the mix was a stroke of genius,' he said gleefully. 'Your participation has made it much more interesting. You've brought a real edge of danger to proceedings.' He looked at me sympathetically. 'It must be very dull for you when you know that you won't die. As far as you're concerned, the stakes are always low.'

'Except, as you've already pointed out, I don't only care about myself. I care about others, too.'

'Oh, detective.' He clicked his tongue. 'That's so mundane. The games at Fetish were becoming like that, and one must take care never to live a mundane life. I knew it was time to make things more interesting. I wanted to see how far I could go if I truly applied myself as games master. This has been the greatest competition this country has ever seen. I even helped you because I wanted to keep things fair. I wanted the competition to be *pure*.'

Jesus.

Colquhoun's lips parted. 'Nah,' she whispered.

Jonas jerked. 'What?'

'Nah,' she repeated.

I glanced at her and suddenly I realised she was right. 'I agree. *Nah*. This wasn't about any kind of competition, pure or otherwise. This was about your own selfish needs. Peter Pickover was first. He was winning too much money and you didn't like that. Am I right? You told Harris and Lyons who to kill because you had an agenda that served your own ends. You tied almost all the killings to Fetish to draw in future customers, not to heighten the danger that you might get caught. You wanted your club to appear risky, in the same way it did when everyone believed it was illegal. People who enjoy risk enjoy gambling, and gamblers can spend a lot of money at a place like Fetish.'

Jonas's eyes narrowed.

'Gilchrist Boast was probably nothing more than a convenience,' Colquhoun said, warming to the theme. 'But you wanted the vampire out of the way. Christopher was complaining about your club and you wanted him gone.'

'Presumably,' I added, 'Samuel Brunswick's root canal simply gave you the opportunity to include him. Again, he was merely a convenience to mask your true intentions.' My voice hardened. 'But Zara had nothing to do with Fetish. You had Zara killed because Murray told you about her. He told you there was a Cassandra involved, and he told you her name. How did you find out where she lived?'

A surge of fury sparked in Jonas's eyes. 'I know people who knew of her,' he hissed. 'I know a lot of people. I wanted to test the Cassandra to see if she could play her own game and foresee her own death.'

'Bullshit,' Colquhoun said.

'Yep. Because then you set yourself up as the final victim,' I told him. 'But you were careful never to put yourself in real danger. That's why you called me first. You wanted rid of Lyons because he'd become a liability. You knew we'd track him down sooner or later, so you decided to make it sooner and in a way that would seal his fate and prevent him from talking. None of the murders were about competition or risk taking.'

'They were about money, ego and fear,' Colquhoun finished. 'Concepts that are about as mundane and run of the mill as it gets.'

Jonas's anger was getting the better of him. A vein was bulging in his forehead, and his legs were visibly trembling beneath his flimsy hospital gown. 'Fuck you,' he said. 'Fuck the both of you.' His hand tightened around the scalpel and he pulled it back to gain enough momentum to strike.

That was all Colquhoun needed. Her head jerked down and she bit hard on Jonas's arm. His scalpel sliced into her skin as he reacted, but it was little more than a nick. He screamed aloud as his own blood spurted and he released her, dropping the scalpel at the same time. Stripped of all his flash and glamour and silver-tongued lies, Kevin Jonas was a pushover.

I surged forward and grabbed Jonas's right arm as Colquhoun grabbed his left. Together we pushed him back against the wall and held him. He struggled briefly, then he relaxed. Once again he started to smile. He simply didn't know when he was done.

'Let's make this more interesting, girls. You can still have your fun and I'll come quietly, but let's play a game first. I hold a deposit box in the Talismanic Bank. Inside that box is a large amount of money.' He paused. 'Untraceable money. Release me, count to ten, then the pair of you can come after me. Whoever reaches me first gets the key to the box.'

He blinked earnestly. 'Normally DC Bellamy would win easily, but she's not in great shape. You're evenly matched, but the odds against me are stacked. You know I won't get away, even with a head start. Allow me ten seconds and everyone wins.'

He seemed to be under the impression that we were both completely stupid. I raised my eyebrows at Colquhoun. She matched my expression.

'Money,' Jonas said with a seductive edge. 'Lots of money.'

Colquhoun leaned forward and murmured in his ear. 'I'm not playing,'

'And that means it's game over,' I added, Finally.

I couldn't say we'd won; too many people had died for this to be counted as a win. But justice would be served and that was prize enough. I glanced around. It was time to find a chair. My knees were getting ready to buckle.

'DCI Murray is really going to enjoy his press conference,' I murmured, spotting a stool behind the nurses' station.

Colquhoun pursed her lips. 'Do you know what? This time

I'm going to enjoy his press conference, too.' She drew out her handcuffs. 'Kevin Jonas, you are under arrest. You do not have to say anything but it may harm your defence if you do not mention when questioned something which you later rely on in court. Anything you do say may be given in evidence.'

EPILOGUE

A SHAFT OF SUNLIGHT SQUEEZED IN FROM THE CURTAINS AND dappled Lukas's shoulder. I reached across and traced its path with the tip of my index finger. He opened his eyes and smiled at me. 'Morning.'

I smiled back. 'Morning.' I gazed at him. 'How are you?'

'I'm okay. I'm still processing what Marcus did, but we'll learn from it. All of us will. Mistakes have been made, and those mistakes will be corrected. This kind of thing won't happen again, not with any of my vampires.'

I believed him. 'I know,' I said quietly. 'I know.'

Lukas brushed a lock of hair from my cheek. 'How about you?' he asked. 'How are you feeling?'

'Sore,' I admitted. 'But definitely better than yesterday.'

He looked relieved. 'Good. You won't...'

I shook my head. 'No. I won't kill myself for a quick resurrection and an easy way back to health. Sometimes pain is good. It reminds me that I'm still alive.'

He leaned across and kissed me. 'Amen to that. I'll make breakfast so you can eat before you take any painkillers.'

'Yes, doctor.'

Lukas smirked. 'I always enjoyed playing doctors and nurses.'

I gave him a playful shove. 'Maybe in a few days when I'm properly healed.'

'I might hold you to that.' He sat up and allowed me a moment to admire his naked body before he grabbed a dressing gown and went through to the kitchen.

I lay back and listened to the muffled sounds of clattering from the kitchen. I thought of Rosie and Peter and Gilchrist and Samuel and Zara. And yes, of Marcus, too. I allowed the heaviness of what they'd been to sink into my bones as I remembered them. They deserved that much. Then I pushed the thoughts aside, because this wouldn't be the only darkness I'd face. In this line of work, there would always be more. I didn't know if I'd manage to deal with it all. I could only hope that I would.

A few moments later, I heaved myself out of bed and pulled on a gown. I picked up my phone from where it was charging and checked the messages. There was one from Grace: Thistle was on her way to the airport, and Alan Harris was still in the ITU but his condition was stable. He added that the werewolf clans were meeting later to discuss Robert Sullivan's fate.

I couldn't begin to guess the outcome of that, but I fired off a text to all four clan alphas informing them that the attack on a human, regardless of who that human was, meant that Supe Squad had to be involved. We didn't have a choice.

I nodded, satisfied for now, and wandered into the kitchen to join Lukas.

'Mushrooms?' he asked as soon as I entered. 'Eggs? Tomatoes? Fried bread?'

'Yes, yes, yes and yes. I'm absolutely famished.'

Lukas handed me a mug of steaming coffee. 'Good.' He watched me as I took several long gulps.

'What?' I asked, as he continued to stare, his gaze warm but also faintly anxious.

'Before we eat,' he said, hedging his words in a manner that was most unlike him, 'there's something I need to say. Or rather ask.'

'Uh-huh.' I squinted. He was starting to worry me.

Lukas took the mug from my hands and put it on the kitchen counter. I glanced at it, then stiffened when I saw the scrawled red script emblazoned on its side. *Bite Me.*

'That mug,' I whispered.

Lukas chuckled. 'I know. It's terrible, isn't it? It was a gift – I didn't buy it myself. I usually keep it hidden away at the back of the cupboard, but we've not been home much lately and all the other cups are in the dishwasher.'

He gave me a crooked grin, reached into the pocket of his dressing gown and took out a small box. He carefully lowered himself onto one knee.

I looked from him to the mug and back again. 'Lukas—'

'You know the worst parts of me as well as the best,' he said. 'You see me in a way that nobody else has, and I know that every time I look at you my heart sings. We've been on a long road together, Emma, and I don't want it to end. When I think of the future, I can only think of you. I know there will be plenty of challenges ahead. I know there will be struggles. But I also know that if we're together, we can face anything. You're all I've ever wanted. I don't want this to be a happy ending, I want it to be a happy beginning.' He drew in a shaky breath and opened the box. 'Emma Bellamy, will you marry me?'

I stared at the purple velvet lining the box's interior. The ring's blue sapphires and white diamonds glinted at me. And for an instant I was transported back to Zara's kitchen and the brief sensation I'd felt when I'd touched her hand.

What had she told me when we last spoke? Her words echoed in my mind. *I'm sorry. I'm so very sorry. It's not what I would have wanted. I can't control it, you see.*

And then the same nausea I'd felt in the restroom at Supe Squad surged through me. Oh no.

I said it aloud. 'Oh no.'

ACKNOWLEDGMENTS

As always, I can't express my thanks enough to all the people behind the scenes who've helped make A Killer's Kiss a reality. Karen Holmes worked her editing magic and Clarissa Yeo of Yocla Designs and now Joy Covers continues to bring Emma's character to life with her book cover.

Lynne Thompson-Hogg provided excellent advice on all aspects on English police procedures and investigations, although it goes without saying that any and all mistakes and poetic licences are down to me.

Finally, a huge thank you to my wonderful team of ongoing beta and ARC readers who keep me on track and on my toes.

ABOUT THE AUTHOR

After teaching English literature in the UK, Japan and Malaysia, Helen Harper left behind the world of education following the worldwide success of her Blood Destiny series of books. She thanks her lucky stars every day that she's able to do so.

Helen has always been a book lover, devouring science fiction and fantasy tales when she was a child growing up in Scotland.

She currently lives in Edinburgh with far too many cats – not to mention the dragons, fairies, demons, wizards and vampires that seem to keep appearing from nowhere.

ALSO BY HELEN HARPER

The *WolfBrand* series

Devereau Webb is in uncharted territory. He thought he knew what he was doing when he chose to enter London's supernatural society but he's quickly discovering that his new status isn't welcome to everyone.

He's lived through hard times before and he's no stranger to the murky underworld of city life. But when he comes across a young werewolf girl who's not only been illegally turned but who has also committed two brutal murders, he will discover just how difficult life can be for supernaturals - and also how far his own predatory powers extend.

Book One – The Noose Of A New Moon

Book Two – Licence To Howl

A *Charade of Magic* series

The best way to live in the Mage ruled city of Glasgow is to keep your head down and your mouth closed.

That's not usually a problem for Mairi Wallace. By day she works at a small shop selling tartan and by night she studies to become an apothecary. She knows her place and her limitations. All that changes, however, when her old childhood friend sends her a desperate message seeking her help - and the Mages themselves cross Mairi's path. Suddenly, remaining unnoticed is no longer an option.

There's more to Mairi than she realises but, if she wants to fulfil her full potential, she's going to have to fight to stay alive - and only time will tell if she can beat the Mages at their own game.

From twisted wynds and tartan shops to a dangerous daemon and the magic infused City Chambers, the future of a nation might lie with one solitary woman.

Book One - Hummingbird

Book Two - COMING SOON

The complete *Blood Destiny* series

"A spectacular and addictive series."

Mackenzie Smith has always known that she was different. Growing up as the only human in a pack of rural shapeshifters will do that to you, but then couple it with some mean fighting skills and a fiery temper and you end up with a woman that few will dare to cross. However, when the only father figure in her life is brutally murdered, and the dangerous Brethren with their predatory Lord Alpha come to investigate, Mack has to not only ensure the physical safety of her adopted family by hiding her apparent humanity, she also has to seek the blood-soaked vengeance that she craves.

Book One - Bloodfire

Book Two - Bloodmagic

Book Three - Bloodrage

Book Four - Blood Politics

Book Five - Bloodlust

Also

Corrigan Fire

Corrigan Magic

Corrigan Rage

Corrigan Politics

Corrigan Lust

The complete *Bo Blackman* series

A half-dead daemon, a massacre at her London based PI firm and evidence that suggests she's the main suspect for both ... Bo Blackman is having a very bad week.

She might be naive and inexperienced but she's determined to get to the bottom of the crimes, even if it means involving herself with one of London's most powerful vampire Families and their enigmatic leader.

It's pretty much going to be impossible for Bo to ever escape unscathed.

Book One - Dire Straits

Book Two - New Order

Book Three - High Stakes

Book Four - Red Angel

Book Five - Vigilante Vampire

Book Six - Dark Tomorrow

The complete *Highland Magic* series

Integrity Taylor walked away from the Sidhe when she was a child. Orphaned and bullied, she simply had no reason to stay, especially not when the sins of her father were going to remain on her shoulders. She found a new family - a group of thieves who proved that blood was less important than loyalty and love.

But the Sidhe aren't going to let Integrity stay away forever. They need her more than anyone realises - besides, there are prophecies to be fulfilled, people to be saved and hearts to be won over. If anyone can do it, Integrity can.

Book One - Gifted Thief

Book Two - Honour Bound

Book Three - Veiled Threat

Book Four - Last Wish

The complete *Dreamweaver* series

"I have special coping mechanisms for the times I need to open the front door. They're even often successful..."

Zoe Lydon knows there's often nothing logical or rational about fear. It doesn't change the fact that she's too terrified to step outside her own house, however.

What Zoe doesn't realise is that she's also a dreamweaver - able to access other people's subconscious minds. When she finds herself in the Dreamlands and up against its sinister Mayor, she'll need to use all of her wits - and overcome all of her fears - if she's ever going to come out alive.

Book One - Night Shade

Book Two - Night Terrors

Book Three - Night Lights

Stand alone novels

Eros

William Shakespeare once wrote that, "Cupid is a knavish lad, thus to make poor females mad." The trouble is that Cupid himself would probably agree…

As probably the last person in the world who'd appreciate hearts, flowers and romance, Coop is convinced that true love doesn't exist – which is rather unfortunate considering he's also known as Cupid, the God of Love. He'd rather spend his days drinking, womanising and generally having as much fun as he possible can. As far as he's concerned, shooting people with bolts of pure love is a waste of his time...but then his path crosses with that of shy and retiring Skye Sawyer and nothing will ever be quite the same again.

Wraith

Magic. Shadows. Adventure. Romance.

Saiya Buchanan is a wraith, able to detach her shadow from her body and send it off to do her bidding. But, unlike most of her kin, Saiya doesn't deal in death. Instead, she trades secrets - and in the goblin besieged city of Stirling in Scotland, they're a highly prized commodity. It might just be, however, that the goblins have been hiding the greatest secret of them all. When Gabriel de Florinville, a Dark Elf, is sent as royal envoy into Stirling and takes her prisoner, Saiya is not only going to uncover the sinister truth. She's also going to realise that sometimes the deepest secrets are the ones locked within your own heart.

The complete *Lazy Girl's Guide To Magic* series

Hard Work Will Pay Off Later. Laziness Pays Off Now.

Let's get one thing straight - Ivy Wilde is not a heroine. In fact, she's probably the last witch in the world who you'd call if you needed a magical helping hand. If it were down to Ivy, she'd spend all day every day on her sofa where she could watch TV, munch junk food and talk to her feline familiar to her heart's content.

However, when a bureaucratic disaster ends up with Ivy as the victim of a case of mistaken identity, she's yanked very unwillingly into Arcane Branch, the investigative department of the Hallowed Order of Magical Enlightenment. Her problems are quadrupled when a valuable object is stolen right from under the Order's noses.

It doesn't exactly help that she's been magically bound to Adeptus Exemptus Raphael Winter. He might have piercing sapphire eyes and a body which a cover model would be proud of but, as far as Ivy's concerned, he's a walking advertisement for the joyless perils of too much witch-work.

And if he makes her go to the gym again, she's definitely going to turn him into a frog.

Book One - Slouch Witch

Book Two - Star Witch

Book Three - Spirit Witch

Sparkle Witch (Christmas short story)

The complete *Fractured Faery* series

One corpse. Several bizarre looking attackers. Some very strange magical powers. And a severe bout of amnesia.

It's one thing to wake up outside in the middle of the night with a decapitated man for company. It's another to have no memory of how you got there - or who you are.

She might not know her own name but she knows that several people are out to get her. It could be because she has strange magical powers seemingly at her fingertips and is some kind of fabulous hero. But then why does she appear to inspire fear in so many? And who on earth is the sexy, green-eyed barman who apparently despises her? So many questions ... and so few answers.

At least one thing is for sure - the streets of Manchester have never met someone quite as mad as Madrona...

Book One - Box of Frogs

Book Two - Quiver of Cobras

Book Three - Skulk of Foxes

The complete *City Of Magic* series

Charley is a cleaner by day and a professional gambler by night. She might be haunted by her tragic past but she's never thought of herself as anything or anyone special. Until, that is, things start to go terribly wrong all across the city of Manchester. Between plagues of rats, firestorms and the gleaming blue eyes of a sexy Scottish werewolf, she might just have landed herself in the middle of a magical apocalypse. She might also be the only person who has the ability to bring order to an utterly chaotic new world.

Book One - Shrill Dusk

Book Two - Brittle Midnight

Book Three - Furtive Dawn